Magic
IN
THE
Air

ADRIANNA SCHUH

RISING ACTION

Text copyright © 2024 by Adrianna Schuh

Cover Illustration © Cover Ever After
Distributed by Simon & Schuster

ISBN: 978-1-998076-60-4
Ebook: 978-1-998076-62-8

FIC027440 - Romance/Paranormal/Witches
FIC027230 - Romance/Multicultural & Interracial
FIC027000 - Romance/General

#MagicintheAir

Follow Rising Action on our socials!
Twitter: @RAPubCollective
Instagram: @risingactionpublishingco
Tiktok: @risingactionpublishingco

Mom, thank you for teaching me there wasn't anything I couldn't do. I wouldn't be me without you.

Magic
IN
THE
Air

Chapter 1

Pushing through the front door of Sugar Spells Bakery, Olivia Ayala glanced up at the clock that hung behind the counter. The scent of coffee and sugar washed over her. 8:29. One minute to spare. She took her time getting here this morning, enjoying the mild chill and feeling of magic that always seemed to permeate the air this time of year. Fall was definitely on the way and she wanted to enjoy her favorite weather while it lasted.

Because soon it would be winter. Winter meant icy sidewalks and ice was never kind to the uncoordinated.

"There you are. I thought you might be late for once," Jill said from behind the counter as Olivia came around and dropped her bag off.

"There's always tomorrow," she said, grabbing hold of her favorite apron from the hook on the wall. It was bright purple and covered in pumpkins and black witch's hats. A Mother's Day present from Daniel last year, his way of making a joke at his mother's expense. For a nine-year-old, her son could be hilarious.

Because Olivia *was* a witch. One who used magic and created spells and recorded them in a book. If she had to compare herself to those witches in books and on TV, the closest thing she could think of was Winnie from *Hocus Pocus*. Except she was a good witch.

This town was a kind of haven for people like her. A place where she and all the other witches could learn and practice their magic freely and safely. In return for that, she and her fellow witches were charged with protecting the magic that flowed through the town.

She tied the apron snuggly around her waist and turned to survey the bakery.

Almost every table was full this morning. Parents grabbing a coffee after seeing their kids off to school and gearing up for the workday ahead. The same table of older gentlemen who were here every morning, drinking their weight in coffee and swapping war stories.

She breathed in the scent of vanilla and cinnamon that mingled with the slightly chilled air that flowed through the door as customers came and went. It was almost impossible for her to feel anything other than happiness when she was here. The bakery was a home away from home, and she had worked hard to get the cozy and welcoming vibe in here exactly right. A few tables took up the main space, with a comfortable couch near the big front window. Near the back were the counter and cases for donuts and other pastries. The walls were painted a bright white with pink and yellow accents.

"I've known you for ten years," Jill said. "I could probably count the number of times you've been late to anything on one hand."

Olivia rolled her eyes at the look on her friend's face. Her dark green eyes twinkled. She wasn't wrong. Olivia hated being late and Jill loved teasing her about it.

Jill was her oldest friend and for a long time, her only friend. In the past, she had tried to make others. Other kids in her foster homes, kids at school, and when she was older, coworkers and other moms who had kids Daniel's age. But she could never get too close. It was tough to make friends when she could never really be herself and the fact that she was a witch wasn't exactly the kind of thing she could tell just anyone.

Jill added more muffins to the case. "So, how was Daniel feeling about going back to school today?"

"He actually seemed excited. Fourth grade is apparently a very big year for him. His excitement surprises me every year. I feel like most nine-year-olds want summer to last forever."

"Give him a week," Jill said with a laugh. "I'm sure the excitement will wear off."

She returned the laugh. "You're probably right. I'm definitely excited. You know how much I love Fall. Cozy sweaters, cute boots. I even started sorting through my clothes last night and don't even get me started on the food."

Colder weather meant soups, pot roast, tamales, and drinks like apple cider and hot chocolate. As a baker, she loved creating treats that went with the seasons: pumpkin pie, cider donuts, cookies with orange frosting, and her favorite Mexican treats like pan dulce, tres leches cake, and Mexican hot chocolate. She wasn't a fan of the popular flavors like pumpkin spice and peppermint, though.

Jill grinned. "Yeah, Liv, I know. We all know how much you love the cold weather. September first, like clockwork, you start yammering on about hot chocolate and tamales and soup. But as soon as it snows ..." Jill trailed off, giving her a pointed look.

She pursed her lips. No one appreciated a good chicken noodle soup like she did and no one had a greater disdain for snow and ice than she did. "Did I miss anything so far?" she asked, scanning the customers currently sitting in the shop again and then leaning down to scan the cases—one side for magic-infused goodies and one side without.

This town may have been home to magic and witches, but not everyone wanted or needed magical baked goods. So, even though the bakery was called Sugar Spells, they always had a good selection of regular old baked goods. Still delicious, of course.

One case was filled with cookies and muffins of various kinds. Another held a few select cakes and pies that tended to be made to order. The last case held all kinds of donuts. Those were most popular in the mornings, for obvious reasons. No one could resist one of her old-fashioned, glazed donuts.

Sugar Spells Bakery was her other baby and she was very proud of it.

"Nothing major. Simon came in with a headache, so I added a hint of mint and willow bark to his usual tea. Mostly just coffee and donuts so far. Oh, and the Jensens were looking a little tense, so I pushed those brownies of yours on them. I think we're going to need another batch of those soon. Nothing inspires a little honesty or makes someone open to forgiveness like those brownies."

"I'm aware. I did create the recipe and the spell myself. Along with quite a few others."

That was one of her favorite things to do with her magic, add spells to her sweet creations. It was often the easiest way to give someone a spell they wanted or needed and it was fun to see the kinds of things she could come up with.

It provided a good distraction from the snooze fest that was her own love life and on the days when she found herself frustrated by her Cerebral Palsy, a disability that sometimes made everyday life very difficult, it helped to know that there were some things magic could help.

Jill laughed. "That's what's so funny to me. You're basically a master at creating these recipes for helping with people's relationships. Want some openness and honesty? Have a brownie. Need a little courage to ask out your crush? Try these cupcakes. But you absolutely refuse to entertain the idea of having your own relationship."

"I like helping people. There's nothing wrong with that *and* I do more than just help people with their relationships," she said around a yawn.

"I know that and I'm not saying there's anything wrong with helping people. I'm just saying, would it kill you to give love a chance?"

She sighed, shaking her head. "Oh? So now I'm supposed to fall in love? I thought we were talking about relationships?"

Jill grimaced "Okay, I guess I got a little carried away there. How about some good, old-fashioned, hot sex then? That's what you need. I mean, really, Liv. When's the last time you got laid?"

Her eyes flew up to Jill's and she fought against the urge to shush her friend. She wasn't exactly being quiet. But that would only rile Jill up further. She tried out her best withering stare and hoped that would prompt a laugh and a change of subject. Unfortunately, Jill was like a dog with a bone.

"You know all you have to do is say the word and I can get one of Malcolm's friends to take you on a date. They always ask about you. Heck, all the single men in this town ask about you."

She rolled her eyes. They had some variation of this conversation every other week. If it weren't for the fact that Jill was her very best friend and business partner, she probably would have told her to shove it a long time ago. But Jill only pushed because she cared, so Olivia kept putting up with it. That didn't mean she had to like it, though.

"Well, they can ask all they want, but your answer better be 'she's not interested, thanks.' You know how I feel about blind dates or any kind of date, for that matter. I just don't have the time. Between taking care of Daniel and running this place, it's just not a priority."

She hadn't been on a real date in years. She had the occasional hook-up in the past. But everything always ended before long. There was no one she could be open and honest with, and she already had trust issues thanks to her Cerebral Palsy and the problems it caused in her past. Add being a witch to that and the idea of trying to maintain any kind of romantic relationship was exhausting.

Besides, the last thing she needed was another one of Jill's setups. She meant well. But she was terrible at choosing partners for other people. How she managed to find her husband, Olivia would never understand.

The last time she had tried to set Olivia up was almost a year ago now and it all went horribly wrong, because the guy had believed Jill's jokes about how desperate she was.

Her friends had talked her into giving the guy a chance. A friend of a friend of Malcolm's. She had arranged a sitter for Daniel. She had geared up for the inevitable conversation that would occur when he noticed how she walked differently. She had done her hair and her makeup. She had even bought a new outfit. All for the guy to show up and say to her, "That outfit looks so hot on you. Bet it's even hotter off you." The whole thing was mortifying. Jill was still making it up to her, in the form of a free dinner whenever Olivia asked.

Jill scoffed. "I did not say date. I said sex. You do remember what sex is, don't you?"

She groaned. "Yes, I remember what sex is."

If Jill was going to keep talking at her, she was going to do some actual work. They had an order come in late yesterday for two dozen lemon cupcakes for a retirement party tonight. The customer had also asked for a calming spell to be added to the recipe. Apparently, this retirement was a source of contention.

"Okay, good! So, am I making a call or not?"

Ignoring Jill, Olivia headed to the back and pulled out the ingredients for the first batch of cupcakes, setting everything on the stainless-steel countertop. Flour, sugar, butter, eggs. She added a couple of lemons and a sprig of lavender for the calming effect. Making cupcakes was something she could do in her sleep. She did not have to focus until she measured the final ingredients, so she let her muscle memory take over, sifting and stirring, her favorite wooden spoon bouncing off the side of the stainless-steel bowl.

"Come on, Liv. Please," Jill whined from behind her.

"No, Jill. No sex. No dates. No random guys. None of Malcolm's friends. No relationship. Nothing. Those things only lead to trouble and I'm not interested."

"Fine, fine," Jill muttered, her face forming a full-on pout. The woman was used to getting her way. "But someday, Liv, someday you will meet someone who will make you change your mind."

"In this town? Not likely. I've known everyone here for years. So, if someone hasn't caught my eye by now, I doubt they ever will."

What she didn't say to Jill, what she couldn't say, was that she hoped that was true.

She had a wonderful life here, a place where she could truly be herself. Her son was happy and healthy and even though she had a disability that sometimes made life hard, living here, owning her own business, made life things easier.

But secretly. Quietly. In the deepest part of her heart, she wished she had someone to share it all with. Maybe someday, she would be brave enough to admit that out loud.

Chapter 2

G rief was a funny thing. Some days it sat quietly in the background, a gentle reminder of the person who was gone. Other days it was a roar that drowned out all the good in the world. For the past six months, Draven James had been living within the din.

The loss of his mother was a specter in the shadows stalking every moment of every day since he had held her hand in his for the very last time.

But today would be different. Today he had a purpose and that purpose was exactly how he found himself in the town of Addersfield, Rhode Island, four hours and over 200 miles from home.

The kind of place you would see on a postcard that instantly evoked thoughts of salt and sun and sand. The quintessential coastal town.

His mother was from here and according to the journals he found tucked away in her nightstand, she was a witch.

At first, he thought it was a joke. But the more he read, the more he believed. Dozens of journal entries that described in detail his mother's early life as a witch: meeting his father, the eventual loss of her magic, and his father leaving them. It was all connected. He read and re-read amid countless sleepless nights. Until finally, a few weeks ago, he made the decision to confirm the truth for himself by paying a visit to this small New England town that, according to his mother, was full of witches.

All he had were these journals and his own instincts to guide him.

He tried to Google the place before just showing up, but he found nothing. No advertisements, no address listings, no websites for local businesses. No way to look for housing. Not even an auto-generated Facebook page and in the age of the internet, that was very strange. But in a town that was home to witches, maybe it was a weird safety measure? It made sense— small towns tended to be very close-knit and in a town that was home to witches, they would probably be even more so.

He was almost certain that his apartment building alone had more people living in it than the whole of Addersfield, which boasted a population of only 6,000. If he had to guess, the impending culture shock would not be insignificant.

He had lived in New York his entire life, a place where anonymity was no problem. But here? He would stick out like a sore thumb. He wouldn't be staying forever, just long enough to get what he needed and that required fitting in. This town was like something straight out of a quaint movie. There were people out walking their dogs, old men sitting in the park playing cards and exactly one main street.

It looked like that was where all the action was, if he could even call it that. He spotted a diner, a pharmacy, and a grocery store right next to the other. People waved hello and called out greetings as they passed each other on the street. This was definitely not New York.

A quick drive around the town square revealed an inn just off the main street. It looked like as good a place as any for a temporary living space, while he looked for a more permanent situation. He wasn't exactly sure how long he would be staying.

He was a journalist for one of the bigger papers back in New York and he was good at his job, which was why his editor had let him take some time off to come here. He had promised her a big story and he planned on keeping that promise. A magical town full of witches? It would be huge. He just needed proof.

Pulling his car into the small parking lot, he killed the engine and sat back in his seat. Glancing around at the buildings and people, the intimacy of it all was completely foreign to him. Who had his mother been here? Did she have a happy childhood? Did she have any remaining family here? Would anyone remember her? Where did she fit into the history of this town? And where did that leave him? He was determined to get answers to his many questions.

There were only two other cars in the lot beside his own—probably employees. How a place like this stayed open in a town this size, he wasn't sure. Especially considering they seemed to be going to great lengths to keep tourists away. He grabbed his bag from the passenger seat and made his way up to the entrance.

Stepping inside, he was instantly hit with the comforting and familiar scent of roses. It reminded him of his mother. The inn itself was like stepping into the pages of a travel magazine, the kind with one of those articles listing "The Top 10 Inns in Rhode Island." The whole place was, in a word, 'cutesy.' Dark wood throughout and lots of floral-patterned furniture. There was even a fireplace off the main room surrounded by books. Maybe he could borrow a few. He'd had to leave the majority of his collection behind.

As he approached the front desk, a woman greeted him with a wave and a bright smile.

Her tone was cheery. "Hi, can I help you?"

"Yes. I was hoping to rent a room. For the week?"

"Sure thing. Are you visiting someone?"

"Nope. Just looking for a quiet place to relax and work on my book. I'm a writer. A little town like this seemed the best place."

Not exactly a lie. But that was part of the job, telling people what they wanted to hear to make them feel more comfortable. No one here needed to know what he was up to. At least not yet. Once the article was published, he could give two shits if anyone found out. If anything, it would make the whole thing just that much more satisfying.

Her brow furrowed, questions brewing in her eyes.

"Is something wrong?"

She blushed. "It's just a little weird. We don't get many visitors, or rather, we don't get many strangers," she said. "I mean, obviously, people visit the town sometimes. We're not like barring people at the town line or anything. I mean ..."

"It's just that this isn't exactly a town on the beaten path."

"Exactly!"

He shrugged. "Well, it seems like a lovely place for what it's worth and I needed a change, so it works for me."

Another trick of the trade. Pile on the compliments.

She seemed satisfied with his answer and didn't pry for more information, thank goodness. Instead, she worked diligently, charging his credit card and having him fill out some paperwork. It was a relatively painless process, considering most places like this would normally be using a computer.

Maybe the whole town was a little behind the times? Was that a reflection on the kind of people who lived in this town? Were witches naturally averse to technology because they had magic to help them out? Or was that supposed to add to the charm of this place? Another question to add to his ever-growing list.

"Well, here's your room key," she said as she handed him an actual, physical key. "Number four. Just up the stairs and to the left. I hope you enjoy your stay. My name is Parker, by the way," she said, pointing to herself. "My family owns this place. Let me know if you have any questions or if you need anything."

"Nice to meet you, Parker. I'm Draven James," he said, resisting the urge to extend his hand. If she'd wanted to shake it, she would have. He paused. "Actually, could you tell me: is there a beach nearby? Or somewhere you can see the ocean?" He held his breath. He was desperate to be near the water.

"Oh. Umm, yeah," she said, looking a little surprised. "Just take Main Street all the way down past the grocery store," she pointed with her finger in the direction of the store. "Turn right and there's a boardwalk path to the beach. You can't miss it."

"Thanks. I appreciate it," he said with a nod. "I'll see you around."

"See you around," she said, again with that same bright smile.

He grabbed his bag and, clutching his honest-to-God metal key, went in search of his room.

It was a standard hotel room, if a little antiquated. Decent-sized double bed, small bathroom. TV, mini-fridge, dresser, even a microwave, *and* more floral furniture. Even the curtains had flowers on them. Not exactly his style, but it would do for now.

He did not have much to unpack. Most of his belongings fit into a few bags and boxes, which were currently taking up space in his trunk. The stuff he had been unable to bring along had been donated, books, a few pieces of small furniture, and some of his larger kitchen appliances. In the bag he brought with him were the necessities, toothbrush, toiletries, and a week's worth of clothes. Hopefully, he would be able to find a place to rent quickly.

But first, there was one part of this town that beckoned to him: the ocean. Grabbing his wallet and keys, he ventured back out into the sunshine, its brightness a stark contrast to the way he was feeling inside.

The town was certainly picturesque, that much he could admit. Walking the quiet streets was incredibly surreal, like something out of a dream. Had he really packed up his entire life and come here on what could arguably be considered a total whim?

What if things didn't work out and he wasn't able to write his story? What would he do then? This was all he had. The fact that this place could have been his home in another life perhaps should have stirred some kind of connection or positive feeling. Yet, he had never felt so disconnected from anything or anyone in his life.

When he arrived at the beach, there was no one else around. Not surprising given the fact it was a Monday afternoon, but he preferred it that way.

In addition to his mother's journals, he had found an album of old pictures, one of which was of her sitting on the beach, presumably the same beach he was standing on now. The dark blue water loomed in the background. Had she ever intended for him to end up here, to discover her secret? Would she have told him everything if she had had more time?

Cancer was a bitch. It came for his mother swiftly and silently. One of those types that was a death sentence before you even knew it existed. One day she looked perfectly healthy and the next, she was sitting him and his brother Lucas down to tell them she was dying. From that moment on, he had tried to distance himself from anything that made him feel too much. His mother, his brother, and the few friends he had.

Between endless doctors' appointments and hours spent sitting in hospital waiting rooms, he withdrew further and further from the person he used to be.

Instead, he focused on work, never letting up. It helped to distract him from the pain and in a way, it paid off. He had too many bylines to count and he was always going after the most controversial or hard-hitting stories, never letting up until he got every piece of information available for a story. He wasn't sure that particular approach would work here. But, whatever it took, he wouldn't stop until he got his story. The pen was mightier than the sword, as the saying went.

Reading her journals was almost like reading a family history with his mother right there with him.

They revealed that she had descended from a family of witches that had made their home here in Addersfield. But she eventually ended up settling in New York City with his father. They met when she was on a trip to New York City to celebrate her turning twenty-one. He was a bartender and had spent the night flirting with his mom while serving drinks and wiping tables. Fast forward to a year later: she told him she was a witch and he was fascinated and more in love with her than ever.

In the journal, she didn't go into much detail beyond that she had decided to share her magic with his father. Only that wasn't allowed and as a consequence, her magic was taken from her. She didn't explain how or why.

His father had wanted her to fight to get it back. But she had felt there was nothing that could be done. Her magic was gone, she'd made a mistake and she would live with the consequences.

For a few years, they'd tried to carry on with their new life in New York. Draven was born two years later and his little brother Lucas the year after. But his father wasn't happy and one day, he left for work and never came back. Over the years he had made very little effort to stay in touch with his sons.

Reading this straight from his mother's own hand had sent him reeling. A lot of things made sense now. The stories full of magic his mother used to tell him before bed. Why she never talked about her past and why they never knew any of her family.

Maybe he could blame his father for all of this, because he'd wanted magic that didn't belong to him.

But to Draven, it boiled down to one thing: his mother had been let down by his father, by the people here in her hometown, by her sons who were now barely speaking to each other and by magic itself.

As far as he was concerned, magic was the problem. Then and now. Magic was the thing that had pulled his family apart, a fact he spent his adult life trying to reconcile with alone. The existence of magic wasn't something everyone knew about and he wanted to make things right for his mother. To prove how much she meant to him and how sorry he was that he hadn't always been there for her, the way he should have been—choosing to let his career become the most important thing in his life.

Even if all he could do now was tell her story, it would have to be enough. He would tell the world about this town, the witches who lived here, and the way they turned their backs on his mother, so many years ago. It wasn't right that they would go on living here, possessing magic while his mother's was taken away.

The slow laps of the waves on the shore were a balm to his raging emotions, embodying a rhythm that was familiar for him. Evocative of home and his childhood. An endless summer day full of sand and sunshine. His mother loved the water, the beach and the warm weather; and she passed that love on to her sons from a very early age. They lived in the city, but every summer was spent in a rental cabin upstate. They fished, they swam, and they sailed for hours every single day. Until their fingers turned wrinkly and they were exhausted from the sun beating down on them.

At night they would lay in the tall grass together, counting the stars and making wishes and Lucas would insist that they try and catch fireflies. The air so warm and sweet. Those summers were everything to him and Lucas, something they looked forward to every year.

The tradition continued right up until the summer before his junior year of high school. At this point he was suddenly too cool to spend time with his family. Of course, looking back now, he would change that if he could. He'd remind himself that he would never get another chance to make memories like the ones they made each summer.

His mother had passed away before either of her sons had children to pass on the traditions to. He had so many regrets where she was concerned. But maybe what he was about to do would make up for that in some way.

Bringing out his phone, he snapped a picture to send to his brother. He made sure to include the passing sailboats in the distance. When he was satisfied that their crisp, white sails were visible enough, he sent the picture and a short message to Lucas.

I miss you.

They hadn't spoken in so long. Time and grief did all they could to keep them apart. But he wanted to change that. It's what their mother would have wanted. If she could see them now, it would surely break her heart.

They used to be best friends, he and Lucas. One of his earliest memories was of a day spent on a beach, a lot like this one, with six-year-old Draven teaching four-year-old Lucas how to build a sandcastle.

Their mother watched on with the biggest smile on her face, laughing along with them each time a wave came to wash the sandcastle away and each time they would hunker down and build a new one. Each one was better than the last.

She had given them so many special moments. Losing her was devastating, the only parent he had left. He missed her every single day.

Being here made him feel so close to her. Just imagining that she might have stood in this very spot, watching these very same waves.

He could not save her from her disease. But maybe he could make this one thing right for her. And he would try like hell, no matter what it took.

Chapter 3

The front door to the bakery flew open, nearly slamming into the wall behind it. Olivia jumped back, fully expecting the person who caused the commotion to announce some kind of terrible news.

Instead, her friend Parker came running in and made a beeline for the counter, her usually flawless light brown hair disheveled from running and her bright hazel eyes glowing with mischief.

Parker was a good friend of Jill's, and Olivia had grown close to her over the years. Parker, like Olivia, was Mexican-American and her family had really taken Olivia under their wing, teaching her aspects of her heritage she never had the chance to learn while growing up in foster care with exclusively white families. Parker's family also owned the inn in town and they really helped out while Olivia and Jill were learning how to run their business.

"Jeez, what's with you?" Jill asked.

Parker rushed to give the details. "There's a hot guy!" she proclaimed, loud enough for the whole bakery to hear.

"Yeah, Parker, there are lots of them," Olivia said. "There are more than a few billion people in the world at last count."

"Haha, very funny," Parker said with a roll of her eyes. "I meant here, in Addersfield."

"Oh. Well, that *is* interesting. He must be new in town. There's no way you would be this frantic over someone we already know. Unless that someone suddenly got better looking overnight," Jill said as she leaned against the counter, eyes wide and waiting for more details.

Parker rolled her eyes again. "Yes, it's a new guy. Way to ruin the moment, Jill."

"A new guy in town? What's he doing here?" Olivia asked, a sense of foreboding tingling at her spine.

"He's staying at the inn," Parker announced, her face breaking out into a big smile again, her eyes bright and shining. "I checked him in this morning, actually."

"What?!" Olivia and Jill yelled but with vastly different tones. Jill was clearly thrilled. Olivia, however, was completely panicking. Her chest grew tight and her palms were now slick with sweat.

Her friends were obviously delighted, if their loud squeals of joy were anything to go by. But what did they know about this guy? What did anyone know about him?

No one moved here unless they were a witch or knew someone who was, like Olivia had. Everyone else had been born and raised here. The town's founders, three witches and their families, had placed a protection spell on the town. You could not find it unless you already knew it was there. So, this new guy had to know about the existence of magic and witches. Which meant he had to know someone in town.

Olivia did not trust people she didn't know. She had never been good at that. Kids did not exactly want to hang out with the girl who walked funny and who weird things happened around. She now knew that those occurrences, shattering a glass when she was angry, pulling a book from the top shelf without a ladder, being able to grow flowers out of season, were her magic making itself known. But at the time, everything was so confusing. Add to that the fact that she never had a permanent home and she had been a very skeptical little girl. Her trust was hard to earn and even harder to keep.

She had learned long ago that letting people in meant they could hurt her. If she liked the family she was placed with, they were sure to give her up sooner rather than later. If she made friends with the new kid at school, they eventually noticed she wasn't like all the other kids and that her disability could be limiting, so they preferred to make friends with the more popular kids. So, she was always careful who she let into her life.

"He's a writer from New York. Or at least that's what it said on the paperwork," Parker said, sitting down at the counter and looking mighty pleased with her bit of gossip. She was always a fan of a good story and this definitely made for one.

"How did he end up in Addersfield?" Olivia asked.

"He didn't say. But he did say he was writing a book and that he needed a change."

"And that doesn't seem strange to you? He should not have been able to get in unless he already knew the town was here. But this guy turns up out of the blue, claiming he's here to write a book. Did he say anything about magic? Or maybe that he knows someone here in town?"

"He did not," Parker said, her voice rising in pitch as her eyes narrowed. "But we do get the occasional visitor from time to time."

She shook her head. "Right. But he would have to know someone here. So, he's lying."

"Or maybe he just didn't want to tell a stranger all of his business," Jill said.

Why was she the only one that seemed really concerned here?

"Oh my God, that's him!" Parker yelled, moving to the window to gape at the guy. Olivia stayed put, not liking the idea of spying on someone like a teenage girl with a crush.

But Jill did not give her a choice, pulling her by the hand over to the window. They probably looked very strange to the customers.

"You guys are being ridiculous; you realize that, right?" Olivia said, looking at her friends instead of staring outside.

"Maybe," Jill said. "But he does make for quite a view."

She finally looked outside, and her eyes landed on the one stranger walking along Main Street.

She froze.

She took him in, totally unprepared for the sheer attractiveness of this man. He was dressed in all black and was tall with dark hair and the shadow of a beard gracing his face. Even from here, he seemed to ooze confidence, like nothing and no one, fazed him. Who knew that kind of attitude would turn her on? Holy shit.

She was about to turn away when he shifted closer to the window, making room for an older couple walking the other way and she caught sight of his eyes, striking and bright; it was as if she had looked into those impossibly blue pools countless times. Her hand raised of its own volition as if to reach for him, when he suddenly glanced their way. She jumped from the window and out of sight, not wanting to be caught ogling the guy.

How embarrassing would that be?

Unfortunately, her friends had absolutely no sense of self-preservation. They continued to stand there gaping.

"Oh crap," Parker muttered. "What do we do?"

"Just smile and wave, kiddies. Smile and wave," Jill said.

"Aww, looks like he's going into the grocery store," Parker lamented. "I was kind of hoping he would come in here."

So was I. Olivia cringed. There was no way she could be interested in this guy, no matter how good-looking he was. His presence in town could pose a threat to everyone's safety. One video recording of magic, and suddenly it's all over the news and they're being studied like animals in a zoo.

"I could go get him if you guys want," Parker offered and Olivia's heart clenched at the prospect.

"No worries, friends," Jill said. "All we have to do is have Parker suggest he stop by the bakery the next time she sees him at the inn and then we can get to know him a little. Maybe do a little harmless flirting. Find out exactly why he's in town."

She was happy to hear she wasn't the only one curious about this guy's intentions.

"Oh, good idea!" Parker agreed, clapping her hands together. "I'm sure Draven would love to visit some places around town."

"Draven?" Olivia asked, brow furrowing. The name did not exactly roll off the tongue.

"Yeah," Parker said with a grin. "Draven James."

His name hung between them, and Olivia tried to think of a way to change the subject. But she came up empty. She was too distracted by her frenzied feelings and shaking hands. Why the hell was she so affected by him? They hadn't even met, and she absolutely could not be attracted to this guy. But those eyes. She could drown in those eyes.

"Wait! He's coming this way!" Parker yelled.

Her face was suddenly hot. Was her hair a mess? Did she have flour on her nose? Why the hell did she even care?

Shit. She could not stop fidgeting.

"Breathe, Liv. You need to breathe," Jill said as the two of them moved back behind the counter.

"Shut up, Jill."

"I'm just saying, you look like you're about to have a heart attack."

"Will both of you shut up?" Parker said, still standing by the window stifling a laugh. "Here he comes."

The bell over the door sounded, signaling a new customer.

Don't look. Don't look. Do not look.

He walked up to the counter, stopping right in front of her.

She looked up.

His eyes, so intense and focused, seemed as if they could see into her soul. Words. She should be making words now.

"Hi!" Jill practically yelled. "Welcome to Sugar Spells Bakery. You must be Draven."

He glanced towards Jill, his brow furrowed in confusion. "Yes, how did you—"

"Oh! That was me," Parker said as she ran over to stand next to him. "Sorry! It's just like I said. We don't get a lot of visitors around here. So, you are big news."

Olivia cringed. Could they be any more small town if they tried? Now he knew for sure they had been talking about him. Was it possible to die from embarrassment? She really should say something. Pretend like the three of them absolutely were not just ogling him through a window.

He laughed. "I see. And you are?" he asked, quirking a brow at Jill.

"I'm Jill. Jill Montgomery."

"Well, it's nice to meet you, Jill. But I'm afraid you'll be disappointed. I'm not that exciting."

"Oh, I don't know about that," Jill muttered.

Dear God. They were ridiculous.

"Anyway ..." Olivia finally said, trying to keep the grimace off her face. "What can we do for you, Draven?"

He was looking at her again. But this time, she was determined to keep her cool. He was just a guy. A very hot guy, sure, but just a guy nonetheless.

He smiled at her, all crooked grin and perfect teeth, his pale-pink lips plush and inviting. This was a guy who knew what he wanted and exactly how to get it.

His lush, obsidian hair stopped just above his ears and the light scruff on his chin only added to the sexual charm rolling off his countenance. She glanced down the length of his strong forearms, at his black T-shirt exposing corded muscles. She spied a dark tattoo etched onto his right shoulder peeking out from underneath his sleeve.

"I didn't catch your name."

Keep it together. "Olivia. Olivia Ayala," she said with a wave. "Jill and I actually own the bakery."

"Is that right? Well, I was on my way back from the beach, when I saw this place and realized I could use a cup of coffee. I haven't had my customary second cup yet."

"Sure thing. Small? Medium? Large? Would you like a latte? Cappuccino? Frappuccino? Mocha? Espresso?"

She was rambling now.

He laughed again, a deep rich sound as smooth as honey. It sent her imagination running wild with thoughts of his lips on hers. His hands in her hair. That rough and raspy voice whispering her name. It sent her blood pounding and her heart racing.

Shit. Where the hell had that come from?

"I'll take a large black coffee, thanks."

She grabbed a cup from the counter behind her, filling it to the brim with their house roast, before capping it off and handing it to him.

His hands were soft and warm. The hands of a writer. That's what Parker said he did, right?

"Cream and sugar are just over there to the right."

He nodded and then proceeded over to where she had indicated. Once his back was turned, Olivia faced her friends, both of whom were watching her with rapt attention.

"Holy shit," Jill mouthed as she fanned herself.

"Go talk to him," Parker whispered.

"No. What would I even say? Hey, you need help tearing open that sugar packet? No. He probably already thinks I'm ridiculous."

Parker rolled her eyes. "Oh, he does not. We want to know what he's doing here, right? So, keep him talking. Go over there."

"No. You do it, Parker!"

Jill groaned. "Oh, for the love of God. Hey Draven," she called out.

He spun around, cup of coffee raised to his lips. "Yes?"

Jill grinned. Olivia knew that look. She was up to something. "You know Olivia was just working on a batch of brownies," she said. "They're probably almost finished if you—"

Olivia cut in. "No, I don't think those are ready yet," she said through gritted teeth, shooting a glare at Jill. She could see Parker biting back a grin.

Olivia had added a little spell work to this particular batch of brownies. It just so happened to be a spell encouraging honesty, a request from a customer who was convinced their partner was cheating. The plan was for the customer to serve the brownies to their partner and then ask some very pointed questions. Normally she and Jill did their best not to use magic like this on someone without their consent, but Olivia knew for a fact this person had cheated. Parker had seen them going into a room at the inn, with someone who was definitely not their partner. Apparently, there was lots of groping and kissing as well, before they even made it to the room. Not exactly discreet.

She was going to get Jill for that one.

Draven walked back to the counter, stopping directly in front of her again.

Olivia pointed at the display. "How about a donut instead? I know it's a little late in the day. But you can never go wrong with donuts and coffee."

"Sure. I'd love one. Glazed, please."

She grabbed a bag from beneath the counter. "Parker said you were in town to write a book? What's it about?"

"History, mostly."

A writer from New York coming here to write a book on history? Surely he could come up with a better lie than that?

"Really? What kind of history?"

He shrugged. "Family history. Sort of a biography."

Family history. Maybe he did know someone from here? But then why not just come out and say so?

She narrowed her eyes. "Why would you pick here of all places to write it?"

He looked away. She took the moment to grab a donut from the case and place it in the bag.

His eyes returned to hers. "Well. I sort of just stumbled on the town and it seemed as good a place as any."

He was lying. She did not dare risk a glance at Jill or Parker to see if they had caught it. But he was 100 percent lying. He knew the town was here and he knew about magic. The question was, how much did he know? And what exactly was he doing here?

"That was lucky. Parker mentioned you're from New York? Seems like quite the drive to write a story."

"I wanted a change of pace. Hoping to gain some clarity." He smiled like he was trying to put her at ease.

Her cheeks heated.

Shit. She was trying to play it cool. But the man was definitely charming.

"Well, I hope you're not too disappointed. Not much happens around here." She shrugged as she handed him the bag. "Let me know if I can help with the book in any way," she said with a smile she was sure did not reach her eyes.

If he hadn't known she was suspicious before, he probably did now. Her friends always said her face was like an open book.

But maybe that was a good thing in this case. Let him think she was onto him. Make him sweat a little.

"I uh ... I'll keep that in mind. Thanks."

He waved to both Parker and Jill before heading out the door. He didn't look back at her.

"Did you guys catch that?" Olivia asked.

"Oh yeah," Jill said, nodding her head.

Parker spoke up. "He said basically the same thing to me when I met him earlier. He's definitely up to something. I'll talk to my abuelita about it. Maybe she'll have some insight."

"Let's make sure the book is safe, just in case," Olivia said quietly. "We don't want any surprises."

They both nodded in agreement. This book contained spells from every generation of witches that had lived in this town. As the most current generation, it was their job to keep it safe. Olivia took that responsibility seriously. She would not be taking any chances where Draven was concerned, no matter how cute he was. The man had no right to have a jaw that chiseled. And the stubble on his face? How might that feel against her skin?

Shit. *Down girl. You only just met the man.*

"You have to admit it though, that man is gorgeous," Parker said with a grin.

Olivia groaned. "So not the point."

Draven laughed as he walked out of the bakery and crossed the street, heading to the grocery store. He'd meant to go before but the bakery had caught his eye.

Olivia and her friends obviously had no idea he could hear them talking while he was fixing his coffee.

It wasn't like he was trying to eavesdrop or anything, but the whole bakery had gone eerily quiet when he walked in. The chatter only started up again when he was walking out the door. Thus, every person in the place had been able to hear not only his conversation with Olivia but also allowed him to hear the subsequent "whispered" conversation between the three friends.

From what he gathered, Olivia was suspicious of him, while Jill and Parker seemed to be focused more on his romantic prospects. Funnily enough, the fact that Olivia found him suspicious was something he found incredibly endearing. It meant she had good instincts. As a journalist, he certainly could not fault her for that. But it also meant he needed to be careful. If even one person got too suspicious, his whole plan could be compromised and he certainly could not have that. Not only was he doing this for his mother, but he had basically staked his career on this exposé. He'd uprooted his life for this.

He would not let one suspicious person ruin that for him, no matter how gorgeous she was.

If the situation were different, he might have considered starting something with her. She intrigued him with her flowing brown hair that just kissed the top of her shoulders, the kind he could easily bury his hands in as he kissed her full, dark-pink lips. Not to mention those eyes, so sharp and assessing, but still warm at the same time. She was just his type.

As he browsed the shelves of the grocery store, clutching his cup of coffee and donut in one hand, her face flashed in his mind. What was she thinking right at this moment? Was her suspicion merely based on the fact that he was a stranger? Parker had said they did not get many visitors. But maybe there was more to it than that—something he wasn't seeing.

Stopping in the bakery was a spur-of-the-moment decision. It wasn't like he needed a third cup of coffee. He definitely did not need a donut. But something had compelled him to go in. If he didn't know any better, he would think it was the magic that existed in this town.

He couldn't be sure, but he suspected that the lovely Olivia used magic in her bakery. As soon as he walked in, he noticed an odd scent in the air, like burning wood mixed with sugar and vanilla and he spotted the two different cases of baked goods. He didn't get a good look, but one case appeared to list ingredients under each option, like the makings of a spell, small things that screamed magic.

"You must be the new guy everyone has been talking about," someone said to Draven as he made his way down the cereal aisle.

He glanced over to see a man with a broad smile and kind-looking eyes. He would guess they were around the same age; Draven having just turned thirty.

"Yeah, that would be me."

The man extended his hand. "Malcolm Montgomery. I own the store."

"Draven James, resident new guy," he offered as he shook Malcolm's hand. "So, the gossip is already in full swing, huh?"

"Oh, most definitely. But don't worry, it gets easier. When I first got here a few years back, the talk was pretty constant. But eventually it fades. Hey, maybe you'll get lucky, and someone else will move here soon."

So much for keeping a low profile.

"What brings you to Addersfield?"

"I'm hell-bent on becoming a cliché, of course," he said with a smile.

Malcolm laughed. "My wife said you were funny."

"Your wife?"

"Jill. She works with Olivia over at the bakery."

"Oh, right. Wow. I literally just came from there. This really is a small town."

Malcolm nodded. "It is and my wife loves to gossip. I'm guessing she texted me as soon as you walked in. New people are big news around here. But you get used to it. Actually, we all have weekly dinners together. Me, Jill, Olivia, and a few other people. On Wednesdays. Maybe you could come this week?"

He was torn. On the one hand, it might be an opportunity to get more information about the town and he couldn't pretend it wouldn't be nice to see Olivia again. But he also did not want to get too close to anyone.

"I appreciate the offer. But I think I'd like to get settled in first. Maybe next time, though?"

"Sure thing. Anyway, I gotta get back to work, but if you ever need anything, I'm around."

"I'll remember that, thanks."

"Good, because Addersfield it's … special. Things will come up and when they do, I'm an excellent listener."

Were people around here always this friendly? First, Olivia offered her help and now Malcolm was inviting him, a complete stranger, to a family dinner just two days from now. People being this welcoming was definitely going to take some getting used to and in his opinion, is a bit naïve on their part. But it certainly had the potential to make his job that much easier.

If these people wanted to help him dig their own graves, who the hell was he to say no?

Chapter 4

The early days of September were probably Olivia's least favorite days. That odd time of year when the early mornings and late evenings necessitated a warm jacket, but the middle of the day was still warm enough for shorts and a tank top.

She was used to being outdoors in all kinds of weather, since her Cerebral Palsy prevented her from being able to drive. The walk over here tonight was nice, even if it was a little chilly. Her cheeks warmed as she smiled at the scent of tamales, spices, and cheese that wafted from the house as they approached.

The sound of voices carried through the kitchen and to the front door. Not bothering to knock, she and Daniel stepped inside and hung up their jackets before kicking off their shoes to join the pile on the floor.

Wednesday night dinners at Rosa's were a tradition long before she had arrived in town. She was so privileged to be a part of them now. These were the kinds of traditions she had always dreamed of having as a kid.

The fact that this was what Daniel would grow up knowing, made her feel so proud.

This was the only family the two of them had and it was a good one. On nights like this, she often found herself remembering the time right after Daniel was born. How lonely she'd been and how different her life was now.

"Alright, bud. I'll be in the kitchen if you need anything. Okay?"

"Okay, Mom," Daniel said with a smile before taking off towards the living room. "I'm gonna go find Malcolm. I've got my story all picked out for the week."

She watched him go and then walked down the hall and into the kitchen. Parker and Jill were already here, along with Parker's mom Janella and Abuelita Rosa.

"Hola mijita," Rosa said when she spotted Olivia and pulled her in for a hug. "I've missed you."

Olivia breathed in the scent of amber and spices, the soothing combination of Rosa's signature perfume and her constant presence in the kitchen. Her hugs were the best. They always felt like coming home.

"Come and help me with the guacamole and you can tell me all about your week."

Olivia stopped to give Janella a hug. She was a lovely woman who always had a kind word to say to everyone. She would sometimes help Olivia with new spells and recipes, as once upon a time, she and her friends were the ones responsible for protecting the town and the book.

But it was Rosa that she was closest to. From the day she arrived in town, Rosa was there, welcoming Olivia into her family and into her heart. She was so different from the families and relatives who only seemed to tolerate her presence and had never tried to help her understand her background. Maybe it was partly her fault, as she had always been afraid to get too close to anyone in case they realized she had magic and became fearful of her.

But Rosa was just the kind of person she'd always needed in her life. Rosa was the one who encouraged her to really lean into her powers and her love of helping people.

At first, the idea of putting spells and charms in her recipes hadn't sat well with her. Was it right to offer someone a piece of cake that would help them relax? Or a cup of coffee that soothed an anxious mind? Especially if they hadn't asked for it?

But Rosa had helped her see that as long as she wasn't hurting anyone, there was no harm done. Even so, she made no secret of which recipes contained spells and she disclosed that information to anyone who asked. A decision that Rosa also encouraged.

She joined Rosa at the kitchen counter, grabbing a few avocados to rinse and peel.

"So, mija. Tell me what's been going on since I saw you last week. Parker tells me we have an interesting new guest staying at the inn and that you met him a couple days ago?"

"Oh," she said with a laugh, eyeing Rosa's wide grin. "Is that all she told you?"

"She might have also mentioned that he was very good-looking."

She shrugged. "I guess so. I really hadn't noticed." She grabbed a knife from the drawer to slice up the avocados. Meanwhile, Rosa was busy taking the pits out of a few others. They always made two batches. One with tomatoes, cilantro, and lime and the other with just salt.

"You *guess so*. Aye, mijita, you know you cannot lie to me. Parker said there seemed to be something between you two. So come on, tell me what happened."

She groaned. "Not you too, Rosa. Why am I the only one worried about this guy? And why is everyone suddenly so interested in my love life?"

"What love life?" Jill called from across the room.

Olivia flipped her the bird.

Sometimes her best friend got on her nerves, but she owed her a lot. The two of them had met at culinary school in New York City not long after Daniel was born. Jill had approached her the very first day, asking her about her magic. She had explained to Olivia that she could sense her powers, a talent which was one of her 'witch strengths,' as she called it.

Of course, Olivia was wary, having never met another witch before. But once Jill demonstrated her own magical ability, lighting a candle with a wave of her hand and saying *ignitae*, they became fast friends.

They partnered up for every activity and helped each other with projects. Jill spent more time in Olivia and Daniel's apartment than she did in her own. She had spent many hours explaining to Olivia how magic worked. The do's and do not's and all the most useful spells.

Jill told her all about Addersfield and the history of the town. Olivia had no idea who in her family was a witch that could have passed it onto her. So, the idea that Jill was able to trace back her own ancestry so far, was fascinating.

Jill asked her to move back home with her the day they graduated. Having no other friends or family to speak of, she had accepted. Jill introduced her to her family and then to Parker and her family. More people entered her and Daniel's lives than she had ever thought possible.

Then, that was it. For the first time in her life, she and her son had a real family. People who understood the one thing she had spent most of her life trying to hide. They had been here ever since.

"Hey," Rosa said, getting her attention again. "I never said I wasn't concerned. You know me. I'll keep an eye on him too. But that doesn't mean we can't appreciate a good-looking man when we see one, right?" Rosa winked.

They spent the next few minutes mixing the guacamole, while Olivia told Rosa all about her encounter with Draven. She admitted that yes, he was handsome and that he had the most gorgeous blue eyes she had ever seen. But that she was also scared about what his presence might mean for the town.

"I understand your concern and I don't think you're wrong to be worried. But I want to tell you the same thing I always do: don't let the past ruin your future. I'm not saying this man has anything to do with your future. But I hate to see you hide your heart, mijita. You will miss out on so much love and happiness and you do not deserve that."

"How's it going over there?" Parker asked from her spot at the table. She was currently loading tamales into a serving dish.

Olivia sniffed and then quickly wiped away the few tears that had slid down her cheeks. Rosa always knew the right thing to say to make her feel better.

"All done here. How about you?"

"Just about finished. Jill? Mama? What about you two?"

Jill was in charge of the beans and salsa while Janella stirred a big pot of rice on the stove.

Jill gave Parker a thumbs up as Janella said, "Good to go. Just need to pour this into a dish."

Helping with dinner was probably Olivia's favorite part of their weekly tradition. There was something incredibly comforting about cooking, that she didn't really get from working in the bakery. Sure, she loved her job, but it was still a job. Cooking like this was purely for enjoyment.

There were no orders to take or customers asking questions. No handsome strangers that left her feeling hot and bothered. It was just her and her family. Plus, it was nice to have a little one-on-one time with Rosa every week, and she usually came away from the evening with a few new recipes to try.

As everyone grabbed plates of food and made their way to the dining room, Malcolm and Daniel emerged from the living room. Every week those two huddled on the couch together, swapping stories about the funniest thing that happened to each of them since last week. Malcolm's stories usually revolved around customers buying weird things at the grocery store. Daniel always got a kick out of those stories.

"Of course, the boys would show up after the cooking is all done," Jill said, rolling her eyes.

"Hey," Malcolm said, taking a seat and then pulling Jill down into the chair next to him. "I always offer to help, and you always turn me down."

"That's because you burn water."

Olivia grinned. Jill and Malcolm were perfect for each other, in the sense that they were complete opposites. He was calm and steady. She was chaos personified and they loved to tease each other about everything. Jill always called it their love language.

"Alright, you two. Enough flirting," Janella said with a smile. "Let's eat."

They had tamales and tacos with homemade tortillas. Guacamole, sour cream, and shredded cheese for toppings. Beans and rice with some of Janella's homemade salsa on the side. And to drink, there was plenty of horchata to go around.

That was the first thing Olivia grabbed. Which, of course, made everyone laugh.

"I should start making you your own pitcher," Rosa said.

"I would not be opposed to that."

"Only if I get my own too," Daniel said from Olivia's other side.

Everyone filled their plates and cups and for a while, there was only the sounds of forks scraping against glass dishes, while Daniel filled everyone in on his first few days back to school. He was thrilled with his new teacher; a friend of Olivia's that Daniel knew pretty well.

Malcolm set his fork down and cleared his throat. "Speaking of new people, I ran into that guy, Draven, in the grocery store on Monday."

"You did what?!" Jill yelled, practically climbing out of her chair. "And you forgot to mention it until now?"

He shrugged. "I guess it slipped my mind."

Jill scoffed. "Slipped your mind, unbelievable. How could something like that have just slipped your mind? So did he introduce himself to you, or did you initiate a conversation?"

"I approached him. Though I don't know why that matters."

Jill rolled her eyes. "Details always matter, Malcolm."

"Wait," Parker said, her brow furrowed. "That was probably right after he stopped by the bakery, right? How did you even know it was him?"

Olivia already knew the answer to that. "Oh, come on, Parker. You know Jill texted Malcolm as soon as she had the chance. You shouldn't be surprised. You were the one who came running in screaming about how there was a hot guy."

"Hey," Parker said. "I did not scream."

Jill laughed. "Oh, babe. You absolutely screamed."

"New people coming to town is exciting and it's not every day we get a visit from someone who looks like him. Sue me."

Rosa, who had been pretty quiet up until now, spoke up. "But not everyone is as excited as you, mi amor," she said to Parker and then turned to Olivia. "You are worried, right, mijita?"

Olivia nodded before glancing at Daniel, who was now focused on her. His own little face was now lined with worry. "But maybe we can talk about that another time?"

Rosa nodded, and then Jill spoke up again. "So, Malcolm. What did you and Draven talk about?"

"Nothing much. I introduced myself. Apologized for your behavior because I'm 100 percent sure it was warranted," he said, throwing a wink Jill's way. "Told him being the new guy would wear off eventually. Oh, and I invited him to dinner."

Parker, Olivia, and Jill all spoke at once.

"You did what?!"

"Why didn't you tell me?"

"Why would you do that?"

Malcolm just stared at the three of them, seemingly too afraid to speak. Meanwhile, Daniel was looking back and forth between all the adults with a grin, clearly delighted by the chaos.

Rosa and Janella were way too calm for Olivia's liking. Apparently, they were content to let the younger generation freak out enough for everyone. But, if she had to guess, they were both drawing their own conclusions about the situation and would discuss them once they were alone.

Olivia, meanwhile, kept glancing behind her in the direction of the front door, expecting Draven to come knocking any minute. Though he probably wouldn't, right? Surely Malcolm would have mentioned if Draven had accepted his offer.

"He turned down the invitation, Liv," Malcolm said quietly.

She turned to look at Malcolm. "He did?"

He nodded.

She was relieved. The last thing she wanted was for strangers to intrude on their beloved tradition. Besides, she could only imagine the awkwardness of the situation if anyone decided to bring up the fact that she found Draven attractive.

"Why did you invite him?" Jill asked.

"I was trying to be nice. The poor guy looked a little frazzled. I did not expect him to say yes, although he did say maybe next time, though I doubt he meant it. Now I'm thinking it wouldn't be a bad idea for me to try and get to know him. Help keep an eye on things."

"We appreciate that, Malcolm," Olivia said, smiling at her friend. Sometimes she forgot that even though Jill and Parker were her best friends, she also had Malcolm, Janella, and Rosa.

She couldn't exactly fault him for extending an invitation. Malcolm was genuinely a very nice guy. She honestly would have been more surprised if he hadn't invited Draven to dinner.

Draven showing up in town had definitely thrown her off and she really had no idea why. But looking around the table at her family, she was reminded that she wasn't alone. She never would be because they always had her back.

"Well," Rosa said, rising from her chair. "It seems like you all have the situation under control. I think Malcolm definitely has the right idea.

We need to keep an eye on this Draven. But there's no reason not to be friendly while we do it. Kill them with kindness is the right saying, yes? Now, how about some dessert?"

Everyone let out some form of a laugh as the tension in the room defused. That was one of Rosa's many talents. She was able to make people feel comfortable in just about any situation. It was her kind heart. Well, that and her cooking. It was impossible to feel anything besides happiness when you had a belly full of Rosa's food.

"Daniel, will you help me, mijo?"

He jumped up, following Rosa into the kitchen. He was always happy to be her little helper. Rosa adored Daniel. She was the grandmother Olivia thought he would never have.

A few seconds later, the two of them walked out, each carrying a plate of sopapillas, fried dough drizzled with honey. To Olivia, they always looked like puffy little pillows.

Rosa loaded two onto a plate for her with a wink. "Everything is going to be alright, mijita. You will see."

For the rest of the night, there was no more talk about Draven or dinner invitations or what his presence in town might mean for all of them.

There was only food and laughter and smiles. And plenty of leftovers.

Chapter 5

The house next door was no longer for rent. Something about that had Olivia feeling very unsettled.

The day ahead had seemed so promising when she woke up only an hour ago. The sky was clear, the sun shining brightly through her bedroom window. The smell of her apple scented shampoo tickling her nose.

A perfect day.

Until she looked out into the yard of the house next door and noticed the ever-present *For Rent* sign was missing.

She had lived in this town for six years and that house had always been for rent. Now it looked almost like new. For years, the paint was chipping and the lawn was overrun with weeds and unwanted brush, that only ever got cut if she got fed up with the eyesore and trimmed them herself. Now things looked clean and crisp.

She could think of only one person who'd be renting a place right now. The guy moved fast, that was for sure. Only one week since he had shown up in town and suddenly the house next door was rented. This could not be a coincidence. She could not have him living next door to her.

It would make it easier to keep tabs on him, but she was also concerned that his presence would only make life harder for her. Her magic was tied to her emotions and Draven was already playing havoc with hers after one short encounter.

She had not had to be this careful with her magic since before she moved here and she did not want to start again now.

Plates and cutlery flew to the table with a wave of her pointer finger and a quickly muttered *leviato*. This was the way she preferred to wield her magic. No big spells or potions. Just her power flowing through her fingertips. No orders to fill or problems to solve. It was freeing.

But today, she needed a little extra help because her mind was preoccupied with other things. Obviously.

She was getting a new neighbor. She was getting Draven for a new neighbor. She was sure of it and that could only lead to trouble.

Her stomach knotted as she finished mixing the bowl of pancake batter and turned on the burner. She set the newly washed griddle over the flame.

Then she turned from the stove to the open window and with a flick of her wrist and a *collapsa,* snapped it shut. She wanted a little fresh air this morning, but now it was getting chilly. She loved fall, loved the cold, but she hated actually being cold—something her friends loved to tease her about.

Above her, the old wooden floors of her home creaked in a familiar way. The sound calmed her nerves, as it was a signal that Daniel was up and getting ready for school.

The return of the school year routine was a welcome change, at least now that things were starting to feel settled. The first week was always a bit tough with schedule changes, hours spent indoors, and homework. But Daniel always adjusted well.

It had been a great summer, filled with days at the beach with Daniel building sandcastles and growing their shell collection. There were barbecues with her friends where she left feeling full and drowsy, sun-tired in the best way—and quiet nights out on the front porch reading her favorite romance novels.

But it was time to get back to reality. That meant homework, after-school activities, and Olivia pretending that she understood fourth grade math.

Sometimes it could be a bit exhausting. As a single mom, she always had to take on double the amount of work to provide for Daniel. She had to be both the mom and the dad. Yet, there had never been a moment when she resented that. She would rather have to work twice as hard than to have Daniel's father, Shawn, still in his life. Not when he couldn't accept Daniel or her for who they were.

Before moving here, things had sometimes seemed hopeless, as she'd stay up all night with a fussy newborn only to have to work a ten-hour shift at a crappy diner one day and attend classes the next. Financial aid paid for school, but money was scarce. Jill and a very kind older neighbor had helped out when she needed it.

Now things were damn near perfect, with no shortage of love and support from everyone around her. She was proud of the life she had built here for herself and her son.

But lately, she'd started to wonder what it would be like to have a partner in all of this? Someone who not only loved her but her son too.

Someone who could help her navigate the ever-lengthening list of trials and triumphs facing a young boy Daniel's age.

She thought she'd found that life partner in Shawn. But looking back now, she could see how wrong she'd been about that. They had met in detention during their senior year of high school, two lost kids looking for someone to love them. She with her abandonment issues and low self-confidence due to her disability and he with parents who'd always let him know how unwanted he was.

They found acceptance with each other, which was why, when he rejected her magic, it left such a mark on her heart.

At this point, finding someone she could truly love seemed like a fairy-tale. Experience had taught her that romantic love only led to heartache. No matter how much she thought they might be someone she could put her trust in, the fact that she was a witch who regularly practiced magic always held her back.

Because the one man she had shared her magic with had run for the hills and that was that. From then on, she had mostly steered clear of any kind of romantic attachment. She would not risk having her heart broken again.

"You okay, Mom?"

Hand flying to her chest, she jumped at Daniel's sudden voice, nearly spilling the batter as she poured it onto the hot griddle.

She turned to find him grinning from ear to ear, looking mighty pleased with having caught her in the act.

She shook her head, heartbeat steadying as she flipped the pancakes over. Golden brown and perfect. Thank goodness. She nodded towards the table for him to take a seat.

"I'm good—just a little distracted. Pancakes should be done in a minute. What about you? Running late as usual? Pretty sure I woke you up an hour ago, slow poke," she said, eyebrow raised.

Daniel chuckled.

She bit back a smile. It was always good to hear his laugh. It served as a reminder that he was happy and loved.

Those were things she had sworn to give her child when she had found out she was pregnant: love, stability, consistency, all things lacking in the life of a little girl whose birth parents didn't want her. So, she did everything she could to show Daniel how loved and wanted he was, even without a father figure in his life. It was her and Daniel against the world.

Her son had absolutely saved her life. From the moment the doctor had placed him in her arms, she vowed to give him the very best life possible.

That was why Draven being here caused her so much stress. Yes, protecting the town was important. But Daniel's safety came before anything or anyone else. Their life here was worth protecting, whatever it took.

"Can I pour the horchata?" he asked, already moving around to grab the pitcher from the fridge.

"Sure, you can, but be careful not to—"

"Spill. I know, Mom. I'm nine, not two."

She shook her head again, one eye on her son's careful pouring of the drink for each of them. Then he added some cinnamon on top, their special trick.

They both dug into their pancakes quickly, Olivia having served them both a stack each. She smiled as he poured on more syrup with each bite.

She had asked him once why he did that. He said each bite of pancake needed the same amount of syrup to make it taste good.

Daniel only had a few minutes before the bus would arrive. They went through this every morning. She woke him up with plenty of time to get ready and he took his sweet time about it until she was practically vibrating with anxiety.

She hated being late. Her son had no such problem.

"Do you need me to check over your homework before you go?"

"We checked it last night, remember?"

"I know, Daniel. But I also know you tend to lose things."

He was a great kid, but he would lose his head if it wasn't attached.

"I have it, mom, I promise. I put it away as soon as I was done this time."

She narrowed her eyes. "I'm choosing to believe you, bud," she said with a wink.

She had already double-checked his bag, but he did not need to know that.

The sound of the approaching school bus sent Daniel jumping off his chair to hug her tight. She immediately hugged him back, resting her cheek on the crown of his head.

"I love you, Mom."

Daniel would only be a little boy for so long. An 'I love you' from her son was one of the sweetest things.

Soon enough, they would be knocking on the door of teenage angst and rebellion. But for now, Daniel was still her little helper and biggest cheerleader.

"I love you too, bud."

"To the moon and back?"

"To the moon and back."

His eyes lit up, his mouth curving up into a smile. He sprinted from the table with his plate and glass to put them in the sink. He grabbed his bag and headed to the door at full speed.

"See you later, Mom!"

"Are you sure you have everything?" she asked, trailing him to the front door.

"Yup!" he replied as he threw on his shoes as fast as he could before one last quick hug.

"You've got your lunch?"

"Yes, Mom."

"What about your shoes for gym class? And your jacket?"

He rolled his eyes; he had learned that move from her. "I've got everything." Then he was out the door shouting a "See you later, Mom!" over his shoulder.

She waved after him at the door as he got on the bus and her heart clenched at the excited sounds of his peers at Daniel's arrival. She stood, watching the bus until it turned the corner.

The house next door caught her eye again. It didn't look like anyone was there. Now would be a good chance to look around, to see if she could figure out for sure if Draven was her new neighbor or not.

As she stepped forward to do some snooping, her phone alarm rang. Shit. She really had to get to work.

Unsurprisingly, finding a permanent place to live was the easiest part of this whole thing so far. Draven knew that people would be tight-lipped, but the folks in this town took that to a whole other level. He was hopeful that now that he had a permanent residence in town, people would stop seeing him as an outsider and maybe that would loosen their lips a bit. It wasn't exactly easy to get information out of people who were inherently suspicious.

It was made all the more difficult by the fact that he couldn't actually tell anyone why he was here. What was he supposed to say? Yes, excuse me, ma'am. Would you mind telling me, are you a witch? Do you have magic? Would you mind if I wrote an article about you? Not likely.

But things were looking up now. Only one week spent living out of a suitcase. Not bad at all.

The house he had rented was a classic Cape Cod. Everything was clean and fresh, with white paint gleaming from a newly applied coat and the yard appeared immaculate in every way. The shutters and front door had been painted a brilliant royal blue.

It reminded him so much of the cabin they visited each summer during his childhood. A little dusty and a little warn, but full of warmth. All that was missing was the ever-present smell of dirt in the air, as a result of his mother's constant gardening.

He missed that.

He glanced toward the house next to his. While he would not call it messy, the inhabitants had adorned the home with a good number of unusual trinkets. A uniquely decorated wreath hung on the front door and tiny, colorful gnomes dotted the lawn. From the front of the house, he could make out a structure in the backyard that he assumed was an ornate kind of trellis covered in vines, and way in the back in an old oak tree was a treehouse.

On top of that, the whole property was surrounded by flowers. Lilacs, sunflowers, even a few roses were all thriving and growing at a rate he could not imagine. He could have sworn a number of those blossoms weren't in season. He had learned a lot watching his mother and helping her tend to her garden over the years. Yet here they were, all in the apparent peak of bloom.

Magic. This was the first real proof he had seen. Not that he could do much with it, though. Even if his editor was someone who knew what kinds of flowers grew during what seasons, this kind of thing could be explained away easily.

She didn't exactly believe in his claims of magic. The fact that he was here at all with her blessing was a testament to his powers of persuasion.

No. He needed something bigger.

So far, he had gone out each day for the past week, visiting the local diner for dinner and stocking up on essentials at the grocery store while also trying to glean information from the locals.

Unfortunately, he hadn't learned much. Yesterday he had even stopped into the local library to peruse the archives. He was hoping to find any information about his mother's life here and maybe find out when she met his father since Draven knew he wasn't from Addersfield.

But the only thing he had found was an article declaring his mother spelling bee champ in sixth grade. Not exactly riveting stuff, but it was nice to get a glimpse of her childhood.

He did, however, stumble upon the town charter. An interesting document that talked about when the town was founded and why. As a place where magical beings, in this case, witches, could live in safety and peace. That explained why his mother would have grown up here and also confirmed that there was a lot of history in this town. Which also meant that everyone in this town should know what happened to her.

But beyond that, there wasn't much else. The constant sneezing from all the dust was hardly worth it.

In the end, he had checked out a book on the town history and settled on a bench in the park. A few random people stopped to chat. But it was all to ask him questions about himself. Where was he from? Did he like the town so far? Was he just visiting someone? Never once did he get to ask any questions that might lead to real answers for him. He tried, but his questions were always deflected. Another thing to add to his list of reasons to be suspicious.

He asked questions about the lack of Addersfield's internet presence and why the town seemed to be against the idea of tourists. Asked why people kept saying things like, "Addersfield is special." What was so special about it? But he could never get a straight answer.

But really, what did he expect? Unless he came right out and said, "Hey, does this town have magic?" He doubted anyone would be willing to tell him the truth. He was still very much a stranger here. While he could certainly eavesdrop, it wasn't like people would be randomly talking about his mother and he would just happen to overhear it. Anyway, conversations tended to halt whenever he went to any place that was crowded, as if every single person in the place was discussing him.

He was 100 percent certain they were.

Hopefully, the novelty of being the new guy in town would wear off soon. Maybe then people would be more willing to answer his questions.

But no, he needed to ask someone about magic directly. Or as directly as he could without revealing too much of his own history. He needed to talk to someone who might actually be interested in engaging in a real conversation with him—one where he wasn't the only one asking questions.

All he had so far for his story were the journal entries from his mother. He needed some concrete proof of magic. No one would believe him otherwise. He needed help and it came about in a very unexpected way.

When he had asked Parker earlier in the week if she knew of any places for rent, he had not expected to get so lucky.

The only place to rent in this town ended up being the house right next door to Olivia's, and it was perfect. She had offered to help him with his book, hadn't she? She didn't need to know the truth of it, that he would be using whatever she told him to expose the town's possession of magic.

His excitement about being her new neighbor had nothing to do with her wide brown eyes and soft smile. Or the way his chest tightened when she got that calculating look in her eye like she was trying to figure him out.

No, this was all business. He had no time for any sort of entanglements, romantic or otherwise. She was a source of information and nothing more. She looked soft and quiet, the kind of person who would want someone steady and romantic. That just wasn't his style.

It didn't take a genius to figure out why. His father left and his mother never got over it. At the time, being just ten years old, he had assumed his parents just did not get along. That maybe his dad would come back, a foolish notion he held onto for years.

But as he grew up, he realized they had been abandoned. He could count on one hand the number of times he had seen his father over the last twenty years. Eventually, he disappeared for good.

Now he knew there was much more to the story. His father wanted magic of his own. When he realized he would never have it, he left.

These thoughts swirled in his head as he settled into his new home. Unpacking was a quick process. His apartment back in New York had come fully furnished, so he was glad to see this house was the same. It reminded him of something out of a movie, as everything was covered over with big white sheets.

According to Parker, there hadn't been a tenant in over six years. This town really did not get much foot traffic.

It was all a little bizarre. How did they keep the town such a secret? More magic, maybe? He could hardly come right out and ask someone.

The house was surprisingly clean. Not much dust or spider webs to clear out. Was that magic, or just a really dedicated landlord? Would he now, forever, be questioning whether or not things were the result of magic? The thought alone was exhausting. Even the yard was well kept, the grass mowed and the hedges clipped.

The house had three bedrooms, the biggest of which he claimed as his own. It was strange. Even now, as a full-grown adult who was living on his own for more than ten years, taking the biggest bedroom was weird. It should belong to his mother.

One of the smaller two bedrooms would be his office and the third he would keep empty. He had no use for it.

His thoughts drifted to Lucas. Was it too much to wish that one day his brother might use that extra room? Or an extra room in whatever place he ended up after all this was over?

His little brother had yet to respond to a single one of his texts. He had sent one every day this past week—a few containing more pictures of the ocean. But mostly messages about how much he missed him and how sorry he was for the way things had ended up between them.

He wanted to tell Lucas what he discovered about their mother. But it wasn't something you did over the phone or through text. It was a conversation that demanded to be had in person. He owed Lucas that.

Draven could not blame him for not responding. Things had spiraled when their mother died—both of them finding it easier to simply bury their grief. In doing so, they shut themselves off from each other. Draven at least had found an outlet. He wasn't sure who or what Lucas had anymore.

Along with the three bedrooms, the upstairs housed a full bathroom. The claw foot tub gave him the creeps. He had never been a fan. Maybe his new landlord would allow him to do some updates.

The kitchen was a dream. He wasn't much of a cook, but this was a dream kitchen. Stainless steel appliances, granite countertops, a giant island in the middle of the room and a six-seat dining table. Not that he would ever need it. The living room had big bay windows and a wood-burning fireplace.

The furniture was older but well cared for, with not a single floral pattern in sight. An inspection of the outside revealed a fenced-in yard with a shed full of tools.

He hadn't gardened in years. He used to help his mother maintain the garden in the backyard of their cabin. It had been a special thing they did together, but the older he got, the less he helped. At the time, it had seemed like no big deal. There was always later. But now, he regretted every missed moment.

Every spring, in preparation for using the cabin in the summer, they would tend to the roses together, one of her favorite flowers. They'd take a trip to the local nursery, spending hours picking out the best bushes, sometimes filling an entire cart. Then the two of them would spend the rest of the day on their knees in the dirt.

Mom would explain the whole process, even though he already knew it. But he would listen with rapt attention. Lucas would be playing in the sandbox across the yard, not the least bit interested. Once the roses were planted, they had milk and cookies on the porch. That part always got Lucas' attention.

When those roses bloomed and they had settled into the cabin for the summer, he would go out and pick a few—putting them in a vase and leaving them on the kitchen table for his mother to find. She had always made a fuss, telling him how much she loved them and how pretty they were.

He missed her so much.

He glanced over at Olivia's house again. So many roses.

He could go over and reintroduce himself. But it was late morning, so she would likely be at work. He was sure she would have noticed that someone had moved in here. Did she guess it was him? If their first interaction was any indication, she would not exactly be thrilled about his presence here.

Maybe he could pay a visit to his new favorite bakery and a certain brown-eyed baker.

Chapter 6

E asily the best remedy for raging uncertainty was keeping busy.

Olivia learned that lesson early on as a kid. On the days when she would wonder why she was born the way she was. When she became angry because her legs prevented her from doing things that other kids could. She spent so much time alone wrestling with both her Cerebral Palsy and her magic, that she needed a distraction. She would focus on schoolwork or read a book. She also spent an embarrassing amount of time sitting in the New York Public Library reading fiction about magic. As if that would give her any real answers.

Now, as an adult, keeping busy meant making sure her business ran smoothly. Some days that meant balancing the books or checking the inventory. Hell, she had even spent entire days refilling napkin holders and salt and pepper shakers. But most days, like today, that meant a lot of baking.

There was nothing better than her hands in a bowl of fresh dough, the smell of yeast overtaking just about everything else. But despite being non-stop busy since the moment she arrived this morning and the concentration kneading dough took, she could not stop thinking about Draven. It was driving her crazy.

It wasn't just that she was certain he was her new neighbor. It was his very existence. She hated to admit it, but he reminded her of Shawn. Not so much in looks, probably because Draven was a grown man and she'd only know Shawn as a scrawny seventeen-year-old, but their personalities were similar.

They both had that unwavering confidence, like nothing could stop them from getting what they wanted. It scared her where Draven was concerned, because there was no way he wasn't after something. The fact that she seemed to be the only one who cared what he was up to made it that much worse. It wasn't like she didn't trust her friends when they assured her they didn't trust Draven either. But something about him made her feel like this was her problem to take care of.

Maybe it was the similarities to Shawn. Or maybe it was the way he made her feel, flustered and out of control, but also like something inside of him could relate to the lost little girl inside of her. That maybe he, like her, just wanted someone to accept him, flaws and all. Or the way he looked at her the day they met. Like he could see right through her. Like he knew her deepest desires. She couldn't get those blue eyes out of her head. Or that smile. Or the sound of his voice.

All of this made her feel awful about herself. He lied straight to her face and all she could focus on was how good-looking he was.

It was infuriating.

So last night, she had used a reflection spell. It was one that let the caster spy on a person through reflective surfaces.

Not that it had done any good. He spent most of the night in his room at the inn reading. Truly riveting stuff.

She also had Parker let her and Jill know whenever he came and went from the inn. Malcolm mentioned he'd been in the store a few times and he stopped by the bakery at least once a day. She noticed every single time he passed by the window when he didn't stop in. Parker said he'd asked her about the ocean his first day in town. So that must've been where he was headed each time he strolled down Main Street.

What was it about the ocean that drew him there every day? Was he just trying to blend in? Was he spying and visiting the beach was just a convenient excuse?

The fact that her heart always sped up whenever she got a glimpse of him was driving her up the wall. She wanted to see him, even if she couldn't and wouldn't admit it out loud. She was drawn to him and to the air of mystery that surrounded him. To that haunted look, he sometimes had in his eyes.

He was too much.

Now, he was probably moving next door to her.

As if that weren't bad enough, her feelings were causing small outbursts of magic. Mainly that the flowers in her garden out back had doubled in quantity since Monday night, the same day she met Draven.

At first, she thought nothing of it, tried to ignore it. But she couldn't keep him off her mind. It was borderline obsessive the way she was constantly thinking of him. What was he doing right now? Did he know about witches and magic? What was he hiding?

The flowers continued to bloom over the next few days, much to her embarrassment and frustration. She tried using a banishing spell, but they just kept coming back.

She just could not bring herself to confide in her two best friends. They would ask too many questions. Questions she did not even want to think about, let alone answer.

Magic was tied to emotions and hers were all over the place. It worried her. The last time she felt like this was right before she and Daniel moved here. She was restless and on edge for days. Her magic was bursting out of her at odds times, with or without an actual spell to direct it. Like her magic knew something big was going to happen before she did.

The second was when she found out she was pregnant. The first right before that, when Shawn left her. It occurred when she was to go through a big change.

It could not be a coincidence. Which meant Draven's presence in town signaled upheaval for her. It could be good; it could be bad. She was inclined to believe it was the latter.

"Well, someone is really going through it this morning," Jill said from across the kitchen, startling her from her thoughts.

She looked up from where she was currently rolling out her dough for a pie crust. She was usually meticulous and never messy, but at this moment, her station and her apron were less than pristine. Her hair was coming loose from the tie she had it in and she could feel flour tickling her nose.

"What do you mean?" she asked, but she trailed off, realizing that there was no point. In their group of friends, everyone always knew everything. Whether it was intuition or some kind of witch telepathy, they did not have secrets.

"Oh, come on, Liv. Something is happening. We all feel it, so I know you're feeling it too," Jill claimed with an air of definitiveness that Olivia did not dare contradict. There was no point. Not when Jill was absolutely right.

She was determined to keep her guard up around Draven.

Not that it mattered. There was no way anything could ever happen between them. She had no patience for secrets and lies. Especially where romance was concerned. If two people couldn't be open and honest about who they were, what the hell was the point?

She learned that lesson the hard way.

She revealed her magic to Shawn in the hopes of being honest with him so that they could have a real future together outside of high school. It was important to her to be completely honest before heading out into the world.

Thinking something small to start with would be fine; she conjured a few flowers in her hand using a spell she had made herself, *Flora*. Nothing too flashy so as to ease him into things slowly.

At first, he just stared and stared at that flower. Then he stared at her, eyes wide with shock, mouth frozen in what she could only describe as horror. Those were truly the longest ten seconds of her life.

Then he backed away, yelling and screaming, hands held out in defense. He was scared, and it shattered her heart. He ran as fast and as far as he could. A few weeks later, she discovered she was pregnant. When she tracked him down and told him, Shawn said he wanted nothing to do with their baby either.

He made that abundantly clear when he summed up who he thought she was with the single most hurtful word that was ever thrown her way: freak.

It hurt even more because he had never been bothered by her Cerebral Palsy. She thought that meant he would be accepting of her magic. But she was wrong. She was a fool and from then on, she had sworn off any kind of romantic attachment.

Of course, her friends wouldn't hear of it and pushed guys on her every once in a while. But it never amounted to anything. That was probably her fault, as she tended to keep most people at arm's length. But it was just easier that way. The fewer people she let into her life, the less likely she was to get hurt. It could be lonely at times. But it was necessary so that no one would ever be able to hurt her the way Shawn did again.

Plus, she had Daniel to consider. The family she found here was special. They were good people who loved unconditionally. But most people weren't like that and she wouldn't let Daniel feel the pain she had.

"It's okay if you have feelings for Draven, you know," Jill said, pulling her out of her head and back to the current conversation with her bestie. "Not every guy out there is like *him*, Olivia. You can't go holding what Shawn did against every guy you meet. That isn't fair."

Shit. Jill was way too perceptive sometimes.

"Shawn has nothing to do with this." She set the dough aside, pulling the mixer over and attaching the dough hook. "And I'm not interested in Draven at all. How could I be? He's a liar, Jill. No one comes to Addersfield for a change of scenery. You know how the protection spell works. How many times do I need to remind you of that?"

Jill scoffed, her eyebrow arching. "Come on, Liv. I'm not stupid. I know we can't trust Draven. I'm just saying maybe we should give him a chance to earn our trust. In the meantime, we're all being careful. But you know that something is going on. I can feel it. I know you can too and it started when Draven got to town. But you're fighting it so much that you refuse to consider that him being here could mean something good."

Olivia sighed. "I'm not fighting anything. I'm just not going to rush to the conclusion that a new guy shows up and that means he's automatically my soul mate or something. I refuse to put any trust in him until I know his intentions. Just because you've decided to like him doesn't mean I have to."

"Oh, honey, you are so in denial. You know it all means something. Why can't you admit it?"

She grabbed a bowl for the dough and slammed it down on the counter, her frustration starting to boil over. The dough went into the bowl with plastic wrap over the top so it could rise. "Draven being here could threaten the town's safety. But you're so desperate for me to meet someone you're jumping to conclusions. We're witches, Jill, and our magic gives us certain instincts. How can you just ignore them?"

"I'm not ignoring anything. We checked on the book just like you suggested. It's safe and secure as always on the altar. Parker is going to keep a close eye on it just in case and we all agreed at the last family dinner to keep an eye on him. You know that. We can spread the word around town that everyone needs to be on their best behavior. No superfluous magic," Jill said, following her as she moved out of the kitchen and to the front of the shop. "Come on, Liv. As your best friend, I can't let you deny the facts. You like him, or at the very least, you're attracted to him. There's nothing wrong with that. At least admit he's hot and I'll call it a day, a slow unproductive day, but a day nonetheless."

"Jeez, Jill. Yes, he's hot, Okay? I admit it. Are you happy now?"

"I'm getting there. But I'd be thrilled if you admitted there's something brewing between you two."

Olivia rolled her eyes. "Brewing? Seriously, Jill? That is not going to happen; I barely know the man for Christ's sake," she quipped, re-tying her apron and adjusting her hair so she was a bit more presentable. She didn't want to scare the customers away.

"You're no fun," Jill replied with a dramatic sigh.

"And you're just bored. I truly do not understand your obsession with my love life. We do this all the time. Why can't you just let it go?"

"Because Liv. You're my best friend. I love you and I just want you to be happy."

She groaned. "But I am happy, Jill. I love my life just the way it is. Since when did you start thinking I needed a man in my life to be happy? Do you not know me at all?"

"I'm not saying you *need* a man to be happy. I'm saying I think you'd be happier if you had someone to share your life with."

"You think Draven is that someone, do you?"

"No. I don't know. But maybe he could be."

"And I'm saying it's never going to happen. Next subject, please." Olivia turned, getting ready to refill the coffee pots when she had the sudden urge to glance out the window.

There, crossing the street and heading their way, was Draven.

Shit. How the hell did she always seem to know when he was in the vicinity? So much for getting Jill off the subject.

Be strong, Olivia. He's just a man. You can handle this.

But the moment the bell above the front door sounded and Draven stepped in, her resistance fell by the wayside. If this were a cartoon, there would be hearts coming out of her eyes.

He was still frustratingly good-looking. When his eyes caught hers and he offered a warm, friendly smile, her resolve weakened further. Maybe she could give him a chance.

Dammit. Why did he have to be friendly? And charming? And hot?

He approached the counter, his hands coming to grab the edge as he leaned closer to her. There was still some distance between them, but her senses were flooded instantly. He looked amazing in his dark blue jeans and long-sleeved black Henley. He smelled of mint and sandalwood. "We meet again," he said.

Damn him.

"So, it would seem. You stalking me or something?" Was this how flirting worked? She could hardly remember. She wanted to give it her best shot. No better way to weasel information out of a man than to make him think you're interested in him, right? She was flirting to get information. That was all. Not because she was actually interested in him. Absolutely not.

So, she let herself sink into the richness of his laugh and she let herself be charmed by the cute way he ran a hand through his hair in a show of slight embarrassment. She was just playing a part.

"Not exactly. I'm here for more delicious coffee and donuts."

Could this guy be any nicer? In her experience, no guy was this nice for no reason. Although she had limited dating experience, she'd been exposed to some truly cringe-worthy dudes over the years. Which meant he wanted something from her. It was possible that something was actually coffee and donuts, but she was inclined to believe otherwise for obvious reasons.

"Well, I'm happy to oblige. Your usual? Large black coffee and a glazed donut?"

Be nice. Keep him talking and maybe he'll stick around a little longer.

"Yes, please. I guess now that I have my own place, I could buy a coffee pot. But then I thought, why bother? When my lovely new neighbor owns a shop that sells coffee and stopping here every morning is easily the best part of my day."

Did he just say... Shit.

"New neighbor?"

He full-on smirked. "Didn't Parker tell you? I was looking for a place to rent and she mentioned the house next to yours was available."

Dammit, Parker. A little warning would have been nice.

"Did she really?"

"She did. It's perfect, really. Since you so kindly offered to help me with my book. Now that we're neighbors, we'll be able to chat all the time."

Smug bastard. Just when she was starting to think he might be a decent guy. He was enjoying this, putting her on the spot. He probably knew she didn't like him and was just trying to rub the situation in her face that she was stuck with him now.

Why the hell had she offered to help him? It was supposed to be a way to get him to talk to her. She never actually expected him to want her help. Especially with a book she didn't believe he was actually writing.

"It's like it was meant to be," Jill said, failing to stifle a laugh.

She cringed. Subtle Jill was not. Dammit! This was only going to make her more relentless where Draven was concerned.

He only grinned and shrugged.

"How about we get you that coffee?" she asked, silencing Jill with a glare before her friend could say anything else.

She got him his order quickly, wanting him gone as soon as possible. She needed time to think, and she could not do that with him here with his gorgeous hair, sparkling eyes, and a jaw that could cut glass. Honestly, the man was infuriating.

"Thanks. I'll be seeing you around, neighbor."

He winked before strolling out the door like he didn't have a care in the world. The bastard had actually winked at her.

Once he disappeared down the street, she turned back towards Jill to glower at her again. Twice in less than a minute, that had to be a new record.

"Meant to be, Jill? Really? I am totally going to get you back for that; you know that, right?"

Jill practically chortled with glee. "Worth it. Totally, completely worth it."

Chapter 7

O livia's new neighbor was definitely going to be a problem. Nothing she did was able to ease her mind about it.

It had been one day since he moved in and already it was like living under a microscope. What should have been a nice Saturday off was fast turning into an all-out war between her and her magic.

So much for relaxing.

Doing magic, for her, was as easy as breathing. After spending the majority of her life feeling so out of control, learning to wield her magic appropriately was such a great feeling. She had an instinct for casting and creating spells that she worked hard to hone over the past six years, and she took pride in her natural abilities.

But one day with Draven James as her neighbor and all that instinct vanished. She was like a new kid on the first day of school, a little bit lost and a lot confused. Even though she knew Draven couldn't possibly see her, every time she used magic, she felt like he was watching. It made her clumsy and flustered. Nothing was working as it should.

It started again yesterday with the flowers when she got off of work. She picked up Daniel from his after-school program and upon getting into the car, he'd picked a lily out of her hair. Then, when they got home, flowers kept sprouting from weird places. The sink, the couch. Even the bathtub. Daniel was absolutely delighted by the whole thing; she was not.

When she went out to check the garden, it was the same thing. Roses, lilies, and daisies. Daisies weren't even in season. She would not be able to explain that away should Draven happen to notice.

Yesterday, after his visit to the bakery, she kept accidentally sending random things flying around the kitchen. A mixing bowl, a whisk, flour. The latter of which ended up in Jill's face.

Of course, Jill found the whole thing hilarious. As if Olivia was doing it all purely for her entertainment. Why were they friends again?

The whole situation was completely ridiculous. No one had ever made her feel so completely out of control since that day, years ago, with Daniel's father. Draven's presence alone was dredging up too many bad memories. She had to think of a way to get this guy out of her life and out of her town and she had to do it in a way that involved as little magic as possible. She had a feeling if he got even a small glimpse of magic, he would never leave and the town would be at risk of being exposed.

But maybe that was his goal?

She agonized over it all last night, tossing and turning in bed. When she did manage to finally fall asleep, Draven was there in her dreams—looking at her with eyes that were far too sweet, whispering her name, tempting her.

She woke up feeling flushed and uncomfortable in her skin. A shower helped a little. But she'd been so flustered and frustrated about the whole thing she burned breakfast.

She checked in with Parker again about the book this morning. It was still safe and in the same place, as it always was. But she would keep checking in. Part of protecting the town meant protecting that book. She reasoned that if Draven were up to anything, the book would be the first thing he would go after.

She would have liked to put a protection spell around the area of woods the book was in. Something that prevented anyone without ties to the town from getting too close. It would need to be imbued with the blood from each of the three original witch bloodlines. But she was afraid to bring it up to her friends. The book was supposed to be accessible to everyone in town, not just those descended from the original witches. She didn't want to be the one to put an end to that.

Instead, that meant constantly nagging her friends. Sure, she could continue to spy on Draven. She could flirt with him and try to trick him all she wanted. But until he actually made a move? She had nothing to go on but her instincts.

So far, Draven had been in town for a week, and nothing had happened. She should be grateful. But his lack of action only made her more anxious, like she was just waiting for the other shoe to drop, which was what led her to her current plan.

It was her second plan of the day. The first was a deep cleaning of the entire house without the assistance of magic. But even elbow deep in lemon-scented cleaning products, the first plan was a failure.

The second plan was to go outside on this lovely fall day and get some fresh air with a book and a glass of iced tea. She'd considered doing some yard work. But with Daniel occupied up in his room with a video game, it was a great opportunity to catch up on some reading. She had fully intended to do just that until Draven wandered outside in a very tight white T-shirt and started raking leaves.

So, here she was, out on her back porch, watching him while he did yard work, completely ignoring the book she planned to read.

Not that she minded watching him. She took a quick sip of her tea and then leaned back in her chair, just taking a moment to admire the gorgeous day. Breathing deeply, she inhaled the smell of decaying leaves and wood smoke. She took another sip of tea, stretching out her legs in front of her, admiring her shiny leather boots before switching back to watching her infuriating new neighbor.

Not that it *looked* like she was watching him. She had used a look-away spell. It made the user's eyes appear to be pointed in another direction while allowing them to actually see whatever they wanted. Essentially, it was spying. And it wasn't even *good* spying.

Because every few minutes, he would glance over at her. At first, it made her nervous. Had he seen any evidence of her magic? The flowers? The explosion of dirt she had just created when her heart sped up after their eyes met for the tenth time before he quickly looked away?

The whole thing was very confusing. Her emotions were at literal war. It was exciting and maddening.

The most frustrating part? She did not hate it, his eyes on her, the way he made her feel and how she found herself wondering what he looked like underneath his clothes.

Damn him.

When she looked up at him again, he had moved, trading in his rake for gardening gloves. She wouldn't have pegged him for the type. Gardening was methodical, peaceful. At least, that's how it was for her—something she did to bring a little order back into her when life became too much.

But Draven? He screamed chaotic, albeit in a controlled type of way. The kind of person who would uproot their entire life to move to a town he claimed to know nothing about and then lie about why; not the kind of man she wanted or needed in her life. Not to mention Daniel's. Yet, here he was—her freaking next-door neighbor.

Here she was, lusting after him.

It was distracting, to say the least, watching him work. The muscles in his arms flexed as he now shoveled pile after pile of dirt, creating space for a flower bed, the rows neat and even. His grunts of exertion called forth images of their bodies tangled together. Beads of sweat glided down his sun-kissed skin.

It reminded her of the dreams she had last night. His low, rough voice whispering in her ear. His lips on her skin.

She stood from her chair, needing to stretch, needing a little relief.

Her whole body was tight. Her hands gripped the porch railing so tightly her knuckles turned white.

Fuck, he was sexy.

Her attraction to him made zero sense. The one thing she hated more than anything was a liar. Daniel's father had lied. Speaking words of love one minute and rejecting her the next.

Why would Draven be any different? Why did she even care if he was? He was a threat. Who the hell was he really?

The sooner she figured that out, the better off she would be. His very presence was wreaking havoc on her magic.

Flowers. He was potting flowers. Oh, the irony. She could not hold in her laugh.

He looked up. To him, it would look as if she wasn't looking at him but instead at nothing in particular.

Shit. She canceled the spell quickly with a wave of her hand and a whispered *revelo*. He was bound to realize something strange was going on if she was laughing at him without actually looking at him.

Her face grew hot. "Hi," she said with a small wave.

"Hey," he said, wiping sweat from his forehead.

He left a streak of dirt behind. She really wanted to wipe it off.

Focus, Olivia, focus.

She met his gaze head-on. Tension bloomed thick in the air between them. His eyes looked dark blue in this light, dangerous and captivating all at once. They locked on her with such a burning intensity that it stole her breath.

Her mouth parted softly, resting slightly agape as he waited and watched her every move. She flexed her fingers, still holding her now nearly empty glass of tea, as he slowly ran his tongue across his bottom lip.

Was he doing that on purpose? Fuck. She should probably say something now.

"Sorry. I just—I'm surprised to see you gardening, I guess."

Smooth, Olivia. Very smooth. Now he knows you were watching him this whole time.

His brow furrowed. "Why is that?"

She blushed. "Well, it's just, I don't know. You're so, you know, you."

Good God, she was an idiot. Was it possible to die of embarrassment?

What was it about him that made it so hard for her to think straight? Honestly, she was surprised she was able to form complete sentences around him at all.

He laughed. "It's something I learned from my mother, gardening. It's been years since I've actually done it. But it's really just like riding a bike."

"I'm sorry. I didn't mean anything by it."

"Hey, no worries. I see you have quite the garden going yourself."

She smiled. It was her and Daniel's little Eden. "Thanks. Daniel and I work hard to keep it up. Sometimes I think he likes it more than I do, though."

"Daniel?" he asked, brow furrowed.

Just then, the back door flew open, announcing the arrival of her excitable nine-year-old. He came around to duck underneath her arm and stand right in front of her.

She placed her hand on his head.

"Draven, this is Daniel, my son."

"You have a son?" he asked. He groaned inwardly. She just said that, he was such an idiot.

Daniel laughed. "Yup, that's me."

He laughed. "Right, obviously. Sorry. How old are you, kid?"

"Nine, going on forty. Or at least that's what mom always says."

The way Olivia smiled when Daniel said that made Draven's heartache a little. That's something his mother would have said about him. A nine-year-old who liked to garden? This kid could have been him or Lucas.

"Nine is a good age," he said. Shit. He didn't really know how to talk to kids.

"What are you doing, Draven?" Daniel asked, peering over the porch railing and into his yard.

"A little gardening," he said as he held up the trowel still in his hand.

"Cool! Can I help?"

"Oh, Daniel, I don't know if Draven wants any help," Olivia said, narrowing her eyes at him.

"I would love some help, actually," Draven said with a smile. Just like how he used to help his mother.

"You could help us if you want, Mom," Daniel offered.

Draven watched as she took in her son's wide grin; it was clear she'd do just about anything for him.

It was like he won the lottery in getting her to spend time with him. She probably wasn't thrilled at this particular turn of events. But for some reason, he wanted her to be. He liked the idea of spending time with her and her son, even if he shouldn't.

"So, what's the plan here? Are we planting flowers, vegetables, herbs?"

"Flowers. I know a little about gardening from my mom, like I said. But I'm most familiar with flowers. Now, if I remember correctly, roses need a lot of sun. Where do you think a good spot would be, Daniel?"

Daniel ran off, searching the yard for the best spot.

"Thanks for humoring him with this. Once Daniel sets his heart on something, it's impossible to change his mind. Most of the time, it's adorable. But sometimes, he can be a bit much."

"It's no trouble. I'm happy to have the help, really, and he seems pretty great."

"Do you like kids, Draven?"

He laughed. "Honestly? I haven't had much experience with them. I'm not much of a people person in general."

"Aren't you a journalist? Isn't that kind of your job? Getting to know people?"

"In a way? But you don't necessarily have to know someone in order to uncover their secrets."

"Is that what you do, uncover secrets?"

She stared at him straight on, her eyes narrowed and burning with intensity.

He shrugged. "Sometimes. Sometimes the secrets find you; you know what I mean?"

The wind whipped through the trees, sending leaves flying. She laughed, twirling around to watch them as they went. He found himself smiling too.

She looked at him again, her eyes softening. "I do, actually." She stepped closer to him. God, she was exquisite. He couldn't get over it. It wasn't just her looks that were drawing him in. It was her. The way she looked at him. The way she talked. Even the way she walked with a quiet confidence marred only slightly by a pronounced limp. She must have some kind of disability, though it didn't seem the right moment to ask her about it.

She radiated kindness. But also, vulnerability. Like she wasn't quite sure where they stood.

She turned back to him. "How's everything going so far, with your book? After the fast pace of New York, you must be bored. Nothing exciting ever happens around here."

"Oh, I wouldn't say that. An enigmatic nine-year-old offering to help me garden is pretty exciting to me. Definitely not something that happens every day."

They both laughed, glancing over at Daniel, who was still methodically searching the yard for the best spot to plant the roses.

"Hey, Mom, Draven! I found a good spot," Daniel called, waving them over from the very back of the yard.

Not giving Olivia another glance, Draven grabbed a potted rose from the pile he'd made and walked over to where Daniel stood waiting. She watched them quietly, Daniel's face lighting up as Draven talked. Her sweet boy was completely in awe of Draven.

It made sense. Draven was new and exciting. It wasn't that Daniel didn't have any interaction with male figures—he had Malcolm, after all—but Draven was so much more accessible to him now that they were neighbors. It was safe to assume that Daniel was already firmly on Team Draven.

It made her wonder how he would fare if it turned out that Draven was here to cause them trouble or to mess with their magic?

It could be very bad.

Daniel was an amazing kid. He was happy, funny, and so freaking clever. Smarter than she could ever hope to be. But that didn't mean he wasn't affected by not having his father in his life.

Over the years, and especially recently, he asked questions, and she tried to be honest. But it was hard to explain to a little boy why their dad didn't want to be in their life.

She hated the idea of Daniel getting close to Draven, only for him to disappear once he got whatever he came for. Something tickled her leg, pulling her from her thoughts. She looked down. Dandelions. Dandelions surrounded her feet.

She looked over at Daniel and Draven. They were both preoccupied with the roses. But still, her heart raced, her forehead starting to sweat.

Shit. This could not keep happening, especially not where Draven might see. She had to get her emotions under control.

When it came to doing magic, to having magic, control was everything.

"Hey, Mom! Come look at this."

She looked over at them again. Draven's head was still turned in the other direction. Hopefully, he hadn't seen anything.

She quickly vanished the flowers with a wave of her hand and a *vanitae*, sending them into the house. Then she crossed the yard, coming to stand right next to Draven.

"It looks great, bud. You guys did a really good job."

Draven looked up at her. "It was all Daniel, really. I just provided the yard space."

Daniel beamed at the praise. "Should we make some space for more stuff?"

"Daniel, I don't know if Draven wants—"

"That sounds great, kid. What'd you have in mind?"

The three of them spent the next couple of hours making space for a flower bed off the side of Draven's front porch. It turned out that the shed in the backyard had all kinds of gardening tools and even a few random packets of seeds.

In the end, the flower bed turned out pretty good and the three of them were sufficiently covered in dirt.

"I think we're just about done here. What do you think?" Draven asked.

"Yeah. I can't wait to see it once the flowers start growing. Hey Draven, did you know roses are Mom's favorite flower?"

"Is that right?"

"Yeah. Maybe once more roses grow from these ones, you can give her some."

Draven smiled down at Daniel. "Yeah, maybe."

Daniel grinned up at the both of them, before bounding off into the house to get cleaned up.

Draven turned to her, that same crooked grin from yesterday on his face. "So, tell me, Olivia. How did you end up here?"

Draven hoped the question would throw her off and given the way her eyes widened, it

had worked.

"What do you mean?" Olivia asked.

"Parker mentioned you were initially from New York. Something we have in common. I was just curious."

Tell me, Olivia. Tell me if you're a witch just like my mother was. Give me something.

"Jill. She and I met in culinary school. The rest, as they say, is history."

"So, you just decided to follow her? Why do I get the feeling there's more to this story?"

She smirked at him. He shouldn't have found that so charming. It was fun going toe to toe with her in this playful way. "Maybe there is, maybe there isn't. Besides, I could say the same thing about you. Because the thing about this town, Draven? It's special."

Special. That was one way to describe a town full of witches and magic.

"I've heard that a lot."

"Because it's true. We're a family here and we protect our family. Me, Jill, Parker. It means everything to us." Her jaw was set in a determined line, eyes hard as steel.

As frustrating as her mistrust of him was, he had to admire her for it. She had good instincts. It was exactly how he would be if the situation were reversed. Her son was lucky to have her as his mother.

"I can understand that. I'm sorry if my being here upsets you. But in a way, I'm protecting my family too."

Her eyes searched his, looking for what, he wasn't sure. But she did not press for more information, maybe sensing now was not the time. Or maybe she was convinced he wouldn't say any more than he already had.

But he had not expected to find someone here who might get him. Someone who might understand his reasons for why he was doing what he was doing.

He knew she wouldn't condone his actions and would probably try to stop him if given the opportunity. But maybe she might at the very least understand his need to make things right for his mother, to protect her legacy.

She sighed. "Well, then I guess we're at a bit of an impasse. It was nice talking to you, Draven. I should probably go."

Or maybe she wouldn't understand at all.

"Wait," he said as she turned to walk away.

He didn't want her to leave, as odd as that was for him to admit to himself, given that she obviously didn't trust him as far as she could throw him. But something about her made him feel calm. Peaceful. A feeling he hadn't experienced since before he lost his mother.

She looked up at him, eyebrow raised in question.

He sighed. But did it really matter what he wanted? That there was this connection to her? He wasn't here to make friends.

"It was nice talking to you too."

When she reached her porch, she turned back to look at him, offering a sweet smile.

Then again, maybe she felt it too? It was all very confusing. But he'd take a smile over a frown from her any day.

"Chocolate or vanilla?" she asked, taking him by surprise.

"What?"

"It's a simple question. Chocolate or vanilla?"

"Chocolate. Is there any other answer?"

She laughed a low throaty sound that stole the breath from his lungs. Fuck. She was sexy.

"Well, I'm a vanilla girl myself. But chocolate it is," she said before disappearing inside.

What the hell was that about?

He discovered the answer to that a few hours later when a basket arrived at his front door along with a note. Everything inside had one flavor in common—chocolate.

"Welcome to Addersfield, neighbor."

Chapter 8

R ight at this moment, Olivia was okay. Not good. Not great. Just okay. But considering how out of sorts she had been over the last few days and her magic still acting of its own accord, she could appreciate a moment where she wasn't making flowers sprout everywhere or flinging ingredients at her best friend.

The weather was really starting to cool down and that helped a lot. The leaves on the trees that lined Main Street were just beginning to change from green to hues of red, yellow, and orange. This was her time of year, the time when she felt most connected to her magic. It was around this time six years ago that she and Daniel had first arrived in town. She had always thought it was a sign that good things happened this time of year.

But then Draven happened. And she'd started to question that belief. It pissed her off, the fact that he could take that joy away from her.

Not even the fact that it was once again Friday did much to cheer her up. But she supposed she should count her blessings.

She had seen Draven every day this past week and each interaction was pleasant. Nice even. She was beginning to look forward to seeing him standing out on his porch or going to the mailbox every morning. Somewhere over the last week, he had become part of her routine.

That only annoyed her more. It was nearing impossible to dislike the man. He was always in a good mood and he always looked happy to see her. Even when she was glaring at him from her own porch while clutching a cup of coffee and sporting some serious bedhead, it would be so much easier if he was rude or mean or walked around with a scowl on his face. If anything, this whole experience was showing her that life would be so much easier if the evil people of the world looked the part.

They should all have one of those mustaches they could twirl around their finger.

Daniel was thrilled. To him, Draven was like a shiny new toy. Most evenings they would be on their knees in his backyard, planting flowers or vegetables while Daniel peppered Draven with question after question.

Under her watchful eye, of course.

Draven was taking it all in stride, answering every question with kindness and patience. It made her happy to see her son happy.

But each night, when she was alone with her thoughts, the fear would creep in.

Was she a bad mother for letting her son get close to Draven? Was it foolish of her to feel a little bit of joy when she saw them together?

Yes. That was the easy answer. Because no matter how nice he was to her and her son, he was still a liar and he was still hiding a potentially dangerous secret. Each time he dodged a question or wouldn't look her in the eye, she was reminded of that fact and it was that reminder that kept her spying on him.

Each night she cast the reflection spell, the guilt gnawing at her. She justified by telling herself over and over that it was for the safety of the town. The guilt did not abate. Each night she watched him read, watch TV, and write, though she never got a look at *what* he was writing. Maybe at some point, she could try and sneak a peek at it. There was no spell she could think of that would help her do this. But there had to be something.

There were so many things to consider here. The worst thing about all of it was the crippling uncertainty, that maybe Draven did not mean them any harm. That maybe the secrets he was keeping were harmless. That maybe she could give him a chance. That was the scariest thing of all. Hope.

So, in the light of day, she clamped it down, not letting the feeling take root. No matter how much she might want it to.

In the light of day, she could pretend all was well, which meant that she was feeling okay.

The problem? Jill would not let it go, the idea that Draven had now become a permanent part of their lives. She was currently bursting Olivia's short-lived moment of peace by asking the same question she had been asking for days.

"Why can't you just admit that you like him? That you feel something for him other than suspicion and wariness?"

She shook her head. "It doesn't matter how I feel. I know he's hiding something. You can't tell me you don't feel it too."

Jill sighed. "You know I do. We all do and we've told you that over and over again. But maybe, whatever he's hiding is not what we think. Maybe there's a good reason he's keeping it quiet. Everyone has a right to their secrets, Liv. I would think that you, of all people, could understand that, feeling the need to keep a part of yourself secret. Besides, he's been here two weeks now and nothing bad has happened."

"That's not the point and maybe he does have a right to his secrets. But we also have every right to make sure those secrets can't hurt us. I can't just ignore the fact that he continues to lie right to my face—any time I bring up him coming to town. Every time I allude to knowing he's not being truthful, he shuts me down. Or redirects. I can't get past that."

"No," Jill snapped, her tone growing heated. "You *won't* get past that. You won't even try because you automatically assume the worst. You said he told you he's trying to protect his family. That's something I know you can understand."

"It's not the same. This is our home, Jill. Mine and Daniel's and yours. And everyone we love. I'm not willing to risk it. Why are you?"

Jill would not look her in the eye. "Let's talk about it when Parker gets here, okay?"

They made their way upfront and to the table that was reserved on Fridays for Olivia and her friends. They always had coffee and chocolate cake. It was Parker's favorite, and they caught up on each other's lives. They talked about all the things they didn't have the chance to during Wednesday night dinners with their family.

It usually consisted of Jill gushing about how sweet Malcolm was. Parker would go on about whatever spell she'd created that week. Olivia would brag about how well Daniel was doing in school or just how great of a kid he was in general. It was just the three of them living their lives together. She looked forward to it every week.

"I swear Friday could not have come soon enough," Parker said as she pushed through the front door. She shed her coat and then grabbed a cup of coffee before sliding into her usual seat.

She and Jill took the two remaining chairs. Olivia did not waste any time.

"Alright, Jill, Parker is here now. Tell me what's going on."

Parker glanced between the two of them. "What's going on?"

Jill grimaced. "Olivia wants to know why she seems to be the only one concerned about Draven's presence in town. Even though she's totally interested in him."

Olivia glared at her.

"Sorry," she said, throwing her hands in the air. "I admit that was uncalled for."

"Will someone please just tell me?" Olivia asked.

Parker glanced at her and cleared her throat. "My abuelita had one of her feelings. About Draven. About you and Draven specifically."

Both her friends had the good grace to look guilty.

"You both knew?"

They nodded.

Embarrassment welled up inside her. It made sense now why she was the only one on edge about Draven.

Parker's abuelita was a town matriarch directly descended from one of the three original families that founded Addersfield. She had helped the three friends out a lot over the years as they took on the duties of the witches before them. She was known to be psychic, though she claimed there was no such thing. To her, they were just feelings. But everyone knew better than to ignore her premonitions. They were never wrong.

"Please don't be mad, Liv," Parker begged.

She slumped forward, head in her hands. An arm came to rest on her shoulder. The scent of jasmine reached her nose. Jill.

"Please, Liv. Just hear us out."

Sitting up, she looked at the faces of her friends. Concern. Worry. For her.

"I'm not mad. I'm just; I don't know? Embarrassed, I guess and a little upset that Rosa wouldn't just tell me this herself. I trust you guys and I know you both would never do anything to hurt me. But being kept out of the loop just brings back bad memories, you know? Reminds me of when I was the kid in school who got excluded because I walked funny. I know it sounds stupid because you guys are my best friends. But, ugh. Never mind."

Parker grabbed her hand. "Hey. It's not stupid. You're allowed to feel however you want to feel. You know you don't have to pretend with us. We felt terrible about keeping it from you and Rosa wanted to tell you right away. We asked if we could. If it helps, we were going to tell you today, I swear. We just wanted to give you some time to get to know Draven on your own."

"What did your abuelita have to say?"

"The day Draven came to town, remember how you felt?"

She nodded. "Yeah. There was something in the air that day. Like something important was going to happen."

"Right," Parker continued. "We all felt it too. That night, Abuelita asked me about you. She said she had a feeling that Draven would be important to you. That we should help you get to know him."

"That's it? She didn't say why he was here? Or what he might know about us having magic?"

"All she said was that him being here meant good things."

Good things? What the hell did that mean?

"I don't understand. Why wouldn't she have said anything when I asked her two weeks ago? Or this past Wednesday? I don't get it."

Parker leaned towards her. "She didn't want to influence your thoughts or feelings. She didn't want you to not feel how you were feeling. Just because she has these feelings does not mean it's 100 percent accurate. You know that. We don't understand it either, Liv. At least not completely. You know this kind of thing is never clear. But we do trust it. So, when we saw that you and Draven might actually be into each other, we figured we'd just let it play out. We've all been keeping an eye on him, though. We always know where he is and what he's doing."

She wanted to believe that. So far, Draven had been nothing but kind. He was respectful of her boundaries where Daniel was concerned and she liked spending time with him. He was serious, but not in a patronizing way. When she was able to make him laugh with one of her sarcastic comments, she felt so good, like maybe if she showed him some kindness, he would open up to her.

But she didn't even know if he deserved that kindness. Her heart was at war with her head. She couldn't let her guard down. She shouldn't.

And yet ...

"What about protecting the town, you guys? What about the fact that we're witches? The fact that we have magic? That sometimes we put spells in our food. And spy on people. Or how about the fact that this whole town is protected by magic? How could I ever explain all that to him?"

Jill sighed. "We don't know. Maybe you won't have to explain all of that to him. But we're just saying, if you want to try, we've got your back. We know it's only been a couple of weeks. But it just feels right, you know?

She did know. From the moment she first laid eyes on Draven, things felt right, even if she didn't want to admit it. It was like the universe was waiting for them to meet. Being a witch meant you took those kinds of feelings seriously.

"I hear you guys," she admitted. "I really appreciate the support and I will consider everything you said, I promise. But you all have to promise me, no more secrets."

They both smiled, nodding and vocalizing their consent.

Then Jill's eyes bugged out, glancing over Olivia's shoulder. "Speak of the devil," she mumbled.

Olivia turned around to see Draven walking through the door. Her face warmed. He had been coming in once a day, ordering a large coffee and a glazed donut. He was officially a regular. But was he also here to see her? The idea of it sent butterflies fluttering in her stomach.

She glanced at her two best friends. Both of them were wearing shit-eating grins.

"Go talk to him, Liv," Jill whispered.

"What? No!"

Parker leaned in. "Maybe things will feel a little different for you now that you know what my abuelita thinks. Just go and talk to him."

Or she could use the knowledge to her advantage. Her friends wanted her to give him a chance? She would. But not for the reasons they wanted. Because she still wasn't ready to admit her feelings. For now, she would stick to her original plan.

Her eyes met his as he walked towards the counter. Offering him a soft smile, she rose from her chair and walked towards him and then around the other side to take his order. Her eyes staying on his the entire time. It felt like he was saying so much with one look. Like he wanted her to figure him out.

God, she was trying.

Just breathe, Olivia. You can do this.

"You again," he joked as he leaned against the counter.

"Yup, it's me. Just the owner of this place. Your friendly neighborhood baker. Who would have thought I'd be here?"

"Who would have thought? Well, I'm here for my usual order. I've become quite the cliché," he said, shaking his head.

"Coffee and a glazed donut?"

He laughed. "Yeah. You knowing my order officially makes me a regular, right?"

"I guess it does. Well, that and the fact that you've been coming in here every morning for the past two weeks. You must really like the coffee here." She went to grab a cup for his coffee when she realized she had brought her cup of tea from the table along with her and she was still holding it. Apparently, his presence sucked up all of her brainpower.

"Among other things."

Her cheeks heated—smooth bastard. With a sheepish smile, she set the cup next to her on the counter and poured some coffee into his cup before grabbing him a donut.

"Before you go," she said as she handed him the items, "there's something I wanted to ask you." She leaned forward, resting her chin on her hand, eyes wide and beseeching locked on his.

"What's that?"

"Would you like to go on a date with me?"

She waited with bated breath for his answer. She was expecting him to say no right away. But his eyes had flicked over to the cup next to her elbow. She glanced over to see what had gotten his attention and froze.

The spoon in her cup of tea was stirring itself.

Shit.

Her other hand was fidgeting while they talked. That's what must have done it. Dammit. Normally a witch needed a spell to wield magic. But during times of heightened emotion, things could just happen. Like all the damn flowers she kept sprouting.

He had definitely noticed this. Had he also noticed all the flowers around her house? She could hardly ask him. She should have been paying more attention just now. Maybe she could just play it off.

"Draven," she tried.

His eyes snapped to hers. "Yes? Sorry, what were you saying?"

"I asked if you wanted to go on a date with me?"

His eyes flicked quickly back to the cup where the stirring had now stopped and back to her again. His eyes looked bright, almost triumphant. That was odd. She would have expected fear or surprise. She tried not to let hope take hold of her heart.

"Oh, uh ... Yes. Yeah. I'd love to. Tonight?"

She nodded her head slowly. "Tomorrow night, actually. If that works for you? Eight? You can pick me up at my place."

He grinned at her. "Sounds great. But I get to plan the evening. Is that okay?"

That surprised her. "Umm. Yeah, sure."

"I'll see you later then. Thanks for uh ..." he trailed off, holding up his coffee cup before stepping outside.

He hadn't added any cream or sugar to his coffee like he usually did. Which meant he was distracted. Shit. Maybe she'd officially scared him off for good. But then why would he have agreed to go on a date with her?

She rushed back over to the table. "Guys! Draven just saw me doing magic."

"What, how?" Jill asked, while Parker blinked in surprise.

"It was my damn tea," she said, gesturing to the now probably lukewarm cup of tea still sitting on the counter. "The spoon started stirring itself."

"Classic," Jill said, not bothering to hide her chuckle.

"Not helping, Jill," Olivia snapped. "I'm worried that I won't be able to keep things under control around him."

Jill rolled her eyes. "Oh, come on, Liv. You could totally play it off if he asks about it. Or you could use this as an opportunity."

"How do you mean?"

"Well. We all agree that Draven probably already knows about magic, right? It's the only thing that really makes sense, even if he doesn't know about the protection spell. So, this could be your opening. Like hey, Draven. I know you saw that thing with my teacup earlier. Well, I'm a witch and I have magic. Now, tell me what you know about it."

"Jill," Parker groaned. "That's ridiculous. Right, Liv?"

Olivia paused. The wording was all wrong. But the idea wasn't terrible. He seemed unsurprised by the display of magic. Maybe even excited. So maybe she could mention it on their date tonight.

"Okay," she said with a smile. "Maybe you're on to something. So, I'll tell you what; I'll feel Draven out on our date tomorrow. Try to see how he would respond if I did bring up magic. I think it'll be my best chance."

"Date!" Jill all but squawked. "You asked him out?"

"I did. For tomorrow night at eight. Though he might not show up now."

Parker grinned. "Liv, that's great. I can't wait to tell my abuelita. Don't worry! He agreed to the date even after what he saw. That means he likes you."

Olivia shrugged. "I guess that's true. Or he just wants to get close to me to make sure what he saw really happened and then he'll run far, far away."

"Wow," Jill said, her face deadpan. "Way to ruin the fun. It's going to be fine. I know it's hard. But try to see this as a good thing, okay? He likes you. So, where are you going anyway?" Jill asked. "You know, since you pulled that date out of your ass."

"I don't know, actually. He said he would plan it."

Parker looked at her, brow furrowed. "On such short notice?" Her mouth moved into a full-on smirk. "You know what? I bet that boy has been waiting to ask you out and you beat him to the punch. He probably already had something planned."

The idea made her heart flutter. "You think?"

There was that pesky thing called hope again. She could pretend that this date was all business. But in her heart, it was so much more.

"Oh, I do and I can't wait to hear all about it," Parker said, clapping her hands. "Now, let's get down to business. The Fall Festival is in just two short weeks people, and we have got a lot of work to do. How are you both doing with your lists? Jill, everything on track with the booths and games?"

"Yes, ma'am. We've got all your classics: bean bag toss, ring toss, balloons darts, and we've got face painting and the corn maze as well this year."

Parker scanned her checklist. "I'm good on decorations. Lots of twinkling lights and paper lanterns. Hay bales, pumpkins, buckets of apples, etcetera."

Olivia tuned them out. Her nerves were taking over again. She hadn't been on a date in such a long time. Never mind the fact that Draven had seen her doing magic. Even if she was kind of excited, she was also very nervous.

How was she supposed to tell Draven about her magic? Because now it seemed like she might have to do just that, if she expected him to share his secrets with her. The last time she told someone, it hadn't gone well. Maybe it was a little unfair to hold her past experiences against him. But then again, maybe not. She didn't owe him anything and where romantic relationships were concerned, life had not been kind to her.

But she also wanted to be prepared for anything. So, she had to consider every angle here. Like, did knowing what Rosa said really cancel out the fact that they still weren't sure what Draven was doing in town and what he might be up to?

Probably not.

But she did like him, more than she was willing to admit. She was sure he liked her too, and Daniel. Why else would he have spent every night during the past week with the two of them?

Her head said it might be the world's best cover. Her heart whispered something else. She just had to decide which one to listen to.

"Olivia, did you hear what I said?" Parker asked.

"I'm sorry, what?"

She laughed. "I asked how things were going with the food?"

"Oh, right. Sorry. Guess I spaced out for a minute. Food. Well, everyone from the diner will be there to help out. I spoke to Emily and Ian a few days ago. It'll be just the basics though: burgers, hot dogs, corn on the cob, and chili too, I think?"

Jill chimed in. "Yeah, I've been coordinating with them. We'll have all of that. I'll be making my cider donuts too. We'll also have cookies, brownies, and cupcakes."

"How about on your end, Liv?"

"All good. I'm making all of my best stuff. Churros, horchata, Mexican hot chocolate, and Janella said she would get me her recipe for pan dulce."

"Oh, I have it right here," Parker said, sliding a sheet of notebook paper over to her.

"Perfect, thank you. This will be my first year making them. I hope I do them justice."

"I'm sure they're gonna taste great. Mama is happy she doesn't have to do it this year. Alright, that takes care of the festival part," Parker said, smiling. "Let's get to the fun part."

Jill laughed. "You're like a kid in a candy store."

"What? Come on; this is our big event. Of course, I'm excited."

Parker pulled out her family's spell book, taking a minute to find the correct page. While the big spell book, the one that helped fuel the town protection spell was kept on the altar, families tended to keep books as well. Olivia even had her own.

They all knew the spell and ingredients by heart. But they always double-checked everything each year just to be safe.

Jill pointed at the words. "Here's what we need: dried lavender, red rose petals, rose thorns, rosemary, sage, hawthorn berry, sea salt, bay leaves, black pepper, a white-sand shell, five clear quartz crystals, and the blood of a witch."

"Who's turn is it this year?" she asked.

"It's your year, Liv," Parker said.

"Oh, joy. Lucky me."

It was only a small cut, just enough for a few drops of blood. Not a big deal. She just wasn't a fan of blood.

"Don't worry, it'll be quick," Parker said, patting her on the back.

"Anyway," Olivia said, not wanting to dwell on it. "I've got the red rose petals and thorns covered. The damn things won't stop growing. Oh, and the shell. I'll pinch one from mine and Daniel's collection."

"I'll get the quartz crystals from my abuelita," Parker said. "Also, the hawthorn berry, bay leaves, and black pepper."

Jill chimed in next. "I've got dried lavender and sea salt."

"Guess that leaves rosemary and sage," Parker grimaced. She hated picking things from her garden. She had an expert green thumb, but she hated picking things.

"I'll trade you," Olivia said. She was only half kidding.

Chapter 9

As Friday bled into Saturday, her anxiety grew and grew. It was a cloudless and calm day. Not at all a reflection of the way Olivia was feeling inside, where worry roared and gnawed at her gut, leaving her feeling very unsteady.

What the hell had she been thinking, asking Draven out on a date? She was an idiot, a complete idiot.

A million different thoughts were rolling around in her head. She had almost marched over to his house on several different occasions to call it off, but given that seemed a little over the top, she found herself dragging Daniel down to the bakery, to rant to Jill. Because what else were best friends for?

It was times like this, that she was most grateful for this small town's walkability. Because even though she couldn't drive, her best friend was no more than a few minutes away.

"In the kitchen, Liv," Jill called out to her when she called hello.

Olivia faced her son. "Daniel, I need to talk to Jill for a few minutes." She turned to lock the door and flip the open sign to closed. "Front door's locked, so we shouldn't get any customers. Maybe you could refill the napkin holders while you wait? You know where everything is. I'll be in the kitchen if you need anything, and I won't be long."

"Okay, Mom."

"You're the best, bud," she said as she planted a kiss on the top of his head.

He truly was the best kid a mother could ask for.

Rounding the counter, she pushed through the door to the kitchen, searching the space for her bestie.

Jill was standing at the table, elbow-deep in dough. "Hey. I was just getting started on the bread dough for tomorrow. It's been pretty slow today, so I thought I'd get a head start and then maybe close up early. What are you doing here?"

"I have to cancel my date."

Jill's hand slipped, sending flour into her face. Coughing, she sputtered out, "I'm sorry, what?"

Olivia started pacing. "I have to cancel this date. I can't believe I did this. Jill, what the hell do I do?" She paused, glancing up at Jill. "Uhhh, you have dough in your hair."

"Oh, screw this," Jill muttered as she tried in vain to wipe bits of dough and flour from her skin and hair. With a wave of her hand and a *spick and span,* she sent the entire mess off her and into the garbage can. This spell in particular was a favorite of pretty much every witch in town. It was hard not to use it for every little mess. Then she set the rest of the dough to kneading itself with *Rollo.*

Some spells were incredibly complicated, where others were comically simple. That didn't make the latter any less useful, though.

"Desperate times," Jill said as she focused back on Olivia. "Why do you want to cancel the date?"

"Huh?" She was mesmerized by the self-kneading dough—anything to distract herself from the current situation.

"Focus, Olivia. Why do you want to cancel the date?"

She grabbed a strand of her hair and started twirling it around her finger. "Oh, right. I uh—it just feels so awkward. I'm still not sure how I even feel about the guy. On the one hand, he's super hot and I like the way he is with Daniel. When I talk to him, I feel like he really sees me. Yeah, he's flirty and a bit cocky, but he also has these moments of vulnerability. Like when he talks about gardening and his mother—he's a totally different person. I know this probably sounds weird because I barely know him, but it is what it is. On the other hand, he's lied to me repeatedly and I have no idea if I can, or should, actually trust him. Plus, I haven't been on a date in years. What the hell do I do?"

Jill simply stared at her for a moment. "Oh my God, first of all, Liv, you need to calm down. Just please, take a breath."

She stopped pacing and followed Jill's advice. She then exhaled while Jill watched. She did feel a little better.

"Alright. Now that you're a little more relaxed, I feel like I can say this. You like him. I knew it. I knew you liked him. I knew it, I knew it."

Her best friend was an actual child.

"What, no. I do not. I don't like him. I asked him out so I could grill him about his intentions. Not because I want to French the guy."

"Fine, fine. Whatever you say, I know you're lying. You can't have your cake and eat it too. If you really want to find out what's going on, you can't cancel. So, go. Go beat him at his own game. Go on the date and get that boy on his knees."

"Geez. Do you have to make it sound so nefarious?"

"Nefarious?"

She rolled her eyes. "Daniel learned the word in school this week, so he's been using it a lot."

"I'm not saying make him fall in love with you or anything. Just use the date to see what you can find out, like you said."

Olivia went back to pacing. "I mean, that was my plan. I'm just so damn nervous."

Jill turned around to check on the dough. She switched back to kneading with her hands. "Liv, can I ask you a question?"

Olivia stopped pacing again. "Yeah?"

"You say you don't like Draven. You keep reminding me of that every chance you get. But if that's true, then why are you really so nervous about this date?"

"The truth?"

Jill nodded. Concern beginning to cloud her eyes. "Of course."

"It's been nice, spending a little time with him every day, as I said. I guess I just feel really embarrassed about that. When I got the idea to ask him out and he said yes, there was a part of me that was excited. How messed up is that? I started thinking maybe he was just a normal guy who liked my son and me."

"But you don't think that's true?"

"I think he could be both. Maybe he does like me and he does like Daniel. But maybe that's also a way to get me to tell him what he wants to know. But maybe, just for tonight, I want to pretend it's not. Maybe I just want to feel normal for once in my life."

She was on the verge of tears now. She just wanted something normal. But even this wasn't that. Even if they did like each other, she was certain that both she and Draven were using each other. Still, was it so wrong to want to make the most of this, to spend some time with an attractive, charming man?

"What does your magic tell you?"

She closed her eyes, just feeling her magic pulsing inside of her, like a second heartbeat.

"It's been all over the place since Draven arrived in town. Earlier today, I started sprouting flowers again and I'm worried Draven could have seen something. Plus, the thing with the spoon yesterday. I don't know how he'll feel if I do decide to tell him. That's what scares me the most, I think. The uncertainty. What if letting myself get close to him is a mistake? But the other part of me thinks getting close to him will be the best thing I ever do. I guess what I'm trying to say is that I don't know. I don't know what my magic is trying to tell me because my magic is an extension of myself and I don't know how I feel."

"You want to know what I think?"

"Always."

"I think whatever is happening between you and Draven is good. Or at least it's going to be. We all think so. I understand why you're scared. But I think if you just let everything go for a moment, you'll see."

She walked over to Jill, pulling her bestie in for a hug. "Thank you. You always know just what to say to make me feel better. I really appreciate it."

"Anytime. Now go," Jill said, pushing her away. "I know that you might not think you should. But try to have a little fun. For me."

She rolled her eyes. "Alright, I'll try, I promise. Oh, by the way, can you—"

"Yes. I'll watch Daniel tonight."

"You're the best," she called out as she pushed through the door back to the front of the shop.

"Don't I know it," Jill said as the door swung shut.

Fretting over what to wear had never been Olivia's style. As both a kid and an adult, she had never had that inclination to linger over her fashion choices. Not just because she had never had much in the way of a wardrobe, as she always preferred T-shirts and jeans, but because it had never seemed practical to her. Did it really matter if she chose a black dress over a red one? Or flats over a sensible heel at the end of the day?

Yet, here she was, staring into her closet, completely at a loss and desperate for something appropriate to wear tonight.

It was her own fault, really. She'd asked Draven out completely on a whim, with no thought for what that actually entailed. It was pure luck that he'd offered to plan the evening. Now, she had absolutely nothing to wear. He couldn't exactly help her with that.

"Come on, there's gotta be something in here," she muttered as she looked through the few dresses she owned. They were all nice but way too formal for a date. One was the bridesmaids' dress she'd worn for Jill's wedding, for Christ's sake. Everything else just didn't look nice enough.

The whole thing was even more frustrating when she considered that it probably didn't even matter what she wore. Because she still couldn't convince herself that he really might like her and that it might be okay for her to like him.

Just as defeat was about to wash over her, a dress in the back of her closet caught her eye. It hadn't been there a few seconds ago. It was a deep purple, one of her favorite colors. A halter dress with a sweetheart neckline and skirt that flared out at the bottom. The kind of dress that looked both cute and comfortable. Exactly her style.

But how the hell had it ended up in her closet? She couldn't remember the last time she went shopping.

Then it hit her. *Jill.* She had probably magicked it to the back of Olivia's closet, knowing she wouldn't have had anything to wear.

She quickly stripped down and put on the dress. Not only did it fit perfectly, but it felt so good on her. She felt beautiful in it. And it was comfortable. She appreciated that. The last thing she wanted was something stiff and formal. She found sensible but cute flats on the floor beneath where the dress was and smiled. She could only wear closed-back shoes with a comfortable arch thanks to her Cerebral Palsy and Jill knew that.

Thinking back on all her past experiences when it came to dating, she honestly could not recall a moment when she had ever felt like this. Nervous and anxious, but also excited, with butterflies beginning to get the best of her, filling her with restless energy that had no outlet.

It was all so very confusing, given her very ridiculous feelings about Draven. But she also did not hate the feeling.

It was like being a teenager again, when you found out the person you liked felt the same way about you, followed by those quick moments when you would catch a glimpse of them in the hallway or in the cafeteria during lunch.

But on the few dates she had been on as an adult and even when she was seeing Shawn, there was more excitement at the idea of not being alone than excitement about the man himself. That probably should have been a sign for what was to come.

Leave it to her to feel this way about someone like Draven. Someone who could not be trusted. The phrase "We always want what we can't have" came to mind.

Once the dress and shoes were on, she checked her appearance in the full-length mirror hanging on the back of her door.

She had done a full face of makeup, primer, foundation, blush, eyeshadow, everything—very different from her usual swipe of mascara and lipstick; looking at herself, there was a sparkle in her eye that hadn't been there in a very long time. She didn't want to acknowledge why that might be.

She grabbed a wrap from her dresser drawer just in case she got cold. She had fifteen minutes to spare and she was restless. Grabbing her keys and purse, she perched on the couch, her knees shaking with nerves. It had been a long time since she had been on a date, let alone a date that was really more of a reconnaissance mission. The whole thing was starting to feel very real.

Should she kiss him? Hold his hand? How far was she supposed to push this? It's not like doing those things would be a hardship. But she did not want to give him the wrong idea.

There was so much riding on the next couple of hours and by the end of the night, everything would be so different. Whether that would be a good thing or a bad thing, she could not say.

In the last hour, she had gotten texts from both of her friends wishing her luck tonight. They wanted her to have a good time.

She jumped at the sound of a knock at the door. She rushed to open it, finding Draven on the other side. He was dressed in black slacks and a dark grey button-down, with a black leather jacket to complete the look. She laughed when she spied his shoes.

"Converse?"

There went his hand, straight to the back of his neck. She definitely made him nervous. She found that endearing.

"Ha. Yeah. I was going for a dressy casual vibe. I like Converse so..."

"Well, mission accomplished. You look great."

"And you look stunning, Olivia."

She could have sworn his eyes darkened as he gazed at her. Damn that sexy voice of his.

"Thank you. So uh, should we get going?"

"Absolutely. But first—"

He pulled a bouquet of roses from behind his back. She could not stop the laugh that bubbled up.

"Sorry," she said, her mouth turning down into a frown at the hurt that flashed in his eyes. "I don't mean to laugh. It's just—I can't believe you brought me roses."

"I couldn't help myself," he said, now laughing along with her. "Unfortunately, these are store-bought and not fresh from my garden. But I hope you can appreciate them all the same."

"I do. Thank you, they're lovely. Daniel will be thrilled to know you took his advice."

"Glad to hear it. I definitely owe him one for the good tip."

She laughed again. Draven owing Daniel a favor might seem like no big deal to him. But she knew Daniel would probably milk it for all it was worth. "Do you want to come in while I grab a vase for these?"

"Sure," he said as he stepped over the threshold, closing the door behind him.

She motioned for him to follow her to the kitchen. She could feel his eyes on her every step of the way. Not in a creepy way, but a different way than she was used to. She wasn't used to having strangers, or almost strangers, in her house—especially male strangers.

Having Draven in her home, even for just a few minutes, was a huge step for her.

She went over to a cupboard next to the stove, pulling out the vase that Daniel had made for her two years ago. Well, made was a stretch. His teacher purchased the vase, one for each student, and he had painted the vase in art class, proudly presenting it to her at Christmas time. She loved it and he would get a kick out of her using it for Draven's flowers.

"You grow herbs in here too?"

She turned, seeing Draven eyeing her small collection of tiny seed pots on the windowsill.

She raised a brow at him in question.

"I noticed you grow some out in the garden as well."

"Oh, right." Of course, he would notice little things like that. Wasn't that what journalists did? Noticed things? She really shouldn't have been surprised that he noticed what she did with her tea yesterday. Was he going to bring that up now? "Well, I like to have the ones I use most often nearby."

That was only half true. But he didn't need to know that.

"For cooking?"

She turned on the sink, filling the vase with a little water. She placed the roses inside and moved to set them on the table. "Among other things."

"Such as?"

Why was he so curious about the herbs she grew?

"Oh, you know. Sage for cleansing. Lavender for luck. That kind of thing." As well as a pinch of each herb here and there for different spells. But again, he didn't need to know that. "Alright. Flowers are all taken care of. I'm ready when you are."

He glanced again at the herbs, before leaving the kitchen and making his way back down the hall. This time, she got to watch him. Could he feel her gaze the way that she could his?

She made a quick pit stop in the living room for her purse, keys, and wrap, then joined him at the front door. He simply stood there for a moment, watching her with his intense eyes. The air was thick with tension. The kind that made her eyes drop to his lips. Her sharp intake of breath sounded so loud in the near silence as his tongue darted out to lick his bottom lip.

She cleared her throat, effectively breaking whatever spell they'd just been under. "Where are we going?" she asked as they made their way out the front door and onto the sidewalk.

But he only smirked and shook his head. "Nice try, but I'm afraid that remains a secret, at least for now."

He led her to his car, opening her door as a proper gentleman would. It was incredibly foreign to her, the politeness and good manners. In the past, her previous dates had almost always arranged to meet up somewhere. If they did walk her to her door afterward, it was because they hoped to be invited in.

"Daniel seemed okay with all of this," he said, gesturing between the two of them as they settled back into their seats.

She smiled. When she told Daniel that she and Draven were going on a date, he was ecstatic. "'Okay' is putting it mildly. He's over the moon. He likes you a lot."

"He's a great kid."

"Thanks. I'm kind of crazy about him."

"It shows," he said as they hit Main Street.

"What about you? No kids?"

This was date-like talk, right?

"Afraid not. I've always been more focused on my career. Never really had time for any of that."

"Any of that?" she asked, glancing over at him.

"You know, a wife and kids. The nice house in the suburbs. That kind of thing."

She laughed, shaking her head at him. "Your ideas seem a little antiquated. You don't have to be married to have kids and who the hell says you have to live in a suburb? A cute little New England town works just as well, in my opinion. Call me cliché, but I see no reason why someone couldn't have both a promising career and a family if that's what they wanted. I mean, look at me."

He cleared his throat. "I apologize. I didn't mean it that way. I think you have a great thing going here with Daniel. I guess I just chose to give all my time to my career."

"Would you say you're good at your job?"

He laughed. "I'd like to think so, yes. Or at least I would hope so, considering all I've put into it over the years."

"How long have you been a writer?"

"Gosh. Since I was a little kid, I'd write short stories and make my mom read them with me. I was on the paper in high school. I studied journalism in college and then got a job at a smaller paper. I worked my way up, and now I write for one of the bigger papers in New York."

"Right. I remember you said that. Is that why you're able to be here now, working on your book? Because you're just so good at your job?"

"Among other reasons," he said, eyes fixed firmly on the road ahead.

Just when he was actually starting to open up to her, he would shut down again. What else was he hiding? If he was so set on keeping her at arm's length, why did he agree to go on this date? He was so frustrating. How was she supposed to get to know him this way?

Maybe if she kept talking, he would too. "I was never much for reading newspapers. So, I'm not sure I would have read any of your stuff when I did live there."

He huffed a laugh.

So much for that idea. Her eyes shifted to the window, watching the world go by in a blur. She was so used to walking everywhere, that sometimes being in a car could be a bit disorienting. But focusing on other things helped. It was a lovely night with a clear sky save for a few wispy clouds. The kind of night she loved. The moon looked full and bright. If she were home right now, she'd probably be curled up on the porch with a book, her fuzzy socks on her feet, a blanket on her lap, and a mug of Mexican hot chocolate in one hand.

She was such a homebody that it was weird to actually be out at night.

"This is a destination date?" she asked as they passed the sign saying they were leaving Addersfield.

Honestly, when he said he would plan the evening, she'd expected dinner at the local diner.

"Yes, but we're not going far. I thought it might be best to try something away from too many nosey friends and neighbors."

Thank God. It wasn't that she wanted to be far from home, per se. But she and Draven had been a topic of gossip for days thanks to his daily visits to the bakery. She could only imagine how much more fodder the town would have if their first date was some kind of public spectacle.

Jill would have been front and center for the whole thing.

"Has anyone ever told you you're a genius?"

He laughed. "I wouldn't go that far. I just wanted the evening to go well. I figured we'd have a better chance if we didn't spend the whole night on display."

They sat in silence the rest of the way. She didn't know what to say to that. It was surprisingly thoughtful and it showed that he paid attention to her wants and needs.

But it was also confusing. It's not like she expected him to suddenly be honest with her just because she'd asked him out on a date. He had to have an agenda, right? He couldn't have actually just wanted to take her on a date.

She thought about what Parker said yesterday, that he'd probably been wanting to ask her out for a while.

He probably knew that she knew he was hiding something. So maybe this date was just a convenient excuse to get inside her head. The man was a freaking journalist, for God's sake. It was literally his job to get information out of people. He'd said it himself.

Maybe she should just cast a truth spell on him and be done with the whole damn thing.

But no. She could not do that. She would not do that. They only used their magic for good and in cases of self-defense or defending others. Absolutely no magic for personal gain. Apart from the occasional household chores.

Could she really blame him for using a date as an excuse to get closer to her? She was doing the exact same thing to him.

Twenty minutes later, they arrived in front of Manor House. This was a relief, because having a disability meant that she was sometimes limited in her activities. Anything that required good balance or walking long distances was difficult. This she could definitely handle. But there was also a trickle of dread. This house was the embodiment of Addersfield town history. If Draven knew about it, maybe he really did know more about the town than he had let on so far. Or, at the very least, being here might lead to him asking a lot of questions.

"How do you know about this place?" she asked as he pulled open her door.

"I do now, thanks to a little research and a chat with a certain grocery store owner. I take it you've been here before?"

She nodded, her gaze returning to the structure before them.

Manor House was the home of the town founder, Melissa Adler, a witch who, along with her husband and children, had fled persecution after the Salem witch trials. After Melissa passed away, her children left the home to the town's historical society. Though she had never been inside, she, Daniel, and her friends visited the grounds often.

He left her for a moment, going around to the trunk to pull out a few things.

"I thought maybe we'd have a picnic here on the lawn and then take a walk on the beach," he said as he joined her again.

"Sounds great. I have trouble with my legs, so it's nice to be somewhere familiar to me." She paused, waiting for him to start asking questions. Instead, he just smiled and started walking.

Maybe he was trying to be polite. She wasn't really used to that. Most people stared when they first got a glimpse of the way she walked or when she brought up her disability for the first time.

She didn't believe for one second he hadn't noticed. But if he was giving her some time before broaching the subject, she could certainly appreciate that.

When they reached the house's front walkway, he stopped, took her hand and raised it to his lips to kiss it gently. The action was so intimate it set her heart fluttering in her chest.

He was smooth; she had to give him that.

Chapter 10

Taking Olivia on a date was a means to an end, or so he told himself. She was the best chance he had of getting this story. He'd been planning to ask her soon, which had nothing to do with how much he enjoyed spending time with her this past week. So, when she asked him, he hadn't even thought about it before saying yes.

He had seen what she'd done with her teacup and the spoon. At least he was pretty sure he had. Something so small and sudden, he at first wanted to convince himself it was all in his head. Because, honestly, as much as he believed that magic was real, actually seeing it happen was something that still scared him.

A spoon stirring itself wasn't supposed to be possible, even if he had always wanted it to be. If he hadn't already been looking for something like this, he would have rationalized it away.

The question now was how did she do it? Was it a one-time thing? Was she the only one? Was it magic, or was there some weird explanation? He had to be sure. This was the break he was looking for. Because so far, all he had written of his story was a catchy headline. Not exactly the exposé he was hoping for.

But seeing her dressed up and looking so genuinely happy was bringing on the guilt. Because maybe she thought this was so much more than what it really was. Maybe that bothered him more than he wanted it to.

He would give anything to know for sure why she asked him out. But asking her meant she might do the same and he didn't know how to answer honestly.

Being here with her tonight felt good. So much so that he almost wanted to blurt out the truth. But, at the same time, he didn't really owe her anything. He was here to do a job and she was the best way to get what he wanted because so far, she was the only one he knew for sure was a witch.

He had no idea what to do.

They laid out the blanket he brought along and set about unpacking the picnic basket he had put together. It was nothing fancy, just food from the local grocery store. Chips, hummus, a cheese board, some fruit, and a special surprise for her.

She burst out laughing when he pulled out the desserts and drinks—the special surprise.

"Churros? And horchata to drink? You stopped by the bakery, didn't you? Jill failed to mention that when I saw her earlier."

"Ah, that's my fault. I asked her not to say anything. I wanted to surprise you. Plus, I've never had horchata before, so I thought now would be a great time."

She smiled. "Oh, well, you're in for a treat. I didn't actually know that I was Mexican until I was eighteen and got a look at my file from the foster care system. I guess no one thought it was important enough to mention."

Shit. The foster system? It sucked that he didn't have a dad growing up, but at least he had his mom and his brother. "I had no idea. I'm so sorry, Olivia."

She shrugged. "It's okay. It's not something I like to talk about. It's in the past now, you know? Anyway, the food is definitely one of my favorite things about it."

"What else do you like about it?"

"The strong sense of family. I never experienced that before, obviously. But Parker's family is also Mexican, so I've picked up a lot from them. They helped me to feel more connected to that part of myself and I've tried to instill that sense of family in Daniel."

She smiled and then turned to grab one of the horchatas.

For a moment, he simply admired her as she quietly sipped her drink while staring up at the night sky. The moonlight cast an ethereal glow and the sound of the waves from the nearby ocean was a comforting melody. She was beautiful and kind, and a damn good mother.

He had no right to want her this much. Seeing her like this, so at ease. The feelings he pushed away since the moment he first laid eyes on her were suddenly there in front of him, begging to be acknowledged. He wanted to tell her. To be the one to put a smile on her face.

He grabbed her hand closest to him on the blanket. Her eyes locked onto his.

"You've done a great job with Daniel. The family you've created for yourself here, well, it's certainly something I envy. It reminds me of my mother. She raised my brother and me alone, but she always made sure we were loved. Even without my dad in the picture, I never felt like I missed out."

It was still so difficult to talk about his mother.

"She died six months ago."

"Is she why you came to town?"

He should just tell her. She might understand—at least part of it.

He nodded. "Yes. My mother never went far from home. Not after my dad left us; I think she wanted to stay where he left her in case he ever came back. I wanted to venture out the way she never could."

Not exactly a lie. But definitely not the truth. What would his mother think of his motivations? He could pretend that he was doing this for her, in a way. But being here with Olivia now, letting her see this part of him? It was one of the more selfish things he had done in his life. That's what his mother would say. He should at least admit that to himself.

"She sounds like she was an amazing person."

He smiled. "She was. But enough about me and my sad story. Tell me about you."

For a moment, he could swear there was fear in her eyes, but then it was gone.

"Oh, well, there's really not much to tell. I'm a mom and I run the bakery."

She stood up from the blanket, straightened out her dress, and reached down to pull him up beside her.

"Let's go for a walk," she said.

Was she nervous?

"Uhh, okay, sure."

The night air had become chilly, but not unbearably so. He had an extra blanket in the car, should they need it.

But she was only in a dress. She stood with her arms wrapped around herself, shivering. Wordlessly, he pulled off his jacket, handing it to her. She accepted it with a grateful smile.

"Sorry. I didn't even think to give you a heads up that we'd be outside," he said.

She laughed. "That's okay. I kind of sprung the date on you. I should have grabbed something warmer than a shawl. I'm always on Daniel to bring a sweater everywhere. Apparently, I forgot my own advice tonight. Thanks for the jacket."

"It's my pleasure. You don't have any other family?"

He could have kicked himself. Smooth, that definitely wasn't. But he felt this almost desperate need to know everything about her. Maybe because he felt a connection, their complicated pasts. He wanted to understand her. To see her and be seen by her.

She shook her head. "None but the family I've made here. But I'm lucky. They accept all of me. My disability, my background, and all the other parts of me."

"What about Daniel's father? If you don't mind me asking?"

"No, it's fine. Shawn just wasn't interested in being a dad and, well, there were things about me he couldn't handle. So, he's never been in the picture. I do my best to make sure Daniel feels that absence as little as possible."

"Seems like you're both doing alright for yourselves. I know what it's like to have an absentee dad and a mom trying her best. You should be proud."

She blushed. He wanted to place his hand over that spot on her cheek, to feel the heat of it against his palm.

"Thanks. I do have help, though. From Jill and Parker and everyone here, really. Life is easier here. Not just for raising my son but also for managing my disability. I mean, I'm sure you noticed my legs, the way I walk, and my lazy eye. I swear I'm always making eye contact with you, even though it looks like I'm not," she said with a laugh.

She seemed nervous. His heart ached for her.

He nodded. He had noticed and he was curious. But she would explain when she was ready. It didn't change the way he thought about her. As for Daniel's father not being in his life? The kid did not seem any worse for wear.

"I did notice. I think your eyes are gorgeous and neither of those things seem to slow you down. Can I ask? What is it that you have?"

She laughed. "I have Cerebral Palsy. While I've learned to live with it, it slows me down occasionally. Mainly it affects my balance. I need to always use a railing on stairs and I'm more likely than most to slip on ice in the winter. But I'm still a regular person, you know? Just living my life."

A beat passed, and the air between them grew thick with everything they were both leaving unsaid, the good and the bad.

He hadn't expected the way she opened up to him. He'd prepared for suspicion and deflection, as she had to have some idea of what he was really doing here. Maybe she knew about his mother? Or at least had some idea of his connection to the town. But then, what did she hope to gain by humoring him like this? Was she trying to do to him what he was trying to do to her?

Were they both in an endless cycle of trying to catch the other one out?

By now, they had reached the edge of the lawn surrounding the house. There were two directions they could go. One was the beach and the other a tree-lined path towards the gardens.

"Where to next?" he asked.

She hesitated at the crossroads for a moment before silently bending down to take off her shoes. That was all he needed. His shoes and socks were pulled off and they were out on the sand.

"Daniel and I have a tradition," she said as they moved towards the water, taking in the view. "Every time we come here we have to find a shell to bring back home."

"Any particular kind we're looking for?"

"Nope. Any shell works, but it has to be whole. That's the only rule."

"I take it you've been here many times. How big is this collection you two have?" His focus split between looking for a suitable shell and gazing at Olivia. Her hair fluttered in the wind, sending the sweet scent of roses and vanilla his way.

"Oh, we've got dozens of shells at the house. We come here a lot. It's always been a special place for Daniel and me."

"If you don't mind me asking, what is it that makes this place so special for you specifically?"

She laughed before bending down to pick up a purple shell that, while almost pristine, had the tiniest chip on the upper rim. She tossed it back to the sand gently.

"This was one of the first places Daniel and I ever came to when we moved here. It was a week after we got to Addersfield. Let's just say I was overwhelmed by the town and the neighbors and the general aura of happy, open, well-adjusted people. Definitely not like most of the people I knew. Definitely not like me. Everyone here just seemed so content I mean, I know everyone has problems. But in a town like this, the biggest crisis is when the grocery store runs low on vegetables."

He could understand that. He had never experienced a tightly knit small-town community and had been taken him aback when he first arrived in town. He could only imagine what it was like for her to try and assimilate.

"I wanted to believe that Addersfield could be the kind of place Daniel and I needed after relocating from the life we'd had before. Still, I needed proof that if we did this, everything would be as good as people said it would be."

"You're one of those seeing is believing people, I take it," he said.

"How could you tell?"

"I can recognize the signs. In my line of work, you have to see the evidence before you jump to a conclusion. You can't craft the story to suit your tastes. You need every piece of the puzzle to be certain of anything."

"Exactly. My first instinct is always to distrust. I wanted so badly to place my trust in something that would not let me down for once. But I was struggling."

"What ended up changing your mind?"

"Daniel. We came here and he was so happy. It was like Christmas for him, between the beach and the telescopes. I could not understand it, because what started as a sunny day turned into a total wash. There were clouds everywhere and you couldn't even see the stars, so what was the point? But he never let it bring him down. I mean, he was only three, so I shouldn't have been surprised. So, I just followed his lead. Maybe that sounds strange. But it just felt right."

"I've said it before, and I'll say it again. I've never met a kid like him before. He doesn't forget a thing and he's always got another ten questions up his sleeve. I've really enjoyed spending time with him lately and with you."

He meant it. For the first time in a long time, he had a little bit of peace. Even before his mother died, he'd carried around a deep sense of sadness. His father's abandonment of their family left a heavy weight on his heart. A feeling that often kept him up at night. Working was the one thing that was guaranteed to distract him. But lately, simply existing in the same space as Olivia and Daniel made things easier.

Maybe it didn't make sense, but he couldn't pretend that it wasn't true.

"Look, Draven, tonight's been ... well, it's been great. I had no idea what to expect. It's been nice getting to know you more. But I have to be honest with you; I still don't know what to think. I don't trust you. At least not completely. Can you understand why?"

He nodded. He could not blame her for that. They were both keeping secrets and they both knew it. But it seemed like maybe she was willing to give him a chance. Not that he deserved it.

"I have more than myself to think about here. I have to think of Daniel and what getting involved with you would mean for him."

Getting involved with someone had never been part of the plan. Especially not with a single mother. He did not do attachment and what would happen once the story came out? She would hate him; he was sure of that. But maybe this did not have to be a long-term thing. Would she go for that?

"What are you saying?" He needed to be sure. He needed to hear her say the words.

"I'm saying that this scares me—you scare me. I don't do this, Draven. I don't get close to people. I know what it's like to be burned and to have nothing but scars and heartache to show for it. I know what it's like to let someone in, only for everything to go wrong and for people to get hurt. As a mother, I never want to put Daniel through that. I don't ever want him to know what that's like."

Everything she was saying gave him hope. Hope that she would understand his reasons for lying to her. But there was also guilt. She was trying to be honest with him about her feelings. He hadn't expected that from her, hadn't expected anything but more lies and unanswered questions until one of them broke and admitted their truth. But the fact that she was trying at all made him want to try too. It was that feeling that made him blurt out his next words.

"My mother was a witch."

She stared at him for a moment, seemingly dumbfounded by his words. So, he waited. And waited. And waited.

After several very long moments, she said, "I'm sorry. What did you say?"

He took a deep, steadying breath. "I said my mother was a witch."

She narrowed her eyes at him. "Is this some kind of joke? Because if it is, it's really not funny."

Of course, she would think that. But that meant that he was right; she had suspected him this whole time of knowing more about the town than he let on. That thought was oddly freeing.

"No! No, it's not a joke. My mother was a witch. I swear. That's why I'm here. I found out my mother was a witch after she died and that led me to this town. She was from here and I just had to know more about it and her and, well, it's a long story. But the point is, my mother was a witch. So, I know, or at least I assume, this town has magic and other witches and I'm guessing you're one too."

She crossed her arms over her chest. "What makes you think that?"

Her words were sharp and blunt; they made his heart ache. She didn't believe him. Either that or she still felt the need to pretend. His shoulders slumped; defeat threatened to overtake him.

He stared at her, beseeching. "Please, Olivia. I know I lied to you before when I said I just randomly found the town. I know I kept lying to you and I'm sorry for that. But I had to be sure I was right. I needed to see it for myself. I could not just show up here and start asking questions. Because what if I'd been wrong? How would that have looked to all of you? Some stranger shows up in town accusing people of being witches and having magic. That's like the plot of a freaking scary movie."

"You decided to use me instead? You lied to me."

He cringed. "Originally, yes, my intention was to get to know you just to get information But this past week, when we really started to get to know each other and I got to spend time with Daniel, things changed. I haven't felt this happy in such a long time. It brought back so many memories of me and my mom and how happy I used to be. Then, when you asked me out, I convinced myself my feelings for you weren't real. That I was just using you because I figured you were just using me too. I convinced myself that you could not possibly care for me. How could you? But what you said before, about how you want to be with me, but you're scared? Well, I'm scared too, because I don't deserve you. I'm scared to really let go and be vulnerable and I'm scared of how much I already care for you. I'm scared of the way you make me feel. I'm so scared I've ruined this before it's even had a chance to start."

She placed her hand over his mouth. "Shhhh. Draven. I believe you."

His eyes widened, heart pounding as her hand moved to cup his cheek. He had to be sure. "You do?"

She nodded. "Yes. Though, I'm still pissed that you lied to me."

"I can understand that. If the situation were reversed, I'd feel the same way. But I hope you can understand why I felt the need to."

"That doesn't make it okay, though."

"I know."

"But" she whispered as she stepped closer to him. "I can understand it. Finding out your mom was a witch? Not exactly a normal thing. I'd say you're handling everything pretty well, considering. I'm sorry you've had to go through all of it alone. I definitely know what that's like."

Something inside him gave way and a weight lifted off his chest.

"Olivia," he whispered. "I'd really like it if we could keep spending time together. I know this started for the wrong reasons. I know I have to earn your trust. But I really want to get to know you. In whatever way you would be most comfortable," he said, reaching for her hand and taking some comfort in the fact that she didn't resist.

"I like the sound of that," she whispered as she stepped fully into his body. She was so warm and she smelled heavenly, a mix of vanilla and roses and moonlight.

"Can I kiss you?"

He waited, eyes searching hers.

She nodded slowly, chocolate brown eyes wide and burning.

Her whole body quivered as he dipped down towards her lips; she was mesmerizing. Her hands snaked up to wrap around his neck. Her quiet gasp drove him wild as he tilted his head to the side, moving so close to her face that if he spoke again, his words would end on her mouth.

Everything was magnified. The cool breeze chilled his heated skin. The crashing waves pounded in his ears. The moonlight shone on the stunning person before him, lightning her up like a beacon aimed straight to his soul. Another wonderful memory made on the sands of a beach.

He hesitated there, letting the anticipation build for a moment.

One more inch and her lips connected with his, softly at first, like a feather brushing up against his skin. It was barely even a kiss—just a touch, a whisper easily lost in the whistling wind around them. It was everything.

But then, he canted his head to the side and brought his hand up to the sharp curve of her jaw, feeling her smooth, soft skin slide underneath his fingertips. Then he opened his mouth, tongue tangling with hers, tasting her and letting her taste him.

He groaned softly but just loud enough so that she could hear it, so she would know how much he wanted her. She shivered, melting into him and digging her fingertips into the skin of his neck. Her body pressed even harder into him, the heat of her seeping into his bones.

His hands dug into her hair, twirling the loose strands and twisting them around his fingertips. Her hair was soft like silk. A second later, she was doing the same to him, combing her fingers through his hair, nails scraping along his scalp, sending a chill down his spine in the most delicious of ways before pulling away, a satisfied smirk gracing her beautiful face.

"That was..." Shit, why couldn't he think of anything to say? A dozen words went through his mind, all of them good, but none of them perfect. So, he just smiled, big and probably goofy.

She laughed, shaking her head before casting her gaze off for a beat, something drawing her attention. "Hold that thought."

She moved over a few feet and bent to grab something from the sand. When she returned, she had a smooth, fully formed shell; it was an off-white color, with deep veins of purple lining one side.

She slipped it into the pocket of his coat.

She stepped back towards him, burying her face in his chest with a giggle.

"What's so funny?"

She looked up at him, eyes wide and bright. "Life, I guess; being here with you. So much can change in such a short amount of time. It feels good. Which is kind of weird in and of itself."

"That's funny?"

"It's unexpected."

He had no idea what to say to that. But he could understand what she meant. Two weeks ago, this would never have been his life. Yet, here he was, probably making a huge mistake. But looking at her face right now, he could not be bothered to care.

"You are something special; you know that" he said as he bent down to place a gentle kiss on her forehead.

"You're damn right I am."

Chapter 11

The air around them on the car ride home was thick and charged. Her hand on his thigh, sliding up and down, made his skin feel hot and tight.

Was she trying to tease him?

After their kiss, they walked back to their picnic spot, in no hurry and in a comfortable silence. His mind was torn between remembering the feel of her mouth on his and marveling at where the night started to where they were now. It all felt very surreal. Even just parting for a few minutes to get into the car felt like a loss. Now, her hand was on his leg, and it was very intentional. When it came particularly close to his crotch, he jumped, a small groan getting caught in his throat.

Olivia made no move to show that she noticed this, but she had to know. She had to be teasing him.

If she kept going, he would definitely have a situation on his hands and they still had another ten minutes to their drive.

"Uh, Liv?"

"Yes? she asked quietly, as she finally looked over at him, her eyes wide and innocent.

She knew exactly what she was doing to him. He hadn't expected this. But he wasn't going to complain.

When he finally pulled the car up to his house, she removed her hand from his leg and turned to him. "Draven. There's something I want to show you. Would you mind if I came inside?"

She was holding a lock of her hair, twirling it around her finger. Whatever moment they just had between them in the darkness of the car was now over. Had he done something wrong?

"Uh, sure," he said as he turned the engine off. This silence was awkward now.

He exited the car and made his way around to open her door. She slipped her hand in his as they walked slowly up his porch steps. It was a little awkward trying to pull out his keys to unlock the door, but he didn't want to let go of her hand.

Once inside, they stood in his front hallway—Olivia having now dropped his hand and fidgeting with her own.

He waited, wanting to give her the chance to speak up on her own. But after several moments of charged silence, he had to say something.

"What is it, Liv? Is everything okay? Are you still mad at me?"

Her eyes snapped up to his. "No. No, I'm not mad. I'm trying to figure out how to show you this. I guess I'm just nervous because it's not something I have to do very often."

His brow furrowed as she reached into the pocket of his coat she still wore around her shoulders. Pulling out the white and purple shell, she placed it on her palm and held it straight out.

"Purple to gold," she whispered, eyes cast down at the shell.

What was she doing? Was she showing him her magic? It dawned on him that she'd never confirmed her own status as a witch. Not that he'd actually given her a chance.

But it didn't matter now, because the shell was changing colors. His heart thundered as purple slowly bled into gold like watercolors on a blank page.

Magic, white and shining, came from her other hand. She had magic.

She looked up at him, a small smile on her face. "I believe you about your mother, Draven, because I'm a witch too. If that wasn't already obvious."

A second passed with those powerful words crackling between them. The whole world seemed to stand still for a moment. Draven swore the room got brighter, that the light around them shone with an unnatural but transcendent golden hue.

Because yes, he already knew that, but having it confirmed was something else entirely.

"I knew it," he said quietly, staring at her in awe.

"You did?"

He smiled, feeling a little sheepish. "Well, I did notice a few things."

She laughed. "Of course you did."

"I did mention it earlier, you know, right before we kissed."

She glanced away, a blush staining her cheeks. "I remember. I just, I don't know, I wasn't ready to admit it yet. That probably sounds silly."

"Hey," he said, reaching out to turn her face back towards him. "It's not silly. I kind of just sprang the whole thing on you. I want you to tell me things, but only when you feel it's right. There's absolutely no pressure and I hope you know this doesn't change anything. You having magic, being a witch. I think it's amazing; you're amazing. I want you, Liv. I want you so damn much."

"I want you too," she whispered, catching her lower lip between her teeth.

Like a wire pulled too tight, the tension in him finally snapped as he captured her lips with his own, her mouth immediately opening to allow him entry. Her arms looped around his neck, his arms wrapping tightly around her waist, pulling her to him and up off the ground.

Instinctively, as he took a step forward, her legs locked around his waist, and he groaned against her, feeling her ankles lock around him.

The need for air overtook him and he pulled back from her roughly as they both gasped, chests heaving with effort. He did not put her down, and she did not make any motion to move.

"I need you," he breathed.

The wide smile she shot at him was the most radiant thing he had ever seen, lighting up her whole face and she kissed him again slowly and sweetly. Her soft lips moved against his like it was as natural as breathing.

"So, have me then," she whispered.

"Fuck," he cursed, his tone low and gruff.

He started up the stairs as her lips latched onto his neck. She bit and sucked at his skin, sending shivers down his spine.

She was an angel and the devil all rolled into one.

When they reached the landing, he was suddenly being pushed lightly into the wall. Confused, he caught her eyes. She was smirking at him, hands raised, magic at her fingertips.

Fuck. He hadn't expected that to look so hot. "You want to play, baby," he asked, nipping at her ear.

"Yes," she whispered as she ground herself against his stomach. She was so warm. He bucked up gently, the friction causing her to moan.

She let up on him and he kept walking towards his bedroom. Once there, he kicked open the door and stalked inside.

None too gently, he deposited her on the bed, barely keeping his weight off her body as he continued to kiss her frantically. Suddenly, he was being pushed until he was on his back looking up at her.

She smiled impishly at him before fisting his shirt in her hand and lowering her head to capture his lips in a bruising kiss, her teeth catching his full lower lip as her hand drifted, pulling the buttons of his shirt apart. They moaned in tandem as she ran her hand along his bare skin, grazing his nipple.

He was so hard for her it was painful, his cock practically begging for release, as she pulled off her dress in one smooth motion. A strangled whine left his throat when he realized that she hadn't been wearing a bra and his large hand reached up to cup her bare breast, his thumb rubbing her nipple as she whimpered. He groaned as her hand wrapped around the base of him, her tongue darting out to taste.

He forced himself to look down at her, not wanting to miss a moment of her mouth on him. She swirled around his head before lowering her mouth around him, taking him as far as she could before hitting the back of her throat. When she added her hand to the movement, his eyes practically rolled back in his head.

Her hand pumped his shaft, her mouth sucking, cheeks hollowing with the effort.

"I ... I'm not going to last," he groaned, a string of obscenities falling from his mouth.

His stomach muscles clenched, tightening and tingling as he came with a long, low groan, Olivia catching his spend eagerly.

She grinned up at him.

He sat up so that they were face to face. Then he kissed down the column of her throat to her chest, taking a nipple in his mouth. Her back arched with a gasp as he rolled her nipple between his teeth, flicking it with his tongue.

"Draven ... please ... I need you. Please."

"I know, Liv," he breathed, "I've got you. I promise. I'm going to take care of you, baby."

He lowered her gently to the bed. She moaned as he leaned forward, pressing wet kisses down her stomach from her navel to the band of her panties. Her shallow breathing hitched when he grabbed the fabric between his teeth, tugging at it and pulling the slip of fabric away until she was bare before him.

Her body tensed, and he glanced up at her, seeing the trepidation on her face. She was nervous, self-conscious. He smiled at her. He was going to take care of her.

"Relax, Liv," he whispered. "I've got you."

He ran his hand along her leg gently, tilting his head to kiss the inside of her knee softly, trailing a path up her inner thigh. He smiled against her skin as her body finally relaxed under his touch.

The smirk returned to his face as he swiped his thumb along her slit, from her entrance to her clit, swirling around the sensitive bundle of nerves, her hips bucking upwards from the bed at the shock it sent through her body.

"Oh God, Draven."

He worked her slowly, teasing around her needy clit, which was pulsing and desperate for attention, before he licked up through her folds, relishing in her taste. His large hand pressed down on her mound to anchor her twitching hips in place.

When he latched onto her clit, sucking and pulling with delicate pressure, she keened, her thighs clenched around his head. She cried out his name as he worked her through it, moving away from the oversensitive bundle of nerves to lightly trace around it.

"Fuck," she panted, her ragged breathing slowly regulating as she came down from her high.

He grinned proudly, wiping his face of her and licking his hand, a satisfied growl rumbling through his chest.

He palmed himself, sucking in a sharp inhale at the contact as he caught her eyes.

"Are you absolutely sure?" he asked her gently. He did not want her to have any regrets.

"Please, Draven. I need this. I need you."

That was all he needed to hear. Then he was on her. His weeping cock smeared precum against the flat of her stomach as he kissed her, reaching blindly to the nightstand and grabbing a box from the drawer to pull out a condom.

"I'm on birth control," she said quickly. "And I'm clean. I haven't been with anyone else in a long time. So, I'm good if you don't want to use one."

He paused over her, his hand still hovering with the condom between his fingers as he blinked down at her, eyebrows raised. He hadn't been expecting that.

He cupped her face in his free hand, letting the condom packet fall to the floor.

"I'm clean as well. So, if you're sure ..."

She nodded, smiling up at him.

He nuzzled at her neck, encouraging her legs apart. He could feel her shaking with anticipation, her fingers gripping his shoulders tightly. He moaned as he pushed into her.

She was so wet for him that there was little resistance. She was like heaven itself and a little bit of hell. Wicked and wonderful.

"You alright?" he panted, halting his movement to search her face.

She nodded.

"Yeah, yeah, I'm fine," she breathed. "It's just been a while."

She whimpered against his lips as he kissed her, long, slow and tender, giving her body time to relax around him.

She nodded against his lips, signaling that he could keep going. He pushed further, all the way to the hilt, groaning loudly as his head dipped to her collarbone. Her cunt tightened around him, gripping him for all he was worth. He had never felt anything like it, his cock twitching at her heat.

"Move, baby," she groaned. "I need you to move."

Experimentally, he rolled his hips. A choked gasp escaped his lips at the white-hot pleasure washing over him. He was almost giddy, grunting and gasping as he bottomed out in her.

"Fuck, Liv," he panted. "You're so fucking tight ...."

Sweat ran between their bodies as he moved, her leg hiked up over his hip to pull him deeper and he groaned at the new angle.

"Touch yourself," he groaned through gritted teeth, the whole bed lurching with the power of his movements.

Her hands shook as she snaked her fingers between them, flicking her clit with uncoordinated movements. She looked delirious, her whole body tensing as she moaned his name loudly. Almost begging.

"Please, Draven. I ... I'm so close ..."

"Let go, Liv. I want to feel you."

She cried out against his shoulder, her teeth sinking into him as she came, her whole body shaking under him.

He gasped against her neck, his movements becoming sporadic. He jerked his hips against hers with a long, low cry, his cock twitching as he came deep inside her, his hand gripping the sheets.

He rolled off her, his breathing ragged.

She moved into the waiting space of his arms, snuggling against his chest as their unsteady heartbeats slowed.

She smiled lazily up at him, no doubt seeing the sated grin on his own face.

It had never been like this with anyone else. It felt right. He gazed at her, trying to make sense of something that was too incredible to describe. What words were worth a moment when time stood still? When everything he had ever wanted was right in front of him?

He wanted to tell her right here and now just how much she had come to mean to him in only a few short weeks. That yes, he had come to Addersfield to expose its secrets, whatever they might be. But now, everything was different. He wanted to beg her forgiveness.

But she looked back at him with a shy, innocent expression, curling into his chest and holding on with a smile so sweet and so warm he could not bring himself to say anything at all.

"It's never been like that for me," she whispered against him, the confession tugging it his heart as it washed across his skin.

"I think it goes without saying that no one has ever come close to you, Olivia."

"What you're saying is it won't be a one-time thing?" she goaded.

He smiled softly at her. "Not if I can help it. But for now, I was wondering if you would tell me more about your Cerebral Palsy. I've never known anyone who's had it and I'd like to know as much as possible."

She looked up at him, a vulnerable yet determined look in her eyes, took a deep breath, and began talking.

Chapter 12

Olivia woke to sunlight streaming in from unfamiliar windows. At first, there was some confusion. This wasn't her bed or her room or her house. She was aching in places no one had touched in so long. But, after a quick second, it all came flooding back to her and the confusion melted into something so much better: real and unyielding happiness.

The comfort she found in Draven's arms last night was amazing and unlike anything she had ever known. Right now, she was curled into him, feeling all of the warmth and safety he could provide. Her sleeping self had entangled herself here all night.

She had bared her soul to him. He asked her directly about her Cerebral Palsy and she told him everything she could manage. Talking about it was never easy, but she appreciated the way he wanted to get to know every part of her. While her disability was only a piece of who she was, it did impact the way she moved through the world. It was important to her that he understood the limitations she sometimes faced.

She first explained how the doctors hadn't known the exact cause of her Cerebral Palsy, how they assumed she would never be able to walk or have any typical brain function. It was this information, she assumed, that caused her birth parents to surrender her to the state, maybe feeling as if they wouldn't be able to give her the care she needed.

"Did that make it hard to find a family for you?" he asked.

"I would assume so. It's why I had to be moved around so much. I had to be carried until I was three years old. I finally took my first steps after my third birthday with the help of physical therapy through the Birth to Three program. I'm sure it was a lot for a foster family to take on. I was smart though, really smart. Doctors were always surprised by that. Unfortunately for me, it meant I picked up on a lot. I can remember feeling very unwanted at a very young age."

He lay next to her, stroking her cheek. "I'm so sorry, Liv."

She explained how physical therapy was the norm for years, until it was determined her legs would never get better beyond a certain point. She would never be able to extend either leg fully. Her muscles would always be tensed, which was sometimes painful and caused her to walk on her tiptoes. Which, of course, meant she was bullied endlessly as a child.

He listened patiently while she explained that she had a lazy eye, had to wear glasses to read and that her depth perception was terrible. No surgery (though she had gone through several as a baby) or glasses could ever fix that.

He held her hand as she explained that the muscles on the right side of her body were so underdeveloped that she leaned permanently to that side. This was why she could never drive, swim, or ride a bike; she was constantly fighting her body's urge to tip her over.

She cried as she told him how lonely her childhood had been. She always felt like a burden because she could not do things other kids could. She could not walk as far; she could not run as fast. She always needed a railing to go up and down the stairs and when she was pregnant with Daniel, she lived in constant fear that she would lose her balance and hurt him.

Through her recollections, he remained a steady presence at her side, listening to her story and offering comfort where and when he could. She had never felt more beautiful or confident than she had in those moments.

In a single word, last night was fantastic. No other man had ever been able to read her wants and needs so clearly and bring her such pure and unadulterated pleasure. She had never felt a connection like the one she had with Draven. It was so strong and so bright and yet effortless in all of its complexity.

The suspicion was still there in the back of her mind, though, nagging at her that this was too good to be true. Those old doubts and fears were never far away. But she shoved them aside for the moment, choosing to focus on only the good things.

She was still dizzy from it all these hours later. As her eyes gazed at him, trailing first down his body and then back up to his face, which was relaxed in sleep, she could not help but smile. It was a victory for her to still be here.

Sleepovers were never her thing in the past. But this was natural and instinctive.

She stretched around a languid yawn and raised her sleep heavy limbs above her head before turning onto her side. Draven's back was to her, his hair an inky black mess on his head, and his shoulders were dusted with freckles that trailed down the length of his back until they disappeared completely.

Fascinated and intrigued, she extended a hand out to touch them, luxuriating in the warmth and texture of his skin beneath her fingers.

He stirred slightly, the smallest intake of air expanding in his chest before he settled again. She held still until he slipped back into sleep before replacing her hand with the gentle press of her lips. His skin carried the tang of salt and vanilla and amber and something very distinctly him. She inhaled deeply as warmth curled through her body. She loved the way he smelled; she was quickly becoming addicted to this mix of him and her together.

The wet press of her tongue revealed that his freckles tasted simply like him. She sighed happily as his scent filled her nose again before kissing a path across the span of his shoulders and down the shallow knobs of his spine.

She pushed her hair off her face and moistened her lips before leaning back in, trailing her mouth the length of his back while listening to his breathing shift. He stirred again beneath her lips as she continued her gentle ministrations, blazing a path up and over to his arm before gently kissing the tattoo displayed there.

A rose for his mother, he had explained last night. What was it about roses? They seemed to pop up everywhere between the two of them. Maybe that would be their thing.

He stirred again. She should have stopped; she didn't want to wake him. After all that hard work last night, the man had definitely earned a little extra sleep.

She smiled again, toes curling at the memories.

The clock on his nightstand indicated she still had several hours before Daniel would be home.

She wanted to show her appreciation for Draven and she could think of no better way to do that right now than to head downstairs and make them some breakfast. Who knew? Maybe he would wake up and find her and they could fulfill a fantasy she had had a time or two, of her and him together on his kitchen counter.

That thought alone was enough to get her moving. Before she disentangled herself from him, she pressed a kiss to his chest right above his heart, smiling when his lips twitched as if his dream had taken a particularly good turn.

Heading downstairs, she gathered everything she would need for pancakes from the cupboards and the fridge, collecting them together with a bowl, tossing ingredients in as fast as she could. By the time he was in the kitchen, his arms wrapped around her, she was well on her way.

Instinctively, she melted into him.

"You had me worried for a minute when I woke up alone. But now I see you've been making breakfast and my feelings on the matter have shifted."

"Have they?" she asked, her voice charged with want. He made her whole body sing.

"Yes. I've always been fond of pancakes," he said as his lips came to brush the spot just behind her ear. She sighed into the sensation, opening herself up better to him as her hands gripped the counter.

"Is that all you're fond of?" she asked, teasing him as she turned around in his arms. He growled low at the insinuation, his hands coming to hold her more firmly as if he were scared that she would slip from his grasp. Those eyes of his expressed all her feelings back at her and she was caught in them.

"If you have to ask that after last night, I did not do my job right," he replied, and she licked her lips as her eyes moved down to his mouth.

She gulped and shook her head. "No, you did. More than once."

Then his lips were on hers. She opened her mouth for him and the things he did with his tongue were delicious. A tiny moan escaped from the back of her throat and he bit down on her lower lip as he pulled her closer by her waist. It was dizzying, being kissed by him. He acted like he was starving and she was his last meal.

They broke apart after a few heated moments, both pulling in ragged breaths as their hands wandered over each other's bodies.

God, he was so sexy. His body was so hard and warm it left her feeling weak in the knees.

She glanced down; the sight of how much he wanted her called to something deep inside her. How long had it been since she'd felt this desirable?

She wanted to return the favor, so without any hesitation, she pulled his sweatpants down and drew in a sharp breath when she saw him, so hard and red—already leaking. She wrapped her hand around his shaft and began to kneel when he suddenly stopped her with a gentle hand on her shoulder.

She looked up, confused. Had she done something wrong?

His Adam's apple bobbed as he inhaled sharply. "Liv. Wait."

"What's wrong?"

He shook his head. "Nothing, just, you first."

He sunk to his knees on the floor in front of her, his breathing labored as he gingerly tugged at her panties, slowly sliding them off and letting them fall to the floor.

He trailed kisses down her hips to her thighs, hooking his arms behind her legs so he could pull her closer to him and then his tongue is gliding between her folds, drawing a low moan out of her.

"Draven. Fuck."

She could feel his smug grin against her cunt.

He devoured her, licking and sucking at her with the same fevered intensity with which he had kissed her.

He groaned against her like he was somehow enjoying this more than she was.

She knotted her hands in his hair, rolling her hips and grinding her pussy against his face, his nose providing delicious friction against her clit.

"Draven," she whimpered. "Draven, fuck, I'm gonna—"

Her vision whited out and she had to cover her mouth to muffle what was nearly a scream. Her whole body spasmed as her orgasm crashed over her, heartbeat drumming in her ears as she struggled to catch her breath. Wave after wave of intense pleasure coursed through her.

A few moments later, she registered his lips on hers and she could taste herself on his mouth and his tongue.

"You taste so fucking good, baby, so sweet," he crooned, making her shiver.

Now it was her turn to sink to her knees. His cock was only inches from her face. She drew in a sharp breath.

She took it in her hand and stroked it a few times, hesitantly at first. His lips parted, eyes fluttering shut.

She looked up at him as she licked a long, hot stripe down his length, all the way to the tip.

"Fuck," he breathed out.

There was something intoxicating about watching him come apart with a simple flick of her tongue.

She took a deep breath and eased him inside of her mouth. She hollowed out her cheeks so she could take more of him, desperate to taste every inch of him, sucking up each drop of his pre-cum.

She glanced up at him again and he was completely undone, groaning and flushed and so responsive to even the slightest shift of her mouth. His hands came down and knotted into her hair. She bobbed her head up and down his length, sucking fervently, desperately.

She whimpered as she sucked and sucked at him, and he cried out her name in a strangled groan as he came, spilling onto her tongue and down her throat.

He smiled down at her and then helped her to her feet.

"I'm definitely famished now," he said with a laugh.

Olivia breathed a sigh of contentment. She and Draven were currently curled up on her porch swing, waiting for Daniel to come home. All she could think was that she wanted this thing between them to have a chance to grow.

She wanted to be honest with him in every way. She wanted to dare to dream of things she had long given up on.

After breakfast, they showered together. He washed her hair and then kissed her until her lips were swollen and her whole body was shaking. Then he fucked her hard and fast, whispering filthy things in her ear as he did.

Her hands clung to his shoulders and she whimpered softly against his lips as he thrust his swollen cock into her with ease. Her head reclined against the shower wall's cool porcelain tile, focusing on that pleasurable fullness he gave her.

He flourished kisses over the wet skin along the column of her neck as he drove them towards that sweet climax.

Clinging to him like a lifeline, her body trembled and shuddered against his, crying into his shoulder as a feeling of ecstasy flowed through her. He ceased his movement and held her hips firmly to his, releasing his spend deep inside her, planting a sweet kiss on her forehead.

After toweling off, they got dressed quickly so as not to get distracted by each other's nakedness. It mostly worked. Then they made their way over to her house and settled on the porch. She marveled again about how much could change in such a short amount of time. Suddenly Draven living next door was exciting and incredibly convenient, instead of an annoying hindrance.

He had been asking questions about her magic for the past twenty minutes, wanting to know how she first realized she was a witch and what kinds of spells she used most often.

"You don't always have to say a spell to use magic?" he asked.

She laughed. "Nope. My magic comes from me. Spells and casts help with certain things and they help focus the magic. Like if I wanted to find a lost object or maybe make it snow. But other things, like when you saw my spoon stirring itself, that was just me. Sometimes when I'm sufficiently distracted or particularly upset, the magic just kind of comes out."

Draven hummed in response, his eyes growing distant.

She guessed what he was thinking about. "You said your mom had magic."

Draven nodded. "After she passed away, I cleaned out her house. I found a box of her things. Journals, letters, pictures. A few letters from someone who lives here or did live here. That's how I found the town."

"Why didn't you want anyone to know?"

He shrugged. "I guess I just needed to be sure I was in the right place. I couldn't very well just show up and start asking people, hey, are you a witch? Did you know my mother? I also wasn't sure what people would think of me."

She laughed. "No, I guess not and I can understand being scared. Well, I can certainly ask around for you if you want. Parker's abuelita might know something about her."

"That would be great, thanks. She wrote a lot in her journals about her life here. But I'd love to talk to some people who actually knew her. All I really know about why she left is that she lost her magic."

Her brow furrowed. "Lost it? I've never heard of anything like that happening before. It's a part of us. Nothing but a spell from the book could take it away."

"The book?"

She laughed. "Right, sorry, I forgot you would not know about that. There's a book that gives magic to the town. One of the original witches that founded the town put some of her magic in the book to help keep the town safe. There are some pretty hefty spells in there."

"Does the book give you your magic?"

She shook her head. "No. I had magic before I lived here and there are plenty of other magical people out there in the world. But the book does enhance my magic, so I'm able to protect the town."

"What would happen if you didn't have the book?"

"Well, things would certainly be a lot more difficult. We like to think of it as an instruction manual passed down through the generations. It helps guide us. We don't know for sure, but it's possible that without the book, our magic would eventually die out and we wouldn't be able to pass it on anymore. Each of us puts a little bit of our own magic into the book to help keep it going. If we lost it, we let's just say it would not be good."

He looked up from his mother's journal and the light from the small desk lamp burned his eyes. Hours after spending the day with Olivia and Daniel, sleep would not come. The three of them had gone down to the beach, keeping the tradition of searching for a shell. Then he had taken them sailing, borrowing the boat from Jill's husband, Malcolm.

Daniel threw every question he could at Draven about sailing. By the end of the day, the kid had learned the nautical terms for left and right and how to tie a slip knot. He was well on his way to becoming an expert sailor. Or so Daniel said.

But the wonderful day had also brought back a lot of memories of every moment spent with his brother on their little sailboat. Now, they were tinged with so much sadness. As much as he enjoyed watching Daniel, it served as a brutal reminder of everything he had lost over the past six months. What Olivia had said about the book weighed heavy on his mind. He looked to his mother's journals for comfort. The clock on his phone read one a.m.

I've lost my magic. Maybe I should be angry. But really, I just feel free. I don't think Eric feels the same, even though he says he does. But he loves me and I love him, so I think we can make this work.

We're leaving tonight. Off to New York to start over. I'm sad to be leaving my friends and family behind. But I think it's the right thing to do. Because everything is different now.

Somehow his mother had lost her magic and he was sure that book had something to do with it. There was possibility there. Maybe a way to do more than just expose the town's magic, though he could not be sure yet. But he had to keep looking. Because no matter what he felt for Olivia, his intentions had not changed.

Olivia talked about how she had found a family here, how they had welcomed her with open arms. Yet, his mother had lived her life completely cut off from the people here. Whether it was by her own choice or not, she had been wronged. It wasn't right and it wasn't fair. So maybe he could use what was in this book to make it right. Maybe he could take away their magic. Give them a taste of their own medicine. A witch's blood ran in his veins after all.

Maybe he could use that to make some magic of his own.

Chapter 13

Glancing around the central square of Addersfield, Olivia could see that this year's festival would be one to remember.

It had been a long two weeks, getting everything finalized. But it was all worth it. Fall had officially arrived and the air held the promise of magic. Tonight, she and her friends would renew the protection spell on the town.

But before that, they all planned to have some fun.

She glanced down at her dress. She had never much cared for this particular tradition. Especially considering the sun was beginning to set and the temperature approaching fifty degrees. But a quick warming spell took care of that.

"I am warm, warm as fire; keeping warm is my desire."

Each of the three witches wore a cream-colored dress with flowing sleeves and long skirts. They wore silver ballet flats on their feet. They adorned their heads with a laurel wreath, made with whatever they chose. Olivia's was woven with roses, lavender, and a little bit of white lace. Parker's held several different colors of dahlias and Jill's went with all things yellow: sunflowers, daisies, marigolds, and forsythia.

Everyone around her was bundled up—hats, scarves, and gloves. Most people carried cups of hot chocolate or hot cider. Kids ran around waving around caramel apples and Jill's cider donuts.

Daniel was off with his friend Lola and her dad. If she knew her son, he was currently trying to play and win every game there was. He was never one to give up easily.

"Hey, Liv," Parker said, coming to stand next to her. "Everything looks great, doesn't it?"

"It does. We really outdid ourselves this year."

"We absolutely did. Jill is dragging Malcolm through the corn maze as we speak and my mom is running our booth. The tamales are selling like crazy. I figured I'd check out the festivities by myself. I lost my wing-woman this year."

"Yeah. Sorry about that."

"Hey, don't apologize. I'm happy for you. Is Draven meeting you here?"

"Mhmm. He said he had some things to take care of first. Speaking of, did you have a chance to ask your abuelita about his mom?"

Parker winced, slapping her hand against her forehead, "Shit. No, I'm sorry, Liv. We've been so busy and I completely forgot. But based on what you told me, she was probably friends with my mom. Or at least she was a friend of a friend. They probably know something. I'll ask as soon as I have a chance."

"No worries. We've all been crazy busy. He's been busy too and he did not seem like he was in any rush to figure things out."

That was a bit odd. If his whole reason for coming here in the first place was to learn more about his mother, why wasn't he more curious? Why hadn't she clocked that before? Her feelings for Draven were distracting her. But she wasn't sure how much she cared right now. Guilt churned in her gut.

"Liv, are you okay?" Parker asked, eyes wide.

But she could examine all of that tomorrow. She was determined to enjoy tonight. "Yeah, I'm good. Just a little bit nervous about tonight and I'm anxious to see Draven, I guess."

That wasn't exactly a lie. She was nervous about casting the spell tonight. It was a big deal and she took the responsibility of it very seriously.

They hadn't seen each other much over the last two weeks. She was so busy organizing the festival and he was busy writing. She had never actually seen what he was working on, but maybe he would show her when he was ready. She could be patient. If she pushed too much, he might get suspicious as to why she wanted to know.

Spending so little time with him made her realize how much she had missed having someone to be with every day. He still came into the bakery each morning for a few minutes, and they saw each other as much as possible in the evenings. He had even taken her and Daniel out to dinner a few nights ago.

The three of them got burgers and milkshakes. Draven talked about sailing with Daniel, regaling him with stories from his childhood sailing with his brother. Then Daniel had asked them if they were boyfriend-girlfriend.

Draven had looked to her as to how to proceed, which she appreciated. She had found herself nodding without giving it too much thought. But once the idea was out there, it felt good.

Only a few nights ago, Draven had attended his very first Wednesday night dinner. Rosa was probably the most thrilled when Olivia and Daniel had shown up at her door, Draven standing awkwardly behind them.

Draven had joined Daniel and Malcolm in the living room and Olivia had overheard him sharing his own funny story for the week. When they all sat down to eat, he handled Rosa and Janella's question with ease. Neither of them mentioned his mother and Draven did not ask. Maybe he just wasn't ready to talk about her yet. Olivia could understand that. In a way, it would be like getting to know his mother for the first time. Something like that could not be easy.

Tonight, she was excited for Draven to experience the festival. It was the very best that Addersfield had to offer.

"You know what would make me really happy, though?" she asked Parker. "If I did not have my best friends spying on my every move tonight."

"Yeah ... well, that's easier said than done. But how about this—I promise to contain the damage as much as I can. If Jill so much as looks like she's going to make an inappropriate comment, I'll tackle her."

Olivia laughed. "I'd pay good money to see that."

"You have to do the same thing for me when or if I eventually meet someone."

"You will, Parker and when the time comes, I've got your back."

Parker smiled. "I appreciate that. Hey, don't look now, but I think your boy finally made it. I'll catch ya later, Liv," she said as she hurried away.

If only Jill could be that cooperative.

Olivia waved after her and then turned around to see Draven looking right at her.

He was dressed in a black leather jacket, black fitted T-shirt and dark blue jeans. He wore his signature black Converse on his feet. His face held a bit more scruff than it had had in recent days. Good God, the man was sex on a stick. His piercing blue eyes always made her go weak at the knees.

She cut through the crowds of people until they met in the middle, coming close enough to reach for each other's hands.

"Hey. You made it."

He smelled so good, like mint and sandalwood. She had missed that smell.

"Sorry, I'm a little late. You look amazing. Very old school," he said with a wink.

At least her friends hadn't forced her to go full-on witch and wear a pointy black hat. That was a tough sell even for her. But it was fun to put on the crown and pretend for a little while.

"Is that a good thing?" she teased.

He responded by pulling her gently into his arms. "Yes. Everything about you is a good thing. You could say I'm in love with every part of you."

Her breath caught at the word love. Oh, what she wouldn't give to know if he really meant that, for this man to see her as she was and not turn away.

In the past, her magic had been the source of the worst pain she had ever known. It had pushed away people she loved and made her feel too different to be loved or accepted. She did not want Draven to leave, not when she had finally found something real.

Because fuck, she loved him. So much. Maybe too much.

"Is something wrong, Olivia?" he asked, his hand squeezing hers a little tighter as her eyes came back up to meet his.

"No, sorry, I just ... a lot is happening, you know?" she said, hoping that he would understand.

"Yes. I know how anxious you've been to have me as your date tonight. I can imagine that prospect alone would drive any woman to distraction."

She did not bother hiding her eye roll. He was kidding and she knew he had said that to cut through some of her tension. She rewarded him with a genuine laugh and a smirk, grabbing his hand to pull him into the fray.

"Come on, you goof. Let's go have some fun."

She walked up to a booth covered by a red and white striped canopy. There was a wall of balloons in a rainbow of colors stapled to large wooden slats at the back of the booth. She stopped and turned to him.

"Loser buys dinner?"

"You're on," he said with a laugh.

He paid for dinner.

She insisted they get foot-long corn dogs. It was her favorite thing at any fair. He looked less than thrilled, but he finished the entire thing, much to her amusement.

For dessert, she stuck to her roots, opting for horchata and pan dulce.

"What is that?" he asked, pointing at the sugary confection.

"Pan dulce. It's just sweet bread. Usually, it's made for breakfast. But Rosa always makes them for the festival. Although, I actually made them this year, with her recipe."

"Well, then I definitely have to try one."

He insisted on paying despite her protests. They walked around hand in hand, just enjoying each other's company.

"You've got big plans later, right?" he asked as he sipped on a lemonade.

"Yup. We're renewing the protection spell on the town. We do it every year at the festival, Jill, Parker, and me. The task gets passed down from generation to generation when the next group of witches is ready."

"What exactly does the protection spell do?"

"Well, it makes the town invisible. It makes it so you have to already know the town exists to be able to find it. It's to keep people who don't know magic exists from finding us."

He stared at her for a moment. She tensed, waiting for his anger. She had been avoiding telling him about this particular thing because she figured he would be annoyed that she knew he was lying to her from the moment they met.

Instead, he laughed, full-on, hands-on knees, belly laughter.

"Draven," she said, beginning to laugh right along with him. "You're not mad that I didn't tell you?"

He looked up at her, wiping tears from his eyes. "I'm not mad. I just feel like an idiot, though I wish you had told me once I told you about my mother."

She cringed. "I thought about it. But I just didn't want to make you feel bad. I mean, I get why you lied.

He shook his head and cupped her face in his hands. "I appreciate that. But in the future, I'd much rather have all the facts."

"I promise," she said with a soft smile before reaching up to capture his lips in a kiss.

One kiss and she was itching to be alone with him. He was holding her hand now, his thumb rubbing circles into her skin—that small bit of pressure making her ache for more.

He seemed to feel the same way because his arm snaked around her waist, pulling her closer. The heat of his hand through the fabric of her dress was just what she needed, as the warming spell had worn off.

His fingers began to knead at the soft skin of her hip. Her hand drifted under the hem of his T-shirt. His skin was hot to the touch.

He leaned his head towards her, his lips just grazing the shell of her ear. It sent a shiver down her spine. "What are you up to?"

She smirked, feeling his breath hitch as her finger dipped into the top of his jeans. "I have no idea what you're talking about."

"Sure you don't," he rasped out. His grip on her waist was firmer now, more insistent. "I want to get you alone. How much privacy do you think we could expect in a corn maze?"

She shook her head. "It's a good thought, but you would be surprised how little alone time you get in there. The kids hide in every corner waiting for people to show up. To scare them."

They both glanced around, desperate to find somewhere they could be alone. She was about to call it a wash when she spotted a structure in the distance. "But I have another idea."

"The Ferris wheel?"

"Yup. We weren't even supposed to have one, actually. But Jenny surprised us all."

He smirked. "Remind me to thank her later."

He paid for both their tickets and pulled her to the nearest carriage. It was one of those Ferris wheels with enclosed seats, thank God. They settled on a bench together and when the ride began to move, his lips were at her ear. "I'm going to kiss you now."

Please God, yes.

His large hand moved to the base of her neck, cupping, pulling her closer—he drew one lone swipe of his tongue against her lower lip before the heat of his mouth was against hers. He tangled his fingers in her hair as he dipped his tongue past her lips—no pretense, no warming up—a desperate divide and conquer that urged her to open up for him.

He turned his head to deepen the kiss, making throaty sounds somewhere between a hum and a growl, and opened and closed his mouth as if trying to devour her, as if trying to take more. Even when they broke away, his lips were moving across her jaw and he pulled her lightly by the hair to force her head to turn as he kissed down her neck greedily. His hand snaked under her dress, sliding higher and higher, fingers finding the edge of her panties and pushing the scrap of fabric aside.

The ride took them higher, occasionally stopping to let on more people. The cool night air tickled her skin.

"Fucking soaked," he hissed. He reached a little further until he could ease two fingers inside her and then deeper, spreading them a little to stretch her. "Just for me."

"It is," she managed breathlessly. "Because of you."

"Yeah?" His head dipped until his lips could tease her nipple through the thin fabric of her dress. He tugged at it softly, licking it after.

His fingers began to pump in and out of her, sometimes drawing out completely to push up through her folds and circle her clit briefly before crawling back down to dip inside again. She found herself rocking forward unconsciously to ride his hand, closing her eyes as he continued to tease her through her dress.

She cried out loudly when he ground his fingers particularly deep and, in an instant, the hand curled around her neck was over her mouth, staunching the sound.

"Have to be quiet, baby," he rasped. "Can you be quiet for me?" He pumped his fingers inside her slowly, stroking at her inner walls. "I want you to come on my hand."

She gave him a shaky nod, swallowing down the sounds in her throat as she ground down on his hand, seeking more. She could feel the sticky mess she was making, felt the way he spread the slickness of her when he found her clit to stroke there, her head fell back as his hand stayed firmly against her mouth, ensuring that she was quiet.

Her sounds came only as unsteady breath and low whimpers in her chest. She shifted her hips with every stroke, every touch—feeling her orgasm building inside as every facet of her skin seems to throb in anticipation. She kept her eyes shut tight as the pressure built and built—Draven worked her faster, touching her more, and her thighs began to shake with the way she was so tightly wound. Her fingers twisted through his hair to tug and tug. She rocked her hips faster; her breaths came harder—stars bloomed in her vision and blood rushed in her ears.

Her eyes flew open when she began to tremble; she saw actual stars above her as she groaned softly through her release. The slippery wet of her orgasm leaked out over his fingers, but he just kept sliding them in and out, lazily now, kissing up her neck in a similar manner.

Then the ride stopped. Shit. He smirked at her, quickly removed his fingers, and adjusted himself in his jeans.

Pity. She had wanted to reciprocate. They exited the ride and glanced around at the crowds. It had only taken ten minutes. But somehow, it felt like longer, in the best way.

"Hey, Liv!"

Jill was hurrying towards them, her flower crown fluttering in the breeze.

"I've been looking everywhere for you. It's almost time for our thing."

"Right, right. Sorry. We uh, we lost track of time," she said, avoiding Jill's gaze. If she looked at her, she would lose it. There was no way Jill would not be able to tell what she and Draven had just been up to.

"I suppose this is where you leave me," Draven said.

She nodded, wishing that did not have to be the case.

"Just for a little while. It's tradition, you know?"

"I get it. This is such an important thing you're doing. I'll just head on home for the night. But ..."

"But?"

"But if you find yourself feeling a bit lonely tonight, maybe we can get together later."

Daniel was staying over at a friend's house tonight. They could have the whole night to themselves.

"I might be late."

He shook his head, his hand coming up to cup her cheek. "I don't care. I'll go and hang out with Malcolm for a bit, kill some time."

"That's a great idea," Jill said. "It's about time you boys got to know each other a little better."

Olivia moved closer, intending to kiss him, only for the moment to be broken by the emergence of her other friend.

"Jill, I thought you said you were grabbing Olivia and heading out. What's taking so—oh, shoot, sorry," Parker said before giving an awkward wave. "Carry on with whatever this is."

She loved her friends. Really, she did. But sometimes, she wanted to throttle them.

"Meet me at my house in a couple of hours?" she asked, looking at Draven and trying her best to ignore everyone else around them.

"I hope so," he said before giving her one last chaste kiss on her cheek. He bid her friends goodbye as he headed back into the fray.

Chapter 14

O nce he was out of her sight, she turned around to her friends, hands on her hips, face full of irritation. She was faced with precisely what she had expected—two downright gleeful women who looked like they would burst from excitement.

"Don't even start," she counseled them before grabbing one of the lanterns Jill held. They would need them once they made it out to the clearing. "We've got things to do, remember?'

Tonight was the perfect night. A full moon rose in the clear sky. The air around them held a chill and the hum of magic floated on the breeze. Anything was possible.

The only sounds they made as they moved farther into nature were the crunching of leaves and grass under their shoes and the soft swish of fabric from their dresses.

Her friends walked at an easy pace, conscious that unsteady terrain through the dark was a difficult thing for Olivia to manage. They each helped whenever she needed it, holding her hand as she stepped over the occasional fallen branch or allowing her to use their shoulder or arm to steady herself.

The spot for the protection spell was always the same. A clearing in a copse of trees on the very far edge of the town square, far enough from the crowds of festivalgoers. The festival was a celebration. A reminder of what the town was and how it had come to be. Not everyone in Addersfield possessed magic, but everyone celebrated it all the same, the thing that had brought them all together.

On this night, Olivia and her friends would call on their magic and the magic of all the witches who had come before them to place the spell created by Melissa Adler, the original witch.

Over the years, the spell evolved and the wording changed, but the intent remained the same. The town would be protected from outside forces, like destructive weather or major acts of violence. Should a tourist or perhaps a lost hiker stumble upon the place where the town should be, they would find nothing but open roads and empty fields. Only if you already knew of the town would you be able to find it. Or any information related to it.

When they reached the clearing, they immediately set to work. An old oak tree stump provided an altar for everything the spell required. It would be the focal point around which they gathered.

It was also the place they kept the book. It was protected by magic to keep it from weathering with age. It could only be removed from the altar with a spell.

Parker stepped forward. "I release you from the binds that help you stand the test of time. Magic given from the past, help us to complete our task."

She grabbed the book, passing it off for Jill to hold and then pulled a piece of chalk from the bag she carried over her shoulder; she proceeded to etch a star into the wood of the trunk. Five points, one for each element, the fifth for the witches themselves. She then placed a quartz crystal on each point of the star. The largest was placed on the top point of the star. This would be where Olivia stood, as she was the one giving her blood this year.

A sprig of dried lavender and one of sage were placed on opposite ends of the star. A handful of sea salt, black pepper and red rose petals were sprinkled around and over the star. Rosemary and bay leaves were placed at the very center, along with a few carefully laid rose thorns and another handful of hawthorn berries. The white sand shell was placed near the bottom point of the star.

They moved quickly and efficiently, like partners in a graceful dance. Olivia relished in the feeling that she was a part of something so much bigger than herself and that she carried on a tradition that went back hundreds of years.

Addersfield wasn't the only town of its kind. Magic was passed down through bloodlines and there were people who wielded magic in different ways all over the world. But this town? It was her town. She was privileged to be able to protect it.

As she got into position at the top point of the star, Draven's face flashed in her mind. His earnest eyes and charming smile. The thought of him made her heart race and a smile threatened to break free. There was still so much they did not know about each other, things that could break them if they weren't careful. But she wanted him, wanted this imperfect thing they had created for themselves. She needed to be with him. Whatever had brought him here, brought him to her, it had to be magic and magic was the thing she trusted to always lead her where she needed to go. It's what got her here.

"Olivia? You read?" Parker asked, stepping forward to hand her a knife.

She nodded, grabbing it with sure and steady hands. Angling the blade toward her right hand, she cut into the flesh of her palm, the conduit through which her magic flowed. The cut was small enough that it would heal fairly quickly but would bleed enough to serve its purpose. She hissed at the sting, her hand throbbing. Wordlessly, she handed the blade back to Parker before turning to face the altar. She raised her hand, squeezing it so that blood flowed freely from the wound, dark as ink in the night, it splattered on each point of the star and into the center. The last ingredient of the spell.

Jill passed her a small roll of gauze. She wrapped her hand quickly and quietly. They always let this wound heal on its own.

She looked into the faces of her friends, offering each one a nod. Then they began.

"With hearts so true and magic so light, we stand and face the fire so bright," Parker began before Jill stepped in.

"We bring safety and love, and hope and light to the people of Addersfield on this sacred night."

Now it was her turn.

"Protect this town and all who dwell here. Lay prosperity and blessings upon us for another year."

"Grant us the wisdom to always do what's right," Parker continued. "To keep us safe on dark, cold nights."

"With open hearts, we call forth our magic tonight and trust that with love we cannot fall," Olivia stated. "Because love will be what conquers all."

When the last word was uttered, a rush of winds, both cold and warm, blew through the clearing. It was transformative, the feeling brushing over every part of Olivia. When she opened her eyes, she could see it—their magic—moving off to envelop the town and all of their family, friends and neighbors. She was lighter than air. Her magic burned bright in her veins.

"Whoa!" Parker said aloud, her smile growing as her eyes traced over the starry sky. "That was amazing. The best one we've done so far."

"Hell yeah," Jill agreed, squeezing Olivia's hand as their eyes met. "That was all you, Liv. We could all feel it."

"I think it's safe to say we crushed it. I don't think it's a coincidence that it happened the same year that Draven showed up," Parker said, glancing over at Olivia.

She smiled. "You sound like Rosa."

"Hey, I'll definitely take that as a compliment. The woman's never wrong."

"I think you're right, though," Olivia said. "Since the day Draven showed up, things have felt different. At first, of course, I thought it couldn't mean anything good. But it's been a month, and nothing terrible has happened and after learning about his mother, I feel like I understand him. I know what it feels like to want to know more about your family and I know what it's like to not have a family. When I see him with Daniel, I think maybe we could be a family someday."

"Aww," Jill squealed. "Our little Olivia's growing up."

"Oh my God, Jill," Parker said. "Do you always have to be so dramatic?"

"Please, you know you love me."

"Yeah, yeah, yeah. So, what now?" Parker asked.

"Now we clean up and get some hot chocolate because I'm freaking freezing in this damn dress and Olivia goes home to her man," Jill proclaimed.

"Are you sure?" Olivia asked, hoping they would say yes.

"Oh, we're sure," Parker said, a stern look on her face. "Now, go on quick before we make you talk about your feelings and finding true love."

She did not have to be told twice. After hugging her friends goodbye, she made her way through the tall grass, lantern in hand, finding the path that they had made on the way in. She followed it just to the edge of the festival grounds before turning to head down the adjacent street, eager to get home.

He was a complete idiot. From the minute he had walked into this town spouting his lies, he had made a fool of himself. The whole thing was beyond embarrassing, how he'd hid his truth from the very first moment, thinking he had the upper hand. His stomach soured. He really should have known better.

For Olivia to not tell him about the protection spell? He wasn't angry, but he was frustrated. Did this mean there really was no trust between the two of them? Still?

But technically, she shouldn't trust him. Especially considering what he was currently doing. A wave of fresh guilt pooled in his stomach. He really didn't deserve her.

He told Olivia he was going to find Malcolm and maybe he should have done just that at the very least, to avoid raising any suspicion.

Instead, he followed her and her friends as they went off to perform their magic. He needed to see this spell for himself. Because this was the proof he was looking for—magic in action.

The three witches weaved through the tall grass, lanterns in hand, to a small grove of trees just on the other side of the town square, not far at all from tonight's festivities. He walked as quietly as possible, staying several feet behind them at all times, to a spot where he could see all three women perfectly.

The friends chatted for a few minutes. Then they started pulling random things out of the bags they each carried. Components of the spell if he had to guess.

Pulling out his phone, he hit record just as they finished setting everything up. There was the book she had mentioned to him, so exposed. Did they never worry that someone might try to take it? Maybe he could. Maybe it would offer him some answers. Answers he did not dare seek out anywhere else lest he be asked too many questions.

His eyes flew to Olivia, riveted as she sliced into her palm and let her blood drip over everything. She quickly wrapped her hand and then stood straight and tall. They were ready.

It was fascinating and shocking all at once, seeing her magic flow through her, a look of pure joy on her face. She was breathtaking. But seeing her like this made him wonder if he could truly make her happy.

Secret revenge plot notwithstanding, could she be with someone who had no magic of their own?

Was that why she told him what the protection spell did? Did she not think he could handle it? Did his mother ever think the same thing about his father? Is that what eventually drove a wedge between them? He knew it had something to do with her lack of magic. But had they been happy before that? His mother having magic and his father having none at all?

He looked up and the spell was taking effect, pulling him from the thoughts swirling in his head. Clutching his phone in a vice-like grip, he turned to watch the magic spread through the town, a white light seeping into everything around them and beyond. The warmth of it flowed all around him, like the sun on a hot summer day. Was it his mother's blood that allowed him to sense it?

He turned back. Parker was touching the book now, saying something. A spell? Would that prevent him from taking the book?

The three of them were just talking now. He shut off his phone and tucked it away in his pocket. He needed to get home before Olivia did.

But then she said his name.

"Draven showed up; things have been different."

He stepped closer, straining to hear more.

"After learning about his mother, I feel like I understand him."

Her next words made his heartache. His breath caught in his chest. And time stood still.

"And when I see him with Daniel, I think maybe we could be a family someday."

Dammit if he did not want that too, whether he deserved it or not. She had already welcomed him into her family in a big way, when she floated the idea of him joining her and Daniel for Wednesday night dinner a few days ago. He had been nervous, mainly because he guessed that Parker's mother and grandmother knew things about what had happened with his own mother.

While it was tempting to ask them his burning questions, he did not want to give anyone any more reasons to be suspicious of him.

In the end, they had a delicious dinner and talked about normal things like the weather and what Daniel was up to at school. Malcolm extended an open invitation to get a drink sometime and Rosa insisted on sending him home with lots and lots of leftovers. It had been such a long time since he had had an evening like that, surrounded by people who truly cared about one another.

Maybe it was foolish. Maybe it was naïve and maybe he couldn't yet fully let go of his plan, his actions tonight were proof of that. But he wanted more of that. Each day with Olivia lessened his need for answers and revenge seemed less and less important. Right now, tonight, all he wanted was to be with her.

Chapter 15

You can't build anything real on a lie. That's what his mother used to say. Yet, that's exactly what he had done here. It did not matter that his feelings for her were real. It did not matter that he was now questioning his plans. All that mattered was that he had lied to her, let her believe that she now knew his secret.

It was the morning after the Fall Festival and he had gotten no sleep last night.

He was riding high after hearing what Olivia felt for him, how she could see him being a part of her family. He made it home not a minute before she was knocking on his door. When he saw her there in the doorway, hair flowing free, flower crown on her head, the moon shining brightly on her face, he was helpless. She was a goddess and he needed to be with her.

She was everything he had never known he was waiting for. She was funny and smart, always ready with a sarcastic quip to make him smile. She was also kind, kinder than anyone with her background had any right to be. But she was also tough. As a single mom, she had to be. But she never let that toughness harden her heart.

She made him feel things, which was something he had been avoiding for a long time now.

Last night had been particularly intense. Even now, the memory of it assaulted his senses. Olivia stretched out before him on the couch, her bright eyes wide and pleading for him to make her feel good.

"I'd like to take care of you if you would let me," he had said.

"Yes, please."

His hands tugged at the fabric of her dress until it fell to the floor, and she was in nothing but matching tan bra and panties. He gently lowered her to the couch before settling between her thighs. In the next second, he had pushed aside the fabric covering her center, pushing a finger inside her slick heat.

His thumb flattened on her clit with the slightest pressure as he inserted another finger and moved so slowly so that she was agonized and writhing.

Oh God, this is perfect. She's perfect. Maybe we can have it all.

He leaned up, placing kisses on her ribs, along her stomach, her hipbone, her thigh.

The heat of his breath created goosebumps when it reached the insides of her thighs. He lifted one of her legs over his shoulder.

He pressed his face into her cunt to inhale her.

"Draven."

"I've got you, baby," he said before taking his first taste of her.

A full lick up her slit. His tongue nudged her clit. He flicked the sensitive nub rapidly, just a tease, before kissing her cunt. She grew wetter and wetter, his mouth and chin drenched with it.

Using two fingers, he spread her open and lapped at her in heavy strokes with the flat of his tongue. He drew her clit into his mouth and sucked.

"Oh, fuck," she whispered.

Soon, her thighs started to tense up and he released the nub before she could come too quickly.

His eyes flicked up to hers. She was panting, her hands on her tits, pinching and rolling her hard nipples.

He dove back into her cunt, determined to finish her off. Her hips rocked toward his face, chasing her pleasure. He pushed two fingers inside her again and curled them in time with his mouth. She shoved her fist in her mouth, trying to hold back her scream.

"Draven," she rasped.

He paused to glance up, meeting her glazed eyes. "Yeah, babe?"

"Fuck me with your tongue," she asked almost shyly. "Please."

Parting her folds again, he lowered his mouth to her cunt. His tongue circled her entrance before slipping inside. He kept his face pressed close to her, his nose nudging her clit as his tongue licked in a steady pattern.

"Fuck," he moaned into her. "You taste so good."

She writhed under him. "Fuck, don't stop!"

She was getting close. Practically riding his face, her pelvis bones grinding against his mouth. Her moans got louder and louder until her orgasm pulled the air from her lungs.

"Draven," she cried out. Then she fell silent, breathless.

Her cunt pulsed around his tongue and her legs shook from the force of her climax. Her back arched off the couch and then she fell back, her fingers relaxing their grip on his hair.

He'd sat up on his knees, wiping her slickness from his face.

She had opened her eyes as she came down and he knew he had looked at her with something far too tender in his eyes.

He shouldn't have let it happen again. None of it should've happened: getting to know her, getting to know her son and caring about her so damn much. It was all wrong. But last night, when she had shown up at his door, he had lost all sense. She was perfect and he just could not help himself.

You can't build anything real on a lie.

Fuck. He was supposed to come here, learn the truth about his mother, write a story and leave. He wasn't supposed to meet someone, wasn't supposed to fall for her and start questioning every decision he had ever made.

Now that he knew where the book was and what destroying it could possibly do. He was so on edge once they were done and just lying in bed, he couldn't relax. So much so that Olivia offered to leave him alone. He only nodded, guilt and sadness tightening his chest. He had spent the night tossing and turning after she went home. His mind jumped from one decision to the next until he could not stand it anymore.

He had thrown on some clothes and in the early grey light of morning, made his way down to the beach. Everything seemed better when he was looking out at the ocean. But still his stomach churned. He was able to ignore the guilt last night when she was in his arms. He was able to pretend that they could have everything together, that his plans no longer mattered. When he was with her, it was easy to pretend that he was no longer angry over the loss of his mother. That his grief no longer weighed him down. That what he had with Olivia wasn't based on a lie. But the minute she had gone, that dream had vanished.

He remembered all that he had come here to do—write an exposé—and now that he knew where the book was, it was exactly the kind of proof he needed. Guilt ate away at him for wanting to forget the plan and just be with Olivia.

He glanced down at the phone in his hand, it was silent for once. With each passing day his editor had grown more relentless. She had questions that he either had no answers to or did not want to give. She wanted to know where the story was. Was there something supernatural going on in the town, or were they all just a bunch of crooks? What was taking him so long? Was there a story here or not?

The problem was his plans had changed. He might be able to take away magic now and that would certainly do more damage than an exposé in a newspaper—the ultimate revenge for his mother having to go through life alone.

So, he lied, explaining that he had been mistaken in his assumptions. There was no story here after all. She was not happy, not that he had expected her to be. Being fired was something he hadn't expected, though he probably should have. A secret part of him was glad. It gave him a reason to stay here, to be with Olivia and Daniel.

But he could not stay, not if he went through with his plan. There was no doubt in his mind they would figure out his involvement very quickly. Even if he ultimately decided not to go through with it, he still could not stay. Not without telling Olivia the truth.

She would hate him.

He did not know what to do. So, here he was, still standing on this beach, waiting for a sign.

The ocean always calmed him. Breathing in the salty air reminded him of his mother and every summer spent under the sun. Sunscreen and sand coated his skin, as he and Lucas built giant sandcastles. The beach was his childhood and now more than ever, he ached to have his family here with him.

"You can't build anything real on a lie," that's what his mother always used to say.

Whenever she would catch him in a lie, no matter how small, that's what she would say. She taught him and his brother that trust was a privilege, not a right, which is why she was always so open and honest with them about everything.

Except for this one thing. Why had she hidden her history from them? Was it just easier that way?

He wanted to be angry with her, wanted to scream to the heavens that she explain herself. But he just could not. Grief was a funny thing and right now, all it allowed him to feel was hate. Even here, in this place that normally brought so much peace.

He hated the people in this town for letting his mother go. Hated his father for leaving them alone. Hated the magic that seemed to be the cause of all his troubles.

But then he thought of Olivia and that look of pure joy on her face as she helped to cast the protection spell last night. She did not deserve to be punished. But he could not let it go. He had come here to make things up to his mother and now he was ready to just give that up? He had to see this through, for her.

"I'm sorry, Mom. I'm so, so sorry." Then he let himself cry. He cried for his mom and for how much he missed her. He cried for Olivia and Daniel and the deception he'd brought into their lives. Then he cried for himself, wept for the life he was sure he could never have.

If only Lucas were here. His brother always seemed to know the right thing to do. It was Draven's fault they barely spoke. Lucas had tried to comfort him after Mom died, tried to be there for him and Draven pushed him away. It was all too much. The pain of losing Mom was too much, so Draven shut down and locked the world out.

He put everything he had into his career and it paid off. The bosses at the paper loved his work and they rewarded him for it. But it still wasn't enough; he wanted more, he wanted to be the best. At the time, he thought success was the true measure of happiness. What better way to make Mom proud?

Lucas tried to tell him he was wrong. Mom had never cared about money or possessions. She just wanted her boys to be happy and they were. But grief changes us all and Draven was drowning in his. So, things with Lucas grew worse and now they barely spoke to each other.

He wiped the tears from his eyes as he looked out at the ocean again. There, near the horizon, sat a small blue sailboat. It looked almost exactly like the one he and Lucas had sailed as teenagers. They worked and saved for months to afford that boat, with mom chipping in just a little. They had fixed it up one summer and learned to sail the next. Mom would sit on the beach, cheering and waving.

He did not know how the boat had gotten there or why. Maybe it was magic. But he took it as a sign from his brother and maybe his mom too. *Tell Olivia the truth, Draven. You can't build anything real on a lie.*

He would tell her the truth and hope like hell that she would understand.

Now seemed like a good time to reach out to Lucas. He pulled his phone back out from the inner pocket of his jacket, navigating to his text messages.

He typed out a text and hit send, feeling a weight lift off his chest. It wasn't much, but it was a start.

'I miss you. Please call me.'

He reached into his jeans pocket and pulled out the purple and white shell, running his fingers along its smooth surface. He had kept it since the night he and Olivia had first been together. It still had the lines of gold. The truth was staring him right in the face. Acknowledging it would be like leaping off a cliff. He just wasn't sure anyone would be there to catch him after the fall.

But he had to try. It was time to lay everything out on the table. He could only hope Olivia would be willing to do the same. He gave the shell a squeeze for courage and shoved it back in his pocket. He needed to tell her the truth. He needed to tell her, right now. Maybe it was foolish. But maybe she would understand. Maybe she would give him a reason to let it all go.

The weather was affecting Olivia's mood. That had to be it. The sky was gray and overcast, with the threat of rain looming on the horizon.

Normally, this was her favorite kind of weather. It gave her an excuse to sit inside, under a blanket with a good book. Daniel would be curled up beside her, watching a movie or drawing while they both sipped on hot chocolate. But today was different. Today, the weather was an omen. Not the good kind.

She glanced out the front window just as the first drop of rain fell from the sky. A single tear slid down her cheek and she sucked in a breath.

It was her. She was affecting the weather. She was crying and so it started to rain.

This was new. She had read about this kind of thing, talked about it at length with Parker. But no one she knew had ever experienced it.

She wasn't as surprised as maybe she should have been. Sometimes her magic went a little wonky when her emotions were strong and at the forefront. It was a witch's prerogative and right now, she was a complete mess. It had to be Draven. Her thoughts, her feelings, they were all currently unsettled. Apparently, they were so strong she was now influencing the weather. She had no idea what to do about that.

She did not want to think about what that might mean in terms of her feelings for Draven. Because given the current situation, the distance he seemed to be placing between them right now, it was looking more and more likely that his feelings did not match hers. He'd basically asked her to leave last night.

Jill. She needed to talk to Jill.

Reaching down to grab her phone from where it rested on the coffee table, she smiled softly when she clicked on the screen. There was a text from Jill already waiting for her. She was on her way.

That sometimes happened in their group, another byproduct of their magic. "A witch perk," as Parker liked to say. They sometimes just knew when one of them needed the other.

She perched on the couch to wait, crossing her arms over her chest to ward off the chill.

The front door opened. "Penny for your thoughts?" Jill asked from the doorway.

"I think they're worth a bit more than that."

"Okay, fair enough," Jill said as she reached into the pockets of her jeans and pulled out a crumpled bill. "I've got a twenty; is that enough?"

Olivia laughed, the vice in her chest loosening. Where would she be without her best friend? Although she really did not want to talk about everything going on in her head, she knew from experience that those were often the most important conversations. The ones you did not want to have but needed to have. She was glad that Jill was here.

"Afraid not," she said as she walked into the living room with Jill following her.

She waited. Jill was never one to pass up an opportunity to give her opinion. It was one of her annoying yet strangely helpful qualities and in this case, she could really use some of her best friend's wisdom.

"Look, Olivia, I don't want to push you, but I'm concerned. So, let's talk, okay? I can tell how upset you are."

"Upset is an understatement, Jill. I don't know what's going on. I think I freaking caused it to rain. I swear I feel like something really bad is about to happen."

Jill looked at her, brow furrowed. "Wait, you caused it to rain? Are you sure?"

"No, not completely. But it started raining the exact second I started to cry. Hell of a coincidence, don't you think?"

"Well, we can ask Parker about that later. Now tell me, why were you crying?"

"I think something's going on with Draven and I'm scared."

"What kind of something?"

She sighed. "I just have this really bad feeling. We had such a great night together last night. But then he got really weird. So, I asked him if he wanted some space and he just nodded, he wouldn't even look at me. When I woke up this morning, I hadn't heard from him."

"And you usually do?"

"Yes! He always texts me good morning, first thing, even if he's planning on seeing me later that day. But today, nothing and it's already almost ten."

"Where's Daniel?" Jill asked, looking around as if he might be hiding somewhere.

"At a friend's house. He won't be home until dinner."

"Okay, so why haven't you gone over to Draven's to check on him? Maybe he's sick or something."

"I can't, Jill. I've already called and texted. What if he's still sleeping and I go over there all freaked out. He'll think I'm ridiculous."

Jill rolled her eyes. "He will not. Honesty, Olivia. Can't you see how crazy he is about you? I don't understand. What exactly happened between yesterday and today? When you left us last night, you were so happy. You were all "I understand him so much better now, and maybe we could be a family."

She shrugged, feeling completely at a loss. "I don't know. Something just feels off. I can't really explain it. I just feel like I'm losing him."

"Liv," Jill said, stepping forward to place a hand on her arm. "Listen to me. Not everyone is going to leave. Haven't you learned that by now? You're never getting rid of me, for example. Draven is not Shawn. You told Draven you were a witch and nothing happened. How much more proof do you need?"

"I didn't tell him about what the protection spell did until last night at the festival. He said he wasn't mad. But maybe he lied?"

"Why would that matter?"

"Because I kept a secret from him. I just didn't want him to feel bad about all of us knowing he was lying the entire time."

"You think that would make him angry enough to just walk away from you? From Daniel?"

"I don't know, maybe," she said quietly. The reasoning sounded a little pathetic even to her own ears.

"Bullshit! You're letting yourself get caught up in this cycle of fear. Draven's not going anywhere, so why are we still pretending there's a chance that he is?"

She stayed quiet. There was no way to articulate her muddled and messy feelings. Jill might be right, but she could not truly understand how she was feeling. Things were going so well. But she could not help but feel like at any moment, the other shoe was going to drop.

She wanted to be happy for once without some looming threat or deep dark secret scaring her. But that was easier said than done.

"Look, Olivia, I get it—"

"No, you don't!"

No one understood. No one got it. She did not even understand the full extent of her mindset right now, so how in the hell could Jill presume to know? "You don't, Jill. All of this is so precarious. It's not just my baggage and my fears I have to worry about. I have Daniel. I have to protect him, even if it means sacrificing my own happiness. Daniel likes Draven so much. So, what am I supposed to do?"

Jill's eyes softened at the mention of Daniel. Guilt gnawed at Olivia's gut for using her son in her argument. Yes, she did want to keep Daniel from getting hurt. It was part of why she wanted to get involved with Draven in the first place. But it wasn't just about Daniel. Her son was strong and tough. He had a resilient heart and he could make it through anything.

But her? She wasn't as strong as Daniel. She had had her heart shattered and her faith broken in the past. Now that she was finally feeling good and whole and alive, she could not handle the thought of it all slipping away.

"Okay, maybe I don't understand," Jill countered softly but with a strict sense of purpose. "But I'm trying, and I know Draven will try too, if you give him a chance."

"Then why haven't I heard from him? We have this amazing night together and then nothing? That doesn't seem strange to you?"

Jill shrugged. "A little, maybe. But it could be nothing. Maybe he's not feeling well like I said before. Or maybe he's busy writing. I bet he just got distracted and lost track of time. We could do a locator spell if you're worried about him?"

"No!" she yelled. "Magic is the last thing I'd want to use in this situation. Mine is all over the place right now and I'd have to follow an object of his. How would I look to him if he saw me chasing his shirt? Especially if he is just sitting at home right now. It would be too much."

"Okay, okay, I guess you're right, bu—" Jill's eyes narrowed. "Hang on. Why do you have his shirt?"

A blush rose to her cheeks. "Oh. Well, I, umm ... I sort of stole it yesterday before I left. I just wanted to feel close to him even when we weren't together."

"Aww, Liv. That's really sweet."

"Okay, yes, whatever. Let's get back to the actual problem. What do I do about Draven? Am I just making up this bad feeling in my head?"

"Look, Liv. I think you and I both know how much Draven cares about you. Just go over there and talk to him. Tell him how his actions made you feel. I'm sure he'll understand. You'll kiss and makeup and all will be right with the world again. No risk, no reward," Jill said with a wink.

She smiled. No risk, no reward. It's something Jill used to say to her a lot when they first met, back when she still hadn't fully embraced the title of witch. Before the people in this town became her family.

Saying it now was Jill's way of reminding her what could be if only she would let it.

"I get it, Jill. I just have to do it. Today. I just need some time alone first and then I'll track him down."

Jill pulled her in for a hug. "Good. Let me know how it goes. Remember, Liv. Not everyone leaves, you know. The right people, the right person, will stay, no matter what."

Tears welled in her eyes. Jill always knew just what to say. As always, she was eternally grateful for her bestie.

They both stepped away from each other, not bothering to hide their wet eyes and red noses.

"Oh, shit. I forgot. I was actually going to call you this morning, but I got a little distracted when I felt how upset you were. Parker came into the bakery this morning. I guess she finally asked Rosa about Draven's mom."

"What did she say?"

"That Draven's mom tried to share her magic with someone else, someone who never had magic of their own and she tried to use the book to do it."

She cringed. "Oh no."

Jill nodded. "I know. That's against the rules. Draven's mom must have known this. I mean, she grew up here and she was a witch herself. She lost her magic because of it. Apparently, it was the book's way of punishing her."

"There was nothing anyone could do?"

"No," Jill shook her head. "According to Parker, they tried to find a way to get her magic back. But when it became clear there was no way to do that, his mom decided to leave town. No one could really stop her. I guess Janella was a friend of hers. They kept in touch."

"Did Janella have anything to say?"

"Parker didn't ask. I guess she doesn't like to talk about it much. She still feels bad."

"Does she know Draven's mom passed away?"

"I'm honestly not sure. Maybe you could talk to Draven and he could go see Janella? I'm sure it would mean a lot to her."

She nodded. "Yeah, I'll do that. Hey, do we know who his mom tried to share her magic with?"

Jill shrugged. "Rosa wouldn't say. I think she would rather we asked Draven about it ourselves. It is his story to tell, after all."

"But I'm not even sure he knows."

"That's what Parker said. But Rosa would not budge. She must think he does know or that he could figure it out if he had all the information. But we kind of thought it might be his dad."

"Maybe. I'll ask him about it if I ever see him again," she tried to joke, though it fell flat.

"Everything is going to work out, Liv, you'll see. I'll get out of your hair, you witch with a b," Jill said with a wink as she made it to the front door. "Remember, let me know how it goes with Draven when you find him."

She smiled. "I will. Love you, Jillybean."

Jill hated that nickname. But today, she just waved it off. "Love you too."

Then the house was still and quiet again, just Olivia and her messy thoughts. She plopped down on the couch, the familiar creak of the springs an oddly comforting sound. She just needed a few minutes to figure out what to say before she headed over to Draven's.

Chapter 16

The knock on the door nearly made her jump out of her skin. As she moved to rise from the couch, something tickled her feet. Roses. A small pile of pink roses lay on the floor and all around her. She sighed. She must have conjured them without noticing, lost in thought as she was.

"Coming!" she yelled as she ran to answer the knock. She smoothed her hair down as she pulled the door open. She probably looked a mess, eyes red and swollen from crying and tears still staining her cheeks.

"Hi," she breathed out as her eyes met Draven's.

"Hi," he said with a soft smile, though it did not reach his eyes. Something was wrong.

"Are you okay? I've been calling and texting you. I was starting to worry."

He cringed. "I'm okay. But I really need to talk to you about something. Can I come in?"

Worry gnawed at her gut. It had been a long time since she had been in anything resembling a relationship but even she knew someone saying they "needed to talk" was never a good sign.

"Of course." She waved him through, shutting the door behind him. She watched him for a moment as he walked through to the living room. Whatever was about to happen could not be good. Taking a deep breath to steady her nerves, she followed after him.

He was stopped in the middle of the room, staring at nothing.

"Are you okay?" she asked.

"I, um ... I need to tell you something and I'm not sure where to start. Let's sit down."

He perched on the edge of the couch, pulling her down to sit next to him.

"Draven, you're scaring me."

He took a deep breath. It must not have done much to steady him because she could feel his hand shaking. "First, I want to apologize for not responding to your texts or answering your calls. I did not mean to shut you out. But this thing I have to tell you isn't easy and I know once I do, you're going to hate me. I spent the morning trying to decide what to do and I know telling you is the right thing."

A cold chill ran up her spine and dread pooled in her stomach. This was exactly what she had been trying to explain to Jill. Something about today had felt off since the moment she opened her eyes this morning. She had a feeling whatever he was about to say would break her heart.

"I told you why I came to town in the first place. I found out my mom was a witch and searching through her things pointed me here. I found letters from friends, pictures, all kinds of things. But what I was most excited about were the journals. She had dozens of journals where she wrote about her life."

Despite her nerves, she smiled. Whenever Draven talked about his mom, his whole face lit up. It was such a cool thing to see. "That's really amazing, Draven. I'm sure you were able to learn so much about who she was."

He nodded, squeezing her hand. "I did. The bulk of the journals started around the time she left here for New York. She and my dad were together, but my brother and I weren't around yet. One of the first entries was talking about how she lost her magic."

Her brow furrowed in confusion. "Yeah. I remember you told me that on our first date."

"Right. But there's more to it."

The first tear fell down her cheek just as a single drop of rain hit the window. She was definitely making it rain. "I knew it," she said softly, pulling her hand from his. "I knew you weren't telling me everything."

"I'm sorry, Liv," he said. "I just did not know who I could trust. Because the thing is, I know why my mom lost her magic here in this town, but I don't know how. I assume someone had to have taken it away. But I also know that instead of helping her, the people in this town let her leave. I know that losing her magic was something that my dad resented, though I don't know exactly why and I know that he eventually left because of it. My mother wrote it all down. That's how I know that she never got over losing him. Even though she accepted the loss of her magic, I can't."

She narrowed her eyes. What exactly was he trying to say?

"Draven," she said slowly. "Before you say anything else, I want to make something very clear. Magic is good. The witches here are good.

So, whatever you think happened as far as how your mom lost her magic, I can promise you; you are wrong."

He stood up from the couch so fast it startled her. He began pacing back and forth, like a caged animal. Then, suddenly, he whirled around to look her right in the eye.

"I am not wrong. This town is wrong. They use magic for a protection spell, but where were they when my mother was raising two boys all alone, huh? Where were they when she was dying?" He choked out on a sob.

She stood up and hurried towards him. Tears shone on his lashes. "No amount of magic can bring back the dead, Draven. You must know that?"

He stepped away from her, jaw set in an angry line. "I do know that. I may not have grown up in this town, Olivia, but I know that. Anyway, that's not what I'm saying. Magic could not have saved my mother, I know that. But its absence did do harm. The lack of it drove my father away. I'm saying that magic tore my family apart, Liv."

His eyes bored into hers, as if pleading with her to believe him, to take his accusations seriously.

She scoffed. He had no idea what he was talking about, no idea of the consequences his mother would have known about all along. She would have known exactly what she was doing but was willing to risk it. "You would say that. That just proves you have no idea how any of this works. Look at those flowers, Draven," she said, pointing to the pile of roses still on the floor. "That's about as bad as it gets. Me, absent-mindedly creating flowers out of nothing because my emotions were going haywire worrying about you. We use our magic for *good*. Magic did not do anything to hurt you. You said it yourself; the lack of magic did."

He only stared at her for a moment, either not hearing her or choosing to ignore her. Now would be a good time to tell him what she knew.

"Exactly," he said quietly. "If my mother had been allowed to keep her magic, maybe my father wouldn't have left us. If the people in this town had cared more, maybe my mother wouldn't have left behind two broken sons when she died. Maybe we would have found a family here, just like you did."

How dare he use her own experience against her like that? Screw him.

"What is it that you want, Draven? Why did you really come here?" she snapped.

He sighed, his whole body slumping. He looked exhausted, as if he carried the weight of the word on his shoulders.

"I came here to expose magic."

"I'm sorry, what?" Olivia asked.

Had she not heard him?

"I said I came here to expose magic."

Her eyes snapped back to his and the fury he saw there turned his whole body to ice. Ironically, this was one of the things he liked most about her. Her fire. Her fierce determination and protectiveness.

The slap she landed against his cheek echoed throughout the room. Both of them were breathing harshly, chests heaving with the effort. Her warm brown eyes were now filled with disgust.

"I knew it. I knew from the moment I heard your name that nothing good could come from you being here. That's why you lied, isn't it? You pretended you did not know anyone here so you could sneak around and expose us? So, what the hell was I, Draven? I gave you everything you needed the night we slept together. Was it all just a joke to you?"

It hurt so damn much for him to see her like this. Despite everything she said, he still wanted to hold her, to comfort her. But he knew she would not want that now.

"No," he gasped out. "No, Liv. I swear. That night changed things for me. I could see how good you were. Even though I was angry, at the town, at the people here, I never thought any less of you."

She straightened up, wiping the tears from her eyes. Her face hardened, mouth settling into a scowl. "Save it, Draven. How can you justify making such a huge assumption? You only knew one side of the story and yet you were willing to punish innocent people? Do you want to know what really happened with your mother?"

He gasped. "I know exactly what happened. I just don't know *how* it happened. You told me you didn't know anything about it."

"I hadn't. I didn't lie to you. Parker asked Rosa about your mom, just like I told you she would. She came to the bakery this morning to tell me. But I wasn't there, because I was busy worrying about you. So, she told Jill, who told me."

"And what exactly did she say?" he asked. His anger simmered low in his gut. He needed to finally know the whole truth.

"Rosa said that your mom tried to give someone else part of her magic and she tried to use the book's magic to help her. Remember, the one I told you about?"

He nodded, avoiding her gaze. She still had no idea he had spied on the protection spell and that he knew exactly where that book was.

"But it did not work and as punishment, she lost her magic completely."

"I know that. I know she wasn't supposed to do it. But I don't understand how she just lost her magic. How the people here—her friends, her family—could just take her whole life away from her and then just turn their backs like she meant nothing to them."

"Our magic is a gift. It's against the rules to try and give it to someone else. But it wasn't other witches that took her magic away. It was the book itself. The magic from the original witches is like an entity unto itself. It's what keeps magic alive."

No. No, that wasn't right. This could not be right.

"Isn't it possible my mother was the victim here? That my father forced her to do it? Why should she have been punished for someone else's mistake? Someone still should have tried to do something," he was almost yelling now.

"She still chose to try. Whatever her reasons, she made the choice in the end, and people did try," she said, shaking her head. "But there is no spell to bring back someone's magic. Or to give someone magic. Or to stop the book from taking it. Your mother must have tried to create one. Her friends tried to help her. But, in the end, she told everyone she had to accept what happened because she had known the risks., So I don't think anyone forced her hand."

He snapped. "That is such bullshit. She loved my dad and was probably just trying to make him happy. It's not right that she could not choose to share her magic with him. It's not right that she had magic and he did not. It's not right that some people have magic and others don't. You, your friends, this whole goddamn town. What makes you so special?"

She was crying again, but he could not bring himself to care.

"I don't know, Draven. I don't know. It's in our blood. Please try to understand," she begged.

"No. You love it, don't you? You love that you have magic and I don't. You wouldn't share it with me if you could, would you?"

"No," she snapped. "I would not. It would not be right. Magic is a gift, Draven. I would not betray it like that."

He laughed, bitterness coating his tongue. "You don't deserve it. None of you do."

She stalked up to him, poking him in the chest hard with her finger. "Don't you dare tell me what I deserve. You're just afraid to face the truth. I'm sorry that your father left you. Believe me; I understand exactly how you feel. You want answers that make sense and the only people who can give them to you aren't around. But that isn't my fault. It's no one's fault. Can't you see that?"

"All I see is everything I've lost."

"What about me, Draven? Do you see me standing here in front of you? You just admitted to me that you were out for revenge and I'm still here. Do you want to know what I think? I think you're afraid. Afraid of this thing that you know so little about. And because you've been so focused on how magic wronged you, you can't see how wonderful it can be."

Each word she said cut him to the quick. He had thought maybe she would understand. She had lost her own family so very early in life, so she should see the need for justice the way he did. But he should have known. She had a family now and it did not include him.

He would see this through for his mother. Even if it meant turning his back on this woman he had come to care so much about.

She moved closer to him, both hands coming up to cup his face. "Please, Draven. Please try to understand."

He gripped her hands tightly, pushing them away and putting space between them. He could not understand. He had to see this through. But not by writing some exposé. No. He was going to take their magic away.

"I'm sorry, Olivia. But I have to do this."

"Do what? Draven, what are you going to do?"

"You'll know soon."

As he walked out the door, the sound of her sobs pierced his heart.

Chapter 17

He hadn't known his exact plan until a few minutes ago: destroy the book.

Yet, he spent the entire walk from Olivia's house looking over his shoulder. Each time he did, he expected to see her chasing after him, eyes burning, determined to stop him. Each time, there was no one. Each time, his resolve hardened further.

It was funny. He did not want to be stopped, but a part of him wanted her to try. Or at least care enough to come after him. That had been his first mistake, letting himself get this close to her; it only complicated things. His second mistake had been letting her into his heart. In the end, she had chosen magic, just like his father had.

The man had valued magic above everything else, even the love of his family. Where was his father now? What had become of him? Not that it mattered. But the similarities between the two situations were not lost on him—one person with magic, the other without it and magic was the thing that tore them apart. Olivia made that clear when she chose her magic over him.

But his father would not win. Olivia would not win. Magic would not win, not this time.

As he stepped into the copse of trees that housed the book, the rest of the world fell silent. He could feel the change in the air, the charge of magic as if he had just crossed some invisible barrier. He glanced around. He was alone.

There was the book, exactly where he had seen it last—resting on that old tree stump, surrounded by the remnants of the protection spell cast only yesterday. He did not understand how they could just leave it here unprotected. Although, he supposed they had very little to worry about. All the people in this town worshipped magic, or so it seemed—even those who had none.

Let him be the one to teach them all a lesson. Too little, too late.

He walked forward, stopping just before he reached the altar. He could not be too careful. He had assumed they had no spells guarding the book, as Olivia hadn't mentioned anything. But she had lied to him about what the protection spell did and after the way she had reacted earlier, he had no reason to believe she would not lie about this. A lie of omission, maybe, but a lie all the same.

He waited a few minutes, his body tensed and ready to spring into action. But there was nothing.

He took a few more steps until the tips of his sneakers hit the wood of the tree stump. Slowly, he reached down to place his hands on the book.

It was smooth and warm beneath his fingertips. The magic a steady beat. Almost soothing. This was only the second time he had felt it. The first being the night of the festival. It occurred to him now that the magic was likely calling to him, like it sensed that he was now ready to accept its existence, where before he would not have.

Why had this gift, as Olivia called it, not been given to him? He had always believed in magic. His mother had encouraged that belief, telling him stories of witches who brewed magic potions and children who could fly. That last part he knew wasn't real, but that first part, he now knew for sure that it was.

For the first time since this all began, he let himself feel some anger towards his mother for hiding this part of herself from him. He had clung desperately to those magical stories after his father left. He'd have given anything to know that there was some truth to them.

But he could not pretend that this was still only about his mother. Maybe if he had never spoken to Olivia this morning, things would be different.

Because knowing her had shifted something in him. He would not deny that. His intention had been to admit his true purpose for coming to town, beg her forgiveness and hope that she listened. That maybe she would convince him to let go of his plans.

Instead, she had added fuel to the fire. Now he wanted to show her how wrong she had been. His mother was innocent. Maybe she had never wanted magic in the first place. Maybe she had only been trying to get rid of it. Why should she be punished for that?

His anger only made him more determined to see his plan through. Someone else might have seen this as an opportunity to take magic for themselves. But not him. No, he just wanted it gone.

He glanced down at the book, his hands still resting on its cover. It was such a plain thing—brown leather with nothing but an M on the cover. If not for its thick size, it could be mistaken for a simple journal. Maybe that was a type of defense mechanism to draw less attention to itself. He flipped open the front cover.

There was an inscription on the first page that read:

Spell book of Melissa Adler. Town founder, Addersfield.

It was her magic that helped protect the town. From what he understood, based on what Olivia had told him, the book did not give the witches their magic. But it did strengthen it. If the book were to be destroyed, it would be like trying to steer a ship with no sail. They would be lost and eventually, their magic might die out altogether.

He began flipping through the pages. He could see that various spells and potions had been added over the years. There was a spell for everything. Finding lost objects, levitating things, starting fires, locating people, turning reflective surfaces into mirrors. Even things like ways to make your hair grow longer and ways to ward off evil.

Some pages looked well-loved; others looked virtually untouched, as if those particular spells had been created for a specific purpose, used once and never used again. Maybe even not at all. Each page held a signature, presumably of the person who'd created the spell. Some pages held several signatures. On those, there were often additions or changes to the original spell. The pages themselves were an odd juxtaposition. The oldest ones looked almost like leather. Whereas the most recent ones were written on plain old printer paper.

Everything was well documented. But the organization left something to be desired. There were no dates on any of the pages and there was no way to tell where a particular spell might be in the book. A person could probably guess if they knew who had created it. But he would have killed for an index.

He kept flipping, hoping to find something written by his mother, but he did not recognize any of the handwriting. It was possible he had simply missed it; the book was huge. It was possible she had never created a spell, though her journals told a different story. Or maybe losing her magic meant her contributions were erased from the book. He was inclined to believe the latter.

Flipping to the most recent page, he found an entry with Olivia's signature.

Brownies—For encouraging openness and honesty in relationships.

Then a list of required ingredients along with a recipe for said brownies. Flipping back, there were a few more spells involving cakes, pies, and cupcakes. There was even one that could be mixed with lemonade.

Apparently, Olivia liked to weave magic into her recipes. Another thing she had failed to mention to him. He had eaten his fair share of her treats from the first day he had stepped into town. Had she ever used her magic on him? Before he had seen her this morning, he would have said no. He trusted her. Now, he did not know what to believe.

He closed the book and paused to consider his options. He looked, but he doubted there would be any kind of spell in the book to take away someone's magic. A spell hadn't taken away his mother's magic; at least, he didn't think so. It had simply disappeared. Some twisted trick pulled by her witch ancestors from beyond the grave.

He could try creating his own spell, not that he really knew how to do that. But he did not want to use magic. He touched the book, thumbing the pages as he considered his options. Destroying the book would not destroy magic but it would eventually deplete it.

Maybe he could burn it. That would certainly do the trick.

MAGIC IN THE AIR

There did not seem to be any kind of protection on the book. He had been able to come here and look into it. But could he actually take it?

He curled his fingers under the back cover and lifted.

It was surprisingly light for how hefty it looked. He glanced around the clearing again, still waiting for someone to barge in on him. But no one came.

He would not burn the book here. That had the potential to be very destructive. No. He would take it down to the beach. It seemed a fitting place for his time here to come to an end. Once it was done, he would leave and never come back.

As he stepped out from between the trees, the book tucked underneath his jacket, his phone buzzed in his jeans pocket. His heart soared for one brief moment, thinking that maybe it was Olivia. But he quickly shook that thought away.

He had somewhere to be, and he would not stop for anything.

Chapter 18

Cold. That was what she felt right now, that bone-deep chill that comes along with devastating sadness. All the feelings she had for Draven had been replaced with a cold dread. Every happy moment and memory was tainted by the bitterness of a lie. A lie so big, it had the potential to ruin her life if she let it.

She was angry too. At him, at herself. But really, should she have expected anything different? Experience had taught her that romantic love did not last. So, how could this thing between them have gone any other way? Wasn't this how love had always been for her? A thing that always ended in heartache.

She should have known better, should have trusted her instincts. But instead, she had let herself get distracted by pretty eyes, sweet words, and, apparently, empty promises.

Except it really wasn't that simple, was it?

Because she had trusted her instincts and her magic had been trying to show her something; she was sure of that even now. She had felt it in the air on the very day Draven showed up. Everyone had—a change. From the first moment she laid eyes on Draven, there was a connection. She chose to trust that feeling, to trust her magic.

But look where it had gotten her. If she could not trust her magic, could not trust herself, what else did she have?

What the hell was the point of it all anyway?

The universe was cruel to offer Draven to her only so she could lose him in this way. If there was a lesson to be learned here, it only reinforced her belief that caring for someone in this way was a waste of her time.

It was all worthless, getting to know him, telling him about her life and sharing her magic with him. He had said it was all real, that he cared about her and cared about Daniel. But how could she trust anything he had said now?

It did not matter anyway, because he left, just like everyone else. She hadn't been enough to make him stay. She was only good enough to be used as a pawn in his game. She had no idea what to do now.

She should probably be concerned. Draven was so fixated on the idea that no one deserved magic and he was going to do something about that, but what? At the moment, when he said she would know soon and then left, all she could focus on was his retreating figure.

The simple act of him walking away from her had been enough to bring her to her knees.

Would he leave town? Should she force him to? Would he write his article after all? Or did he have something bigger in mind? Should she try and stop him? He had accused her of choosing magic over him. Maybe she should show him what her magic could really do.

But no. That wasn't her. She would never use her magic to intentionally hurt someone.

203

She glanced out the window. The rain was coming down steadily now. The wind was howling. It matched the feelings inside her. Sadness and confusion. Hurt and anger. Loneliness. But at least she had Daniel. Draven had no one.

Daniel? How was she supposed to explain this to Daniel? He adored Draven. She could see it anytime the three of them were together. He would be devastated.

That's what she was most afraid of, how this would affect her son. He was such a kindhearted soul, always willing to see the good in others. She had tried to follow his example with Draven, despite the red flags. She had known better than to let him into their lives and she had let it all happen anyway.

A hoarse and desperate sob escaped her throat. The pain was an aching wound in her heart.

But no. She could not break yet. She walked over to the couch, to the pile of flowers still on the floor.

"*Clineto,*" she muttered and the flowers vanished. That particular spell was one of the oldest from the book and also used very frequently. It was great for cleaning up messes, though they didn't know where all the vanished stuff wound up. She walked into the kitchen, eyeing the vase of flowers that still sat on the counter—the ones Draven had given her on their first date.

She walked over, snatched them up and promptly tossed them in the trash. The way things were going, she would probably never be able to look at a flower the same way again, which was a real shame. Flowers were kind of her thing.

She walked around aimlessly for a few minutes, the house almost eerily quiet. It was getting close to noon, which meant that Daniel would not be home for at least another four hours.

She had no idea what to do with herself now. How quickly she had gotten used to Draven being a constant presence in her life. She should really update Parker and Jill. If Draven was up to something, they needed to figure out what it was and stop him before someone got hurt. Before *anyone else* got hurt

The buzz of her phone pulled her from her thoughts. She walked over to pick it up from the table. A video call from Jill. Why would Jill be calling when they had spoken in person not long ago? She hit the answer button.

"Jill? What's up?"

"Liv, I need to ask you a question. It's going to seem weird, but just bear with me, okay?"

"Okay ..."

"Were you able to get in touch with Draven after I left?"

A video chat did not seem the best way to fill Jill in, but desperate times. "Yeah, I did. I really need to explain what happened. I think Draven's going to try something. He told me he thinks magic ruined his family and he said he's going to do something about it."

Lines deepened on Jill's face. "Here's the weird question. Did Draven mention talking to Malcolm last night at the festival?"

"This morning?"

"This morning or at any point last night."

She shook her head. "No. But he did say he was going to pay Malcolm a visit when we left him last night. Remember, you were there."

Jill nodded. "I know. But the thing is, Malcolm told me he never came by and after what you just told me ..."

"You think he was up to something before I met up with him?"

Jill cringed. "I'm sorry, Liv."

"No," she said, holding up her hand. "I think you're right. But what the hell would he have been doing?"

"Ouch! Shit, this was not where I wanted to end up." The voice came from somewhere in her house.

"What the hell?" Olivia said, looking around for the source of the sound.

"Liv," Jill said. "Are you okay? What the hell was that noise?"

"I have no idea," she whispered. "I'm going to go check it out." She walked as quietly as possible out of the living room and into the hallway. But there was no one there.

The floorboards creaked over her head, like a scene from a horror movie. Her heart raced, her palms going clammy.

"I think someone is upstairs," she whispered to Jill. She held her finger to her lips.

She walked over to the bottom of the stairs. "Hello," she called out, leaning over the railing to peer up the stairs.

A figure appeared at the top and she lifted her hand, ready to use her magic to defend herself.

"Sorry, Liv," a familiar voice called down. "I was supposed to end up in your living room. Clearly, I messed up somewhere."

"Parker," she breathed out in a rush. The fear in her heart melted into a mixture of relief and annoyance.

"Did you say 'Parker?'" Jill asked from the phone clutched tight in Olivia's hand.

She sighed. "Yes, yes I did," she said, holding up the phone so Jill could see their mutual friend coming down the stairs.

"Jesus, Parker," Jill snapped. "You almost gave me a heart attack!"

Olivia let out a quick laugh. "You! I'm the one whose house she just randomly popped into. Parker, what the hell are you doing here? How the hell did you end up upstairs without me seeing you?"

Parker cringed. "Yeah, sorry about that, Liv. I was trying to poof myself into your living room. But somehow, I ended up in your shower. If it makes you feel any better, I hit my head pretty good."

"You poofed yourself? What the hell does that mean?" Jill asked, looking as confused as Olivia felt.

"I came up with a spell the other day to transport myself places—good thing to have in case of an emergency. I needed to talk to Olivia right away. So, I figured now was a good time to try it."

"What's the emergency?"

"Oh right, shit, I got so distracted. The book is missing."

"What the hell do you mean the book is missing?" Olivia asked before turning back to Jill, still on her phone. "Get over here right now."

"On my way."

Thank God for small towns. Five very tense minutes later, Jill was flying through the front door.

"Now, what is going on, Parker?" Olivia asked.

"It was my abuelita. She called me earlier to say she had a bad feeling. She told me I should go check on the book, so, of course, I did and it was gone."

Jill swore. "Who would want to take it? And why?"

Olivia already knew. Maybe she had known all along. "Draven."

Jill grabbed her hand.

She stood numbly and listened while Jill explained everything to Parker.

"What do we do?" Parker asked quietly.

Olivia turned to her friends. "We stop him."

Chapter 19

He pulled a lighter from his pocket. It was the one single thing of his father's that he had kept, a heavy silver thing with a rose etched on the front. It had been left behind on the night he walked out of the house and never came back.

It seemed fitting that it would be the thing to help him end all this. All the anger and fear and grief churning in his gut had compelled him to dig it out of the bottom of his suitcase before leaving the house this morning.

He held it now in one clenched fist, the wind howling in his ears. He lowered himself to the sand, the book in his lap. He was the only one here again. He had come to think of this beach as his place. It seemed right that this would be the place where he executed his plan. It seemed very prophetic—very full circle.

He set the book down in the sand and got to his feet. There was no fire pit here. Didn't beaches usually have a fire pit for bonfires and such? He had never really paid attention before. So, he set about collecting sticks and stones, a pyre to burn the book upon. A fitting end to it all.

Except it would not stop raining and the wind seemed to blow harder every second. But he was determined. Flicking the lighter, he bent down to hold the flame to a small stick in his other hand. He used that stick to then light the pile of wood at his feet. The flame caught quickly. Once he was satisfied the flame would not blow out, he went to collect the book from the spot where he left it, only to find that the wind had blown it open.

He got down on his knees to peer at the pages.

To create the perfect wind (for sailing)

There was a list of ingredients and then the spell itself.

I wish the wind to blow today.

This wish it will not fail.

I wish the wind to blow today.

So that it may fill my sails.

Kelly Grace Reynolds

"Olivia," Jill said softly. "Are you sure—"

She held up a hand to silence her friend. "Jill, please don't. If Draven's planning on doing something to the book, we have to stop him. If we lost it, we could lose our magic. Is that what you want?"

Jill shook her head. "Of course not. But let's just think about this for a second. Could he actually do any damage to the book?"

Parker nodded, eyes wide with fear. "The book can be destroyed. The only spells we used on it were ones to protect it from weather and age. I'm guessing no one ever thought we'd need to protect it from being stolen."

Olivia laughed. She could not help herself. It was all so ridiculous and yet it was happening. The one man she had let herself feel anything for in years turned out to have a vendetta against her town and was intent on taking away their magic. You could not make this stuff up.

"Liv?" Parker asked gently, placing a hand on her shoulder.

"It's all my fault. I let my guard down around Draven. I told him what the book was and what it did for us and last night ..." she whirled to face Jill, tears pooling in her eyes, "last night when he was supposed to be catching up with Malcolm? He probably followed us to watch the protection spell. That's probably how he knew where the book was. He saw it."

"Olivia," Jill whispered. "It is not your fault."

"But it is. When he came to see me earlier, he told me the truth and I snapped. I accused him of being afraid of magic. I told him the truth about his mother. I could see how much learning everything had hurt him. But I lashed out. I pushed him away."

Parker pulled Olivia's face up, cupping it in her hands. "Anyone else would have done the same thing, Liv. Believe me. He lied to you, betrayed your trust. No one would expect you to immediately forgive him, if at all. He did a terrible thing and you reacted accordingly."

She sniffed, wiping the tears from her eyes. "Maybe you're right. But I shouldn't have let him leave. I was so ready to believe he was exactly like Shawn that I ignored his pain. Maybe he doesn't deserve my forgiveness, but I won't let him do this. I won't let him take our magic. Because if he does, I know it will haunt him for the rest of his life. I don't want that for him. There's so much good in him. I won't let him snuff it out.".

She would give him the chance that Shawn never gave her. She only hoped he would take it and if he didn't, she wouldn't hesitate to stop him. She had too much to lose.

"How are we going to stop him, Liv?" Parker asked. "We don't even know where the hell he is."

"Should we use a locator spell?" Jill asked.

"No," Olivia said, shaking her head. "We don't need it. He's down at the beach. That's the only place in town he loves more than anything. The place where he always feels the most connected to his mother. If he was going to try and take away our magic, that's where he's going to do it."

His mother had written this spell. There was no date, but he knew it was likely from before she had met his father. She had still used her family name. It did not strike him as a particularly advanced spell. Maybe something she had come up with as a teenager?

He read it again, laughing at the title. She had loved the water, the beach. He had always assumed she had no interest in sailing, though. Always content to watch him and Lucas venture out. But maybe she had loved it just as much as they had. The idea brought tears to his eyes.

On impulse, he pulled out his phone. He unlocked the screen and navigated to the camera. He moved back just a bit so he could capture the entire page. When he was satisfied, he sent it off to Lucas.

He sighed, feeling the weight of all his decisions on his shoulders. Seeing his mother's name in that book was difficult in a way he hadn't expected. That anger was back, pounding in his heart, pulsing in his blood.

His mother was a witch once upon a time. Before now, it had been this fantastical idea. But seeing that spell put the truth of it right in front of him. His mother was a witch and she made her choice anyway, knowing the risk it posed.

Magic is a gift, Draven. And I will not betray it.

Olivia's words sounded in his head. So sure, so absolute. He had to believe his mother was the same. That despite this one mistake, she too believed that magic was a gift and if she did, then she would not want this for him now. She would not want revenge. Seeing her spell in the book proved that to him. Even if it was just a silly spell, his mother had truly been a part of something here. She would not want him to destroy it.

No. She had to have known the consequences of her actions and he could guess why she did it.

His mother had loved his father more than anything. Maybe that was her biggest mistake, loving someone who only wanted to use you. Maybe his father did love her, but he loved the idea of magic more and eventually, he got tired of pretending.

Draven was no better, using Olivia and her love of magic to further his own agenda.

Shame settled heavily in his bones. It was all so wrong. Because he could see now how his anger and his grief had skewed his viewpoint; he had been so lost. Adrift in a sea of loss and loneliness, discovering his mother's secret had been something of a lifeline for him. His assumptions about magic's role in her life was a distraction from the pain he lived with every day, the ache in his heart that gnawed away at him. The memories he was desperate to never forget and the fear that someday he would.

He looked down at the book, pages now wet from his tears. What would his mother think of him now? Would she be disappointed? Angry? Probably both. How could he have ever thought this would be what she would want? It was clear to him now that this was the sign he had been looking for earlier. Leave it to his mother to wait until the last possible second. He would laugh if he had the energy.

Because while he was incredibly happy that he hadn't gone through with burning the book, he was now faced with another problem. Olivia. She had let him into her heart, sharing the most intimate parts of herself with him. He knew how much trust meant to her and he had betrayed that trust.

The sound of the waves crashing against the shore drew his attention. How many significant moments of his life had taken place with that sound in the background? Just two weeks ago, he had stood on this beach with Olivia and Daniel, the three of them searching for another shell to add to their collection. Daniel had been so thrilled that Draven had been the one to find one this time.

Being out on the boat brought him so much joy, the wind whipping around him, the smell of salt in the air, and how amazing it was to teach Daniel about sailing. The way he and his brother had taught each other.

How on earth was he supposed to fix this mess? Should he even try? Olivia and Daniel both deserved so much better than him.

It was taking incredible strength to keep from going back to her right now and begging for her forgiveness. He wanted to see her, to touch her.

He fluctuated between overwhelming guilt from the way he had handled everything to crippling fear that he had lost the person he loved forever.

He loved her.

It was not something he intended, falling for her so quickly. But it was inevitable. Looking back, that much was obvious—but it was never something that he planned. The more she gave him, the more he wanted and oh how he fucking wanted her. How he still did.

It was like a hole in his chest, one that was gaping, ugly and raw. Everything still worked as it should—his heart beat and his blood flowed—but there was no reason for it now. He found himself wondering what he had done before her. How was it possible for her to have such a hold on him after such a short time?

His phone buzzed again, this time from somewhere near his knee. He had set it down after taking the picture. He picked it up, blowing away a few specs of sand and glanced down at the screen—three unread texts from Lucas. The first two were from earlier. He had been so preoccupied with taking the book, he had never looked at them. The first two were in response to his picture of the ocean from the first day he arrived in town and his picture of the sailboat from earlier today.

I miss you too.

And I'm sorry for everything.

The last was a response to the picture of the book page.

What is that? Draven, what's going on?

He sent a quick reply back, letting Lucas know that everything was okay and that he would call him soon. Knowing that his brother wanted to see him, wanted to talk to him, made the pain in his chest that much easier to bear. No matter what happened with Olivia, at least he still had

Lucas. There was so much they needed to say to each other, so many wounds that needed to heal. They had both taken the first step today.

The pop of a stick in the fire caught his attention. The flames were still going strong. He should put it out. Then he would go talk to Olivia.

He stood up from the sand, the knees of his jeans now soaked through. Dusting himself off, he stooped to pick up the book. He tucked it tightly beneath his arm and walked over to the fire.

"Draven! Don't!"

Chapter 20

The wind howled in his ears, but he was sure he heard his name. He looked up towards the water. The rain had stopped. His foot was still poised above the fire, ready to kick sand into the flames.

"Draven, please don't!"

He turned towards that voice. He would recognize it anywhere. Olivia.

Olivia, Jill, and Parker all ran towards him, hands raised in defense. He looked down at the book in his hands and the way he was standing so near the flames. To them, it must have looked like he was trying to burn the book.

Olivia came closer, slowing her steps as she did. "Draven, please. Give me the book. I don't want to hurt you, but I will if I have to."

Magic flowed from her fingertips. White and gold. Bright and bewitching, just like her. The fire in her eyes was striking. God, he loved her. Probably the most inappropriate time to have a thought like that. But there it was.

"Olivia," he said, turning slowly around to face her head-on.

"Don't move, Draven. Don't take another step."

Jill and Parker were slowly making their way towards them, eyes bouncing between Draven and Olivia.

His eyes locked on Olivia's. In them, he could see fear and determination. But there was also something else. Something he dared to hope she could still feel for him. The way she had approached him, ready to use her magic to stop him, he was sure that meant she hated him. But the way she was looking at him now, with so much love and tenderness. Maybe there was hope for them yet. He took another step away from the fire, holding the book out to her. Too late, he realized his mistake. She lunged, pushing her magic out towards him. The force of it knocked him off his feet and into the sand—the book flying out of his hands and to the sand by her feet.

Olivia screamed. The sound was like something out of a nightmare. Blood pounded in his ears, his heart racing in his chest. His head hurt. His back hurt. Everything hurt. But he supposed he was probably lucky to still be breathing, given the circumstances.

He stared up at the sky; the clouds were starting to clear. Was it a coincidence that the moment he saw Olivia again, the rain had stopped? Or had he hit his head harder than he thought?

He had always believed in magic. Now that he had really seen it in action, sexual foreplay notwithstanding, maybe he had been seeing it everywhere for a while. Like when you bought a car, and suddenly everyone on the road seemed to have the same one.

Now he was just rambling to himself.

He waited a moment for the world to stop spinning. Then he sat up just as Olivia reached him, getting down in the sand to sit near his head.

"Oh my gosh, Draven, I'm so sorry. I did not mean to hit you that hard. I wasn't trying to hurt you, I swear. I reacted on instinct. I just wanted to get the book out of harm's way."

"It's okay. I actually kind of liked it."

Her laugh was weak and watery. "I think maybe you hit your head. You're not making sense." She reached out a hand to help him sit up and then moved away.

He missed her instantly.

Footsteps sounded somewhere nearby. "Is he alright" Parker asked.

"Hey," he said, turning towards her. "I'm good."

She waved at him weakly before grabbing the book where it had landed in the sand. She gave him a small smile and backed away. He could see Jill standing a little further back, her phone held to her ear.

"Draven, I'm so sorry," Olivia said, voice nearly a whisper.

He shook his head. "I'm fine, Liv, I swear. How did you find me?"

"Well, Parker came to tell me the book was missing and I sort of put the pieces together from there. I figured whatever you were going to do, you would want to do it here. I know this place is special to you."

His breath hitched at her words, even amidst all of this chaos. When she had every right to turn her back on him and all they had shared, she proved how much she understood him.

While he found that incredibly touching, it also served as a reminder of just how much he did not deserve her.

"Olivia, I am so sorry. For everything. For lying, for using you, for speaking to you the way I did earlier." Her eyes were filled with so much sadness. It took everything in him not to pull her into his arms and never let her go. But would she want that? After everything, he'd just done.

"What you told me about my mother, I did not understand it. I was angry and scared. I think I was so wrapped up in what I assumed to be true, that I wasn't willing to accept what was actually true. You were telling me that my mother actually did something to warrant punishment, that she chose to do this bad thing. My whole life, I've believed my mom was the good guy and my dad was the bad guy. To hear that might not be true, it gutted me."

She moved closer to him, her hand raising to touch his face. At the last second, she changed her mind, lowering it back to the sand. He hated that he was responsible for her hesitance.

"I can understand that. It hurts when you realize that your parents don't always make good choices. Or that they're not very good people at all. It's something I had to come to terms with about my birth parents. That maybe they did not want to deal with a child that had so many medical issues. It hurt and I'm not saying that what your mom did is anything like that. But I can understand why you were so angry."

"I appreciate that. But that doesn't make what I tried to do any more acceptable."

"You're right, it doesn't. But I feel like I should have tried harder to understand how you were feeling. I didn't even try. I just got defensive, trying to force you to see things my way. I didn't understand how you could have such a skewed view of magic when it has been nothing but good to me. But I realize now that it did not play the same role in your life that it did mine."

He sighed. He truly did not deserve her. "I didn't really give you a choice, Liv. Look. My mom died. It was fast and awful and I never really had a chance to process the whole thing. So, when I found her journals, I felt like I had a piece of her back. When I read what happened, that she lost her magic, I did not understand how something like that could happen. And I felt like she deserved better. I was too lost in my grief."

"What changed your mind?"

He smiled softly. "My mother. I found one of her spells in the book, actually."

"You did?"

He nodded, laughing. "Well, I didn't actually find it. I had set the book down to build a fire. When I went to go pick it up, the wind had blown it open to the page with her spell. It was some silly spell about making a good wind for sailing. But I took it as a sign. Her way of telling me that magic was good. The truth is, I'll never really know why she did what she did."

"But if you had to guess? I'm sorry, I don't mean to pry. But that's the one thing none of us knows. I don't think your mom ever told anyone."

"I really don't know. When I was a kid, before my dad left, he and my mom argued all the time. But I never paid attention to what they were arguing about. In her journals, she just said that magic was always coming between them. But, if she lost her magic trying to give him some, I would think that he left because she did not have magic anymore. In her journals, she talked about him wanting her to try and get her magic back. But she would not. She accepted the consequences of her actions. I'm guessing he left when he realized she would not change her mind."

"I'm so sorry, Draven. I can't imagine what that must have been like for you."

He shrugged; he had come to terms with not having a father a long time ago. Everything he had been working towards over the last month had been for his mother. "It was hard at first. But I had my mom and my brother. We never felt any less loved. If my dad did leave because he could not love my mother without her magic, I don't want anything to do with him. I barely knew him then and I have no idea who he would be now. I don't know how they met or even when they met. I do know that after everything happened, they moved to New York together and then had me and Lucas. I don't even know where he is now."

"You're sure you don't want to find him? We could do that, you know, using a locator spell."

He placed his hand over hers, interlacing their fingers. "I'm sure. I have no idea where my father is or what he's up to these days. I would assume if he hasn't tried anything by now, he probably never will. But Liv, there is something I wanted to talk to you about. I think there should be a protection spell on the book. I don't know if it's my place to say anything, but I think it's a good idea. I mean, look at what I almost did. I don't want anything to happen to you, or this town, or magic."

He glanced back at Parker and Jill. Both of them had moved closer, waiting for him to continue. "I may have been the first to attempt anything, but I don't know if I'll be the last. I think we need to make sure that this never happens again. I may not have magic of my own, but I want to do what I can to help protect it for my mother and her legacy, and for you," he said, turning again to look at Olivia.

"I think it's a great idea," Jill said. "I honestly can't believe we never had a protection spell on it before. Seems like a major oversight."

Parker glared at her. "Don't let my abuelita or mama hear you say that, Jill. We've literally never had a reason to. Not in a town like this."

He could feel his face growing hot. "Sorry, guys."

The three women all turned to look at him before bursting into laughter. At least they could already joke about the whole thing. Honestly, the whole thing was absolutely ridiculous. How could he have possibly been so single-minded and selfish? He really did not deserve their forgiveness. But he was glad to have it.

Jill walked up to him, face set in a determined scowl. "Just promise me you'll never do anything to hurt Olivia again. She really cares about you. I forgive you now, but I won't be so forgiving if anything like this ever happens again."

He looked her straight in the eye, hoping she could see how serious he was. "I promise you, Jill."

She smiled. "Good. By the way, you'll be having words with my husband too. He's not happy with you at all."

He cringed. Hopefully, he hadn't completely burned a bridge with Malcolm. He needed at least one friend in this town if he planned to stay. But that really depended on Olivia. They would need to sit down at some point and really figure out where they stood with each other.

Parker spoke up from behind them. "About that protection spell. I might have just the thing for that, actually."

Olivia laughed. "Why am I not surprised?"

Parker shrugged, a blush rising to her cheeks. "It's a spell I've been toying with for a while. I think it could work for this. Here," she said, pulling a piece of paper and pen from her pocket. She wrote down some words and held the paper out to Olivia.

"You want me to do it? But it's your spell."

Jill stepped forward. "You should do it, Liv."

He gave her hand another squeeze. "Come on I've never seen you use magic before. Well, not for anything like this."

She looked at him, worry clear in her brown eyes. "Are you sure?"

Her concern broke his heart. He wanted her to know that her magic was something he was proud of. He could see now just how miraculous it all was. And he was proud to be a part of it, even in a small way.

He pulled her towards him, arms wrapped around her waist. He lifted her chin and bent down to place a soft kiss against her lips. "I'm sure. I want you to know your magic is amazing. You're amazing. I love you, so damn much."

"I love you too, Draven. More than I ever thought I could."

He laced his fingers through hers and let them hang between their bodies. "Then let's do this. You and me, together."

She winked at him and lifted the paper containing the spell up, holding it out so they both could see it. Parker walked over to Draven and held out the book to him. Slowly, he reached out to place his hand on the cover. Together, he and Olivia began to read:

With magic that burns so light and bright.

Hide this book now from Evil's sight.

We call upon the elements – Earth, Water, Fire, Air.

Guard this book from Evil's touch.

We cloak it now in witch's light.

He felt it the moment the last word left their lips. A rush of power like nothing he had ever felt before—an ethereal glow shining from their joined hands.

She glanced over at him. He was sure his face held a mixture of shock and joy. To be able to do this with her, to help protect the town. It was truly a gift. If only his mother could see him now. Hopefully, she would be proud.

"You're amazing," he breathed as he pulled her in for a hug. Then he pulled back slightly to whisper in her ear. "Who knew magic could be such a turn-on?"

He was pretty sure her laughter could be heard clear across town.

Chapter 21

He lifted the cup of coffee to his lips and took a sip, loving the way the hot liquid flooded his taste buds and spread throughout his body. It was colder than usual for an October day, especially this early in the month, but he could not say he minded, for the most part anyway. He had always loved the cold.

He glanced down at his phone, disappointed to see no message from Lucas again. It had been two days since the big showdown at the beach and everything was more or less back to normal. He and Olivia had worked out the parameters of their relationship. They were in love and he was staying put. Other than that, they were just taking things one day at a time. But he could not pretend he wasn't dreaming of bigger things. Of rings and I do's and promises of forever. He just needed to figure out how she would feel about it all.

"Something on your mind there, stranger?" a voice asked from behind him as he stared out at the water.

He knew that voice. But the owner of that voice should be hundreds of miles away, not here on the beach in this small town. He turned around and sure enough, his little brother was there, a huge grin on his face.

"Lucas," Draven said, not fully believing his eyes as he rushed towards his brother. He pulled him in for a tight hug, tears stinging his eyes. His little brother was here. He had missed him so much.

The last time they had seen each other was a few weeks after their mom died, a meeting to settle her estate between the two of them with her lawyer. He barely remembered that day. Everything was too loud and the world moved too fast when, inside, all he was feeling was the void his mother left. He wasn't even sure he had actually spoken to Lucas.

This had to be the best surprise ever. His little brother was here.

"Miss me?" Lucas asked with a smile.

"Why didn't you tell me you were coming? When I asked you to come for a visit, I figured you would at least give me a heads up. Don't you have to work? I can't remember the last time you actually took time off."

"That's because I didn't take time off. I quit."

"You did what? Why? I thought you loved your job?"

"You heard me. I quit. It just seemed like a good time. Honestly, I've been thinking about it since mom died and hearing from you just gave me the push I needed, I guess."

"Well, that's ... why didn't you tell me? When did you get into town? More importantly, how the hell did you know where to find me?" Draven asked, still somewhat stunned. Though, to be honest, he did not care much for the particulars. He was just glad his brother was here.

"Oh, about half an hour ago. I checked in at the only place in town. Asked that hot girl at the front desk."

Draven laughed. "Parker."

Lucas nodded. "Right, Parker. I asked if she knew you and she pointed me in the right direction. Well, she gave me your address."

"Which begs the question yet again: how did you find me?"

"Well, I knocked for a good five minutes. Just when I was about to give up, I met one of your neighbors and the kid told me where you might be. He's something else, that one. It seemed like he gave his babysitter the slip, the poor woman came out of the house looking scared to death."

He laughed. "That sounds like Daniel. Kid's too smart for his own good. He's always getting up to something. I take it you didn't run into Olivia?"

Lucas shook his head. "Nope. But I'm kind of glad. I really wanted to see you first."

Draven had mentioned her to Lucas in one of his previous texts. But given that it was a late Tuesday afternoon, he knew she would be at work. Hence Daniel's babysitter. Draven still needed to figure out how he was going to spend his own days now that he was an actual permanent resident of the town.

"I still can't believe you're here," Draven said, shaking his head at Lucas's wide grin.

His hair was cut short as always, though a bit shaggy on top. His brown eyes were bright in a way Draven hadn't seen in so long. It was as if leaving his job had lifted a weight off his shoulders. He seemed lighter, happier, more at ease. It was so good to see.

"Well, believe it. I'm thinking of sticking around for a while. If you'll have me."

"You really quit your job then?"

"Yes. It was time. Hell, it was more than time. My career was basically my whole life. You and I have that in common. I just want more than that. Plus, there's nothing left for me in New York now that you're here and I wanted to know what the hell is going on with you. That picture you sent me looked like some kind of spell."

He reached behind his head to rub at his neck. How best to even start this conversation? Probably blunt honesty.

"Yeah. A lot has happened, little brother, and I'm not sure exactly where to begin. But the gist of it is, Mom was a witch."

He spent the next hour explaining to Lucas how he had discovered the secret, what he had assumed happened when their mother lost her magic and what he had tried to do to make it up to her.

"Wait, you tried to destroy magic? All because of something you read in one of mom's journals? Which I want to read, by the way. But, seriously, big brother? It seems like you were missing some vital information."

He cringed. "Yeah. I'll admit it wasn't one of my best decisions. But I was hurting so much from losing mom. Finding all of that stuff made me feel so close to her again."

Lucas placed a hand on his shoulder. "I'm sorry, I didn't mean to judge you. I get it, I miss mom too."

They were both silent for a few moments, just feeling the loss of their mother.

Then Lucas leaned back and smiled softly. "So, she was a witch? I feel like I should be more shocked than I actually am. But in some ways, it totally makes sense."

"That's what I thought too. She was always telling us stories about magic and witches. Who knew they were based on her actual experiences? That picture I sent you of that spell? It was one that mom wrote. It's in a bigger spell book that the town witches use. I'll show it to you as soon as possible."

Lucas nodded before his smile faded and his face turned down into a frown. "How does Dad fit into all of this?"

"I'm still not 100 percent sure. But we're assuming that he left mom when she made it clear to him that she would never try to get her magic back."

"We?"

He blushed. "Me and Olivia."

"Right, Olivia," Lucas said with a smile. "She's a witch too?"

"She is and she's much too good for me."

Lucas laughed. "I absolutely believe that. So, when do I get to meet her?"

"Tonight, probably. She should be off work soon. We can all have dinner together, you, me, Olivia and Daniel. You can go and check out of the inn. I have a spare bedroom with your name on it, little brother."

"Sounds good, big brother. But before we get to any of that, what do you say we build a sandcastle?"

Draven's great-grandmother's wedding ring was something that his mother had kept in her possession since he could remember. It was always sitting in the top of her jewelry box. He had liked to stare at it from time to time and watch the way sunlight reflected off the single diamond. It was one of the few things he had brought with him of his mother's other than her journals, pictures and letters.

She had gifted it to him not long before she died. Making him promise that if the time ever came, he would present this ring to someone. If he never found that person or simply did not want to give that person a ring, he would pass it on to his brother. At the time, he had assumed that's exactly what he would do. But now, now there were possibilities—things he had never wanted before.

Lucas was moving around in the other bedroom, putting his things away. After they built their sandcastle and snapped a picture, they drove back to the inn, grabbed Lucas's things and headed back to Draven's house. They chatted for a bit about nothing in particular and then went off to spend some time alone with their thoughts. It was nice to hear the familiar sounds of another person in his living space. He was excited for tonight when his whole family could be together for the first time. His family. Funny how two simple words could bring him so much peace.

He glanced down at the ring, remembering again the day his mother gave it to him.

"Wait for the right kind of love, Draven. The kind that makes you feel more like yourself. Wait for your best friend. Someone who understands you and doesn't want to change the fundamental pieces of who you are but also makes you strive to be the very best version of yourself. Never settle for less than what you deserve," she had said.

"Did you settle, Mom? With Dad. Do you feel like you settled?"

She nodded, her eyebrows pinched together. She rubbed her chest, as if the admission caused her heart pain. "Sometimes I feel like I did. But it doesn't really matter now, does it? Because whatever else your father did, at least he gave me you and your brother. I just want you to be happy, whatever that looks like for you. It doesn't have to be getting married and having kids. It just has to be something that leaves you feeling fulfilled. Just promise me that you'll keep that ring. If nothing else, then as a reminder of me telling you this today."

He promised her. With tears In his eyes and a kiss to her too pale cheek, he promised her. He had wanted more time with her. Time to show her how much she meant to him. If only she could have known Olivia and Daniel and seen how he and Lucas had found their way back to each other. It wasn't fair that she wasn't here to be a part of all this. But he could not change that. What he could do was live. Live in a way that would make her proud. Thinking about the way Olivia loved him, how she understood him and supported him even after everything he had done, he finally found what his mother had wanted for him.

That alone made the pain of her loss that still lingered in his heart that much easier to bear.

His thoughts went back to that sandcastle, now standing tall on the beach. It was such a silly thing for two grown men to do. But as they had built it, feeling the cold, wet sand between their fingertips, he liked to imagine his mother was watching, a smile on her face and a feeling of peace in her heart. Her boys had finally come home.

Chapter 22

This was a lot of food, even for her. But this family dinner was special, their first with Lucas, so Olivia wanted to make it special. There were going to be a lot of people. Her, Draven, Daniel and Lucas. Parker, Janella, and Rosa. Plus, Jill and Malcolm. Still, she may have overdone it a little. Not that there was anything she could do about that now.

"Wow, Mom. Even for you, this is a bit much."

She cringed. Damn that kid. He was too much like her. Yet, she had to laugh. Hopefully, everyone would be willing to take home plenty of leftovers because she had gone all out. She was making enchiladas with beans and rice—three pans of each—chips, and homemade salsa. Of course, she had mixed up a few pitchers of horchata. She also made two tres leches cakes—plenty for everyone and then some.

"I have to admit, the kid has a point. You sure you made enough for everyone?" Draven asked as he came to stand next to her at the counter.

"Ha ha, you're both absolutely hilarious. So, I went a little overboard, okay? I'm just excited. It's Lucas's first family dinner with us. A new beginning for everyone. Is it so bad that I want it to go well?"

"No," Draven said, pressing a kiss to her hair. "I think it's really sweet of you. I'm sure Lucas will appreciate your thoughtfulness."

"Yeah, Draven's right, Mom. I think everything is going to be great," Daniel said, giving her a big smile and clapping his hands together like he was ready to get to work. "Do you need help with anything?"

She pulled Daniel close, planting a kiss on the top of his head. Always her best little helper. In addition to this being Lucas's first family dinner, this was also the first time she was cooking said dinner. Rosa had graciously agreed to give up her cooking and hosting duties this week. She was also a little nervous. Looking around at her kitchen, every surface was covered with dishes and pots and pans. Maybe next week they could go back to Rosa's. This whole thing was a lot more work than she thought it would be.

The house did smell incredible. But from now on, she would stick to baking and cooking the occasional meal for Daniel and herself during the week. Well, herself, Daniel and Draven.

These last few days with him had been nothing short of perfect. She knew it wouldn't last forever. Eventually, one of them would do something to annoy the other. But that was life. Always a little bit messy. They had the talk about where this was going and what they each needed from each other to make this work: no more secrets, no more lies. Draven would continue living in his own house for the time being, if only to make sure things stayed consistent for Daniel. Though if Daniel had his way, Draven would be moved in tomorrow.

She was grateful. Daniel loved Draven and Draven adored Daniel. There was a time not so long ago when seeing the two of them together terrified her, if only because she was worried that he would leave them. But Draven was committed to their life together and now Daniel knew he was someone they could both depend on.

The three of them spent the next couple of hours cooking and putting the finishing touches on everything. She was more than grateful for the help. She loved seeing Daniel in the kitchen. It always got her wondering if someday he would turn his passion into a career, the way she had. Of course, she wanted him to do whatever would make him most happy, but there was a little part of her that loved the idea of a mother and son bakery. Not that she would ever tell Daniel that. Poor kid would probably be mortified.

About an hour before dinner, Lucas showed up. Draven had introduced the two of them yesterday over a much smaller dinner. She was thrilled to learn that Lucas would be staying in town on a permanent basis. Draven explained about their mother and what exactly that meant for them. Then they had gone to look at their mother's spell in the book. For now, it was being kept at Parker's, protected by the brand-new spell. Eventually, they would come up with a more permanent place for it, but for now, this worked.

Lucas had shed a few tears upon seeing the spell. He had a million questions and Parker and Draven did their best to answer every single one. Draven also mentioned that there seemed to be something between Parker and Lucas, that they were constantly stealing glances at each other and flirting when they thought no one was looking. She didn't want to get her hopes up, but she was excited for her friend. Maybe she could ask

Parker about it at some point tonight. Away from prying ears, of course, and only if Jill promised to be on her very best behavior.

It was also really great to see Daniel and Lucas interact with each other. While Draven was generally pretty serious, Lucas was not. He was constantly cracking jokes and telling Daniel all kinds of funny stories about his life in New York—the G-rated versions, of course. Daniel was a great kid and he could throw a sarcastic comment out there with the best of them. But sometimes, she worried he was a little bit too serious for a kid his age. So, it was nice to see him loosen up that much more around Lucas.

Of course, that endeared Lucas to her even more. The best and easiest way to end up in her good graces was to be good to her son.

"I don't want to jinx it, Liv...." Draven said at one point from his spot beside her in the kitchen. "But I think this is going to go very well."

She laughed, stepping into his arms for a hug. "I think so too. Alright, we've got thirty minutes before the troops arrive. I think everything is just about done. We just need to get the rice and beans into the serving dishes. The enchiladas can stay in the oven; we'll just turn down the temperature to keep them warm. I need to mix up the guacamole, both kinds. The pitchers of horchata can stay in the fridge until everyone gets here. We'll bring out the dessert later, obviously and we need to set the table."

Crap, there was still so much to do. Suddenly thirty minutes felt a little bit like thirty seconds.

"Hey, Liv," Draven said, still holding her in his arms. "We've got this. Everything will be ready to go. It all looks delicious; it all smells delicious and I know everything will *taste* delicious. You've worked really hard today and everyone will appreciate that. It's just a family dinner. I know it's a special one, but you don't need to prove yourself. Everything is going to be great."

She sighed. "You're right; I'm sorry. I don't know why I'm worrying. I mean, I do this for a living."

"Well, technically, you bake for a living. Not cook."

She shoved him away, laughing. "Oh my God, you're starting to sound like Daniel with that damn sarcasm. Yes, I bake for a living. But you know what I mean. I work with food."

He pulled her back into his arms, still laughing at her frustration. "I'm sorry. I just could not help myself. I think you're right, though; Daniel is a bad influence."

Their laughter was interrupted by the sound of the doorbell ringing.

She glanced at the clock on her phone. She still had thirty minutes, right? No one was supposed to be here yet.

She looked at Draven, but he was looking anywhere but at her. Then he was pulling her along behind him and out of the kitchen.

"Come on. Let's get the door," he said, glancing back at her, not bothering to hide his smirk.

He was definitely up to something. Apparently, she was just along for the ride. Passing by the living room on their way to the door, she glanced that way at Daniel and Lucas. They were sprawled out on the floor, each had a video game controller in their hands. She laughed. Daniel had finally found someone willing to play with him. God bless Lucas.

Draven pulled open the door and there was Parker, standing on the porch with a plate of cookies in her hands.

"Parker, hey," Olivia said. "What are you doing here? You know dinner's not until six, right?"

Parker looked confused. "Oh, really? Because yesterday Draven said I should be here at 5:30."

She glanced at Draven. Again, he would not look her in the eye. "He did, did he? Well, isn't that interesting?"

"Umm, yeah. I guess," Parker said, clearly still confused. "Can I come in?"

"Oh, right! Sorry. I'm just surprised to see you here early," she said, sending a pointed look at Draven. He had the good grace to look sheepish, his hand coming to rest against the back of his neck. He was nervous about something.

"It smells amazing in here, Liv. Just like at Rosa's. Like home and happiness and cheesy goodness," Parker said as she took off her coat. She had also donned a scarf, hat, and gloves.

The cold weather had officially taken hold. Not that Olivia minded. Today she was finally able to break out one of her fuzziest sweaters and her favorite suede black boots with fur-lined insides. As far as she was concerned, the weather should always be like this.

"Glad to hear it. I would not want to disappoint your abuelita."

"Oh, you know you could never. She loves you almost as much as she loves me. So, anything I can do to help since I'm *apparently* a little bit early?"

"I could use some help getting everything into the serving dishes. Come with me to the kitchen."

"No, wait," Draven said from where he was standing next to Olivia. "Maybe you could set the table, Parker? Just hold on one second."

He turned and went into the living room, leaving Parker and Olivia more than confused.

"Is he alright?" Parker whispered.

Olivia shrugged. "I can honestly say I have absolutely no idea."

When Draven returned a few seconds later, he wasn't alone. He was dragging a confused-looking Lucas along with him. "Parker, you remember my brother Lucas, right?" he asked her with a smirk.

Parker blushed. "Of course. Hey, Lucas. Nice to see you again so soon. I hope you're ready to get the third degree from my abuelita."

"Hey," Lucas said with an awkward wave, shuffling his feet.

Draven moved to stand next to Olivia again. "I was thinking Lucas could help Parker set the table. What do you think, Liv?"

That sneaky bastard. He was trying to set them up and he didn't tell her?

She nodded, making sure to keep a smile on her face. My God, subtle Draven James was not. "That sounds like a great idea. Parker, you remember where everything is, don't you?"

Parker eyed Olivia, probably catching on to said setup. "I remember. Come on, Lucas. We need settings for nine people. Liv, I'll be having a word with you later."

Once Olivia was sure the two of them had passed into the kitchen, she rounded on Draven.

"What the hell was that?" she whispered, not wanting everyone else to hear her.

"What do you mean?" Draven asked, hand going again to grab at the back of his neck.

She laughed. "Oh, come on, Draven. You were obviously trying to get the two of them alone. Why didn't you tell me? I would have been able to help you do it in a much less obvious way. Baby, that had all the subtlety of a wrecking ball."

"I'm sorry. I panicked. I told Parker to come at 5:30 because I figured she and Lucas would have a chance to talk on their own before everyone else showed up. But I didn't really have a plan for how I was going to do that."

"Yeah, you made that pretty clear. Ugh, Parker is going to be so mad at me."

He grabbed her hand. "You can blame the whole thing on me."

"You bet your ass that's exactly what I'm going to do. Although your methods weren't great, I think getting those two together is an awesome idea. I know you said Lucas might be into her. I'll keep an eye on Parker tonight and see if she is actually interested in Lucas. Otherwise, there's really no point to this whole thing. Now come on, matchmaker, we have to get the food ready. We probably have like ten minutes now."

They recruited Daniel to help dish everything up and between the three of them, they were left with three minutes to spare before the doorbell rang again. They left Parker and Lucas alone in the dining room, hoping to give them as much alone time as possible.

She went to answer the door and was greeted by four concerned faces. Rosa, Janella, Jill, and Malcolm.

"Aye, mijita," Rosa said, stepping inside and pulling her in for a hug. "Have you heard from Parker? I called her to see if she needed a ride over, but she did not answer her phone."

"I texted her and never heard back either," Jill said as she pulled off her coat and scarf. She handed them to Malcolm to hang up with his own coat.

"Oh," Olivia said, not sure how much to say. If they all knew Lucas and Parker might like each other, they would never hear the end of it.

"She's actually already here. She came a little early to help get everything ready."

Just then, the sound of Parker's laughter rang out from the dining room.

Janella smiled. "Well, it sounds like she's having a good time, whatever she's doing."

Another laugh rang out. This time at a lower octave.

Rosa looked around Olivia and towards the dining room. "Who's that with her? Draven?"

Draven poked his head out from the kitchen. "Someone say my name? Oh, hey, everyone. Hope you're all hungry," he said as he held up a dish full of enchiladas.

Everyone looked at Olivia, now with curiosity clear on each of their faces. She sighed. Well, so much for keeping things quiet. "She's with Lucas, Draven's brother."

"Oh," Jill said, a huge smile breaking onto her face. "That is interesting. Does Parker like him? Does he like her? Come on, Liv. Spill."

Olivia groaned. "No, Jill. Do not start. Draven tried to subtly get Parker and Lucas alone together, but it was anything but subtle and I don't think Parker is very happy. Or maybe she is? I'm not one hundred percent sure. But she did not look very happy."

"She sure sounds happy," Malcolm said from behind Jill.

Olivia shot him a glare. "Okay fine, maybe she likes him. But please, the guy just got here. We don't want to scare him off, right?"

Rosa nodded, patting Olivia on the arm. "That's right, mijita. We promise we'll be on our best behavior. Isn't that right, Jill? Janella?" she said, fixing them both with a hard stare.

"Yes, ma'am," Jill said, face turning a little red.

"Si mama," Janella mumbled.

She had to hold in her giggle. As nice as Rosa could be, she could also be equally as stern. You did not necessarily want to be on the wrong side of her temper. But it was especially funny to see her semi-scolding her own adult daughter.

Olivia cleared her throat. "Now that that's all taken care of. Let's go and eat, everybody."

They all made their way into the dining room. Parker and Lucas were seated next to each other at the far end of the table, heads bent towards each other, talking quietly. Parker was twirling her hair around her finger.

"Are we interrupting anything?" Jill called out as she entered the room, throwing a wink at Olivia.

That little brat.

Parker and Lucas broke apart, both glancing anywhere but at each other.

Lucas coughed. "Umm, no. We about ready to eat then?"

Draven and Daniel walked in, each carrying a dish. She hurried out to grab the rest, Rosa hot on her heels.

Once they were all set to eat, introductions were made between Lucas and everyone else. He and Malcolm bonded instantly, sharing a love of major league baseball. Rosa kept commenting on Lucas' impeccable manners, which annoyed Draven to the point where he asked Rosa to give him some pointers. Janella would not stop staring. Every time Lucas interacted with Parker in any way, her whole face would light up. There was no way that Parker and Lucas did not notice. But, if they did, they never let it show.

Olivia felt for them. Although Draven's first family dinner did involve a lot less staring from Janella and a lot more questions from Rosa. She wasn't sure what that meant. She would have to ask Rosa what she thought of Lucas the first chance she got, especially if he was going to be involved with her only granddaughter.

All things considered; dinner went off without a hitch. When the night was over and all the leftovers had been handed out, she could only think of how lucky she was to have all of these people in her life.

But as she put the last of the dishes away and then tucked Daniel into bed before coming to stand in her empty bedroom, what she wanted most of all, was to be alone with Draven.

Climbing through Olivia's bedroom window was not something Draven ever thought he would have to do. But desperate times.

They hadn't had a night together since the fall festival. Four nights was like an eternity after all that they had been through. Tonight would be the first time they were together since there were no secrets between them. He could finally let go.

He and Olivia had agreed that he would leave and sneak back in when Daniel was asleep. It was important to both of them that he did not have to go through too much change all at once.

"This is really more romantic in books," he said as he stumbled over the windowsill and into her room.

"Oh, you poor baby. Come here and let me make it better," she said as she stepped toward him. "Don't worry about being quiet. I cast a silencing spell on the room. We can hear everything outside, but no one will be able to hear us."

He smiled. He finally had her alone. He lifted her up, her legs coming to wrap around his. He wanted her as close as possible. He pulled her into his arms and carried her across the bedroom to set her gently on her bed.

She already looked a bit of a mess, her hair wild from the way his fingers had carded through it and he could see that her skin was flushed. His mouth landed on hers and he kissed her soft, sweet lips. She whimpered at the contact, the sound making him ache. He wanted her so badly.

Her nipples made hard little points beneath her thin cotton sleep shirt, leaving little to the imagination. His eyes alternated from this to her face as he reached forward to tease one taut little bud through the fabric.

He curled his body over hers to reach her lips again and she tilted her head back to meet him just as he plunged his tongue into her mouth, savoring the sweet, warm taste of her. Mint and Olivia. So perfect. His fingers inched down her ribs and to the soft curve of her hip to find the hem of her T-shirt. He curled them under the fabric to slowly pull it up and over her head as she raised her arms to help him.

"You're exquisite," he breathed against her mouth.

He stared at her bare chest, wanting to take her in for a moment. It had never been like this before, as they'd always had secrets weighing heavily between them. He wanted to savor each moment.

She was all golden-brown skin and dusky pink nipples, waiting and ready to be kissed. There wasn't one single part of her that he did not want his lips to taste.

He fell to his knees, bringing him eye level to her chest, which made it easy to lean in and capture one little bud between his lips. There was a soft catch of her breath, as her fingers moved through his hair, before she pulled him even closer. He groaned at the way she was so eager for him, making him painfully hard. He teased her with his lips and his tongue and his teeth—his hands curled around her hips to hold her still even as she squirmed from where she was spread out for him on her bed.

A long, low moan escaped her throat when his fingers curled into the waistband of her pajama pants along with her underwear, the sound making his cock twitch inside his now too-tight jeans.

He pulled them both off quickly, leaving her open and exposed to him. His lips moved to her thigh, the wet warmth of her calling out to him. It was so close to where he wanted to be, but not just yet. He let his teeth graze her soft skin gently at first. Then he nipped at her, soothing the burn with the sweep of his tongue.

How far could he push her? How much control was she willing to give him? He wanted to possess every part of her. Make her his in every single way.

He held her gaze as he lowered his head to her waiting heat. Her eyes burned into his, begging, pleading for his mouth. When he took the first lick, she squirmed, already trying to ride his face. He had to hold her hips to the bed as he dipped his tongue inside her, lightly, still only teasing.

"Please, Draven. I need more, please."

"Shhh," he breathed out, giving an open-mouthed kiss to her mouth before moving down and giving a small lick to her clit. Her thighs tensed under his palms as he sucked lightly around the slick little bundle of nerves.

She tasted like heaven. Musky and sweet and God, he had missed this. She was intoxicating and dizzying, the taste of her on his tongue driving him wild.

She tilted her hips upward, searching for more of his tongue. She pushed closer, seemingly frantic. Another silent plea for more—and he was happy to give it to her. Glancing up at her flushed face, he could see the way her lip was trapped between her teeth, the way she struggled to keep herself upright as she trembled.

"I want to watch you," she panted, rising up higher on her elbows.

He watched her as she watched him mouth at her pussy—wet flicks of his tongue and heavy presses of his lips at her clit that had her gasping softly. His eyes burned into hers, daring her to take every ounce of pleasure as he tugged on her clit. Licking it faster and faster as she moaned louder and louder, his name a constant whisper on her lips.

Her back bowed and her mouth fell open, and there was an incessant shifting of her hips like she just couldn't control her body anymore. She pushed up into his mouth as she begged for more.

"More, Draven. Please, more."

He imagined doing this again with her thighs straddling his face and her hands gripping the headboard—letting her ride his mouth to take whatever she needed from him until she was dripping her sweet nectar all over his face.

But that would have to wait. He was too desperate right now, too eager to be inside her, to have her warm, wet pussy tight around his aching cock. Would this feeling ever fade—this feeling that he would never get enough of her?

Something told him that would never be the case. He loved her, he wanted her, and he would continue to show her just how much for as long as she would let him.

He circled her slick entrance with a single finger before he slipped it slowly inside—teasing in and out as he hummed at the sweet taste of her, now dripping, as he continued to suck at her clit. She was so wet for him and her panting breaths mingled with the squelch of his finger as he swirled it around and around, bringing her higher with every passing second.

He added another finger, curling them inward to find that secret place he knew would drive her wild, grinding them deeper and deeper until she was all but sobbing.

"Fuck. Fuck, Draven, I'm so close."

He groaned. "You're so perfect, Liv. Such a pretty little pussy. Tastes so fucking sweet."

She whimpered, thighs now shaking on either side of his head, holding him in a vice grip.

But he did not mind it, welcomed it, even, because she contracted around his fingers, gripping them tightly in spasming little squeezes. He circled his tongue around her clit before pulling it in between his teeth to suck hard.

"Draven. Oh God," she gasped. "Draven, I—"

Her back hit the bed as she started to come, no longer able to support her own weight. He licked her through it, fingers slowly moving in and out to match the canting of her hips. She moaned, her back arching off the bed again, her chest heaving with the effort, her fingers shoved into his hair to try and push him away.

He came away gasping for breath and turned his face to huff against her thigh, leaving a series of wet kisses there, taking a moment to catch his breath.

He left another soft kiss between her legs that had the lips of her pussy twitching under his mouth and then moved on to quickly press another kiss to her thigh, her hip, just under her belly button—climbing up her still-shaking body until he mouthed just under her jaw where her pulse thumped against her skin.

"I love you, Liv. So good for me. So, fucking gorgeous when you come. So good."

She shivered at his praise, her hands sliding over his shoulders and raking down his back as she turned her face slowly to kiss at his jaw. Her whole body was relaxed under his hands. She looked spent. But he wasn't done with her yet, not by a long shot.

"Turn over," he urged her quietly. "Onto your stomach."

She looked at him for a moment, brow furrowing when he pulled away from her. But he held her gaze unwavering, willing her to put her trust in him. Her eyes darkened the longer she stared until finally she rolled over and glanced back at him from over her shoulder, waiting patiently for what he had planned.

His lips found her lower back, kissing a path up towards her neck as his hands slid around her waist and down her ribs to settle at her hips. He gripped her there tightly and tugged them up and off the mattress, situating her until her ass was high in the air. Her face was still pressed against the sheets.

He moved back a bit to unbutton his jeans, pulling them down along with his underwear to release his throbbing cock. Her ass was in the perfect position to slot himself against her. He took a moment to rub against her, relishing in her quiet whimpers. He wanted her so much.

"Don't move," he murmured, pulling fully away from her to remove his jeans and shirt, leaving them in a pile at the foot of her bed.

Then he just stood there, to drink in the way she looked, just waiting for him—ass high, her pussy soft and wet between her legs. He could see her face even from here, wide-eyed, mouth open and panting as she watched him looking at her, her full lower lip trapped between her teeth as he ran a hand over the length of his hard cock.

"Look at you," he breathed. "Waiting so patiently for my cock." He gave himself a rough squeeze as her pussy clenched around nothing as if begging for him to fill it. "Do you have any idea how incredible you look right now?"

She squirmed, clearly impatient. "Draven," she pleaded.

"Shh," he said as he reached out to squeeze her hip in quiet reassurance. "Stay still for me, baby. I promise I'm going to make you feel so good."

Another soft whimper escaped her lips, but her hips stilled. But he could tell by the slight tremble of her arms that it was not easy for her. She needed him and it did unspeakable things to him to think how desperately she was trying to do what he asked of her. He did not think anything had ever turned him on more.

She was so damn sweet, he wanted to give her everything and more.

He walked up to the edge of the bed, climbing on behind her. He wrapped his fingers around his cock to give it a few short strokes. Then he fisted himself just under the head and rubbed himself through the slick crease of her, smearing his cock in her fluids as his mouth parted of its own accord, drawing in a sharp rush of air at the hot, wet feel of her.

He dipped the head inside once, then again and then again—slowly, purposefully, as her tight hole stretched around the thick head. A sound of surprise issued from her lips as he thrust to sheathe himself fully inside of her, only to pull back out immediately. A cry of protest left her lips at the loss of contact.

He rubbed a hand down her back to soothe her. "Shh, quiet, Liv," he admonished softly.

She nodded quickly even as she tried to push back against him.

He choked out a laugh as his hand moved down to her ass to give it a squeeze. "Needy little thing, aren't you, baby?"

But what he did not say was that he was just as greedy as she was. It was an easy decision to dip back inside her, to fill her entirely with him, his whole body wrapped around hers as if they were the only two people in the world. Her pussy wrapped around him like a glove, snug and wet and warm.

He lingered for only a moment before thrusting into her hard. The force of it sent her body forward. But he had a tight grip on her hip that kept her from going anywhere. She moaned long and loud as her body acclimated to the size of him.

He wrapped his hands around her arms, pulling her upright until her back was flush with his chest so that both of them were up on their knees. "Gonna move now, baby," he said as he kissed along the curve of her neck.

"Yes. Yes, Draven. Please."

This time though, it was a slow thrust, in and out of her as one hand curled around her jaw, turning her head so that he could kiss her lips. Their tongues tangled together as he thrust up into her again. It had never been so intense before. The need to take her over the edge burned through his entire body.

He could not say what it was about her, that pushed this side of him out into the light—something that had always been there but not like this, never like this. He could not seem to let go of this urge to claim her, to own every part of her. He didn't try to because she seemed to enjoy it. But he needed to be sure.

"If this ever gets to be too much for you, you tell me. I promise I'll stop."

"Okay," she panted. "I promise. I trust you, Draven."

Her words were like a brand on his heart. She trusted him to take care of her and he was going to do just that.

His fingers crept up over her bottom lip to dip inside her mouth. Her lips closed around them to suck softly, offering no protest as he pushed them deeper into her mouth, filling it.

He held them there as his pinky and thumb spread out on either side of her jaw, gripping it tightly. The feeling of her hot wet mouth sucking at his fingers mirrored the way her pussy clenched his cock. From the way she clenched around him, he would guess she was enjoying it just as much as he was.

He kept her just like that when he started to move again, her mouth as full as her pussy—her body held tightly against his as he found a punishing rhythm. His lips mouthed at her shoulder and his hips slapped against her ass as he made short, rough strokes up and into her. Every thrust seemed to hit just a little deeper than the last; the slap of skin on skin filled the air as her loud moans and whimpers reverberated around his fingers still firmly inside her mouth, her tongue swirling around them with every thrust.

"That's," he huffed against her throat as he pulled her back further against his cock— "so good. You're doing," he growled into her skin when her pussy contracted around him again, "you're doing so damn good, baby."

He pulled his fingers from her mouth.

"Yes," she panted as she lifted her arm to drape it around his neck, winding her fingers in his hair. "Wannabe good for you."

Her other hand began to snake down between her legs and he quickly batted it away to use his own fingers instead. He found her swollen clit easily, circling it steadily as his lips found her ear.

"You're so beautiful like this, taking my cock so well. I love you; I love you so much," he panted into her ear.

She groaned, bringing her lips to his in a searing kiss.

The fingers of his other hand teased at the soft skin of her throat as he quickened the pace of his fingers on her clit; the pressure beginning to build in his cock made it hard to keep a steady rhythm.

"You gonna come for me?" he asked as he bit gently at her shoulder and then immediately licked to soothe the sting. "Can you come on my cock, Liv?"

She nodded, her lashes fluttering closed. He wrapped his wet fingers very gently around her throat—not applying any real pressure but holding her back against him as he drove into her with wild abandon.

"Come on, baby," he urged quietly, feeling the way she was clamping down on him in short little spasms. "That's it, come for me, Liv. Want you to fucking come."

A scream tore from her lips. He could swear he was never more grateful for her magic than in this very moment. Her body shook and her pussy quivered, creating a slick mess between her legs that made him thrust even harder.

His hand found her hip again to grip her there, holding her tight as he drove into her still-trembling warmth with everything he had.

"Olivia," he called out as he finally tumbled over the edge, his cock seated deep inside her as it twitched to fill her with his spend. His chest heaved against her back as he struggled to catch his breath. It was several long seconds before he was even able to move.

Eventually, he became aware of the mess between their bodies and the uncomfortable feeling of sweat cooling on his skin. He gently lowered her to the bed, planting a quick kiss to her lips before heading to the bathroom to clean himself up.

He returned a few minutes later and waited while she took her turn in the bathroom.

When she got back into bed and under the covers with him, he pulled her into his arms and placed a soft kiss on her forehead. If only he could stay here forever, breathing in the scent of her.

They lay together quietly for a while. It was nice to just be together, feeling no pressure to talk or fill the silence. He'd been caring around so much anger for so long, he couldn't remember the last time he'd let his mind just go quiet.

It was in this peaceful calm and stillness that a thought occurred to him.

"Liv, do you think my mother had anything to do with our meeting?"

"What do you mean?"

He pushed some hair away from her shoulder and settled in behind her, pulling her close. "I mean, do you think magic played a part in all of it. Like wherever my mom is, she made all of this happen?"

"I don't know. But I think anything is possible. I mean, how could I not? I am a witch, after all. I think magic can do things without any of us knowing. I mean, there was definitely something in the air the day I first met you. It felt like it was all meant to be."

He nodded. "I know what you mean. I'd like to think that maybe my mother played a part in all of it."

"I'm sorry that I never got to meet her."

"Me too. She would have loved you. Just like I do."

She smiled back at him, eyes shining brightly with so much love and hope. "I love you too, Draven," she whispered as she drifted off to sleep. "I love you so much."

Chapter 23

Two Months Later

"You're sure you're okay with Draven and me going to this thing together?" Olivia asked Daniel for probably the hundredth time as they stood at one side of the town gymnasium hanging streamers for that night's holiday party.

"Mom, come on. I already told you it's fine. You guys are a couple and that's what couples do, right? Go to these kinds of things together?"

"Yes, you're right. It's just that this will be our first year going where you aren't my date, bud, and I don't want you to feel left out."

"Answer me this, Mom: If I wanted to come with you guys, would you or Draven say no?"

"No," she replied instantly, already seeing his point as he bit back a smile.

Parker appeared then, carrying a very full basket of hand-cut snowflakes for Olivia and Daniel to hang on the walls; Olivia groaned. They definitely needed some more help.

"Hey," she said, turning to Parker after glancing around the room for her boyfriend. "Where are the guys?"

Draven, Lucas, and Malcolm had been in and out of the gym most of the day doing all the heavy lifting and whatever random task Parker handed out to them. But they had disappeared for the last hour or so.

"Oh," Parker said, pulling piles of snowflakes out of the box. "They're working on a special project for me."

"Special project?"

"Nothing you need to worry about," Parker said with a wink.

What could Parker possibly have the guys working on that she did not know about? She didn't bother asking Parker for more details; she wouldn't tell her anyway. The woman was a master at keeping secrets.

The last hour dragged by. They had been setting up since noon, only stopping for a quick snack break. It was now nearing 4:30 in the afternoon.

She and Daniel went home to eat a quick dinner and to get ready.

But her nerves just would not settle. Something about tonight felt important. Maybe it was the fact that this would hopefully be the first of many holiday parties and she wanted it to go well.

She had been pacing around the kitchen for the last twenty minutes, just waiting for 6:30 to roll around. Eventually, Daniel joined her, offering up the solution.

"You know what always helps when you're feeling anxious, Mom ..."

"Horchata," they said at the same time.

Her earlier tension slipped away as they prepared their drinks. In this space, he was just her little boy. She was endlessly thankful for the kindhearted, thoughtful kid he was turning out to be.

"Hey, Mom? Can I ask you something?"

"Anything, bud," she assured him as they each took their glass of horchata and brought it to their lips.

"Are you still scared of being with Draven?"

She and Daniel had a long talk after that whole mess with Draven and the book. She wanted him to know what Draven had considered doing and why he had ultimately changed his mind. She tried her best to explain what her own issues were. He was a smart kid and he could often sense when she was feeling out of sorts. She wanted him to know as much of the truth as was appropriate.

She paused for a moment to consider the question. But she already knew the answer. She wasn't afraid of being with Draven, not anymore. He was committed to her and to Daniel, he loved them both very much.

"No, Daniel. I'm not scared. Not anymore. Why do you ask?"

"I don't know," he said, although it was clear he did since he had asked the question. "It's just that you're always nervous. Like with the dance tonight."

She understood. Her sweet-hearted boy was trying to make sure she was okay.

"You want to know why I'm nervous?"

He nodded.

"I'm nervous because I want tonight to go well. This is another first for Draven, and I want him to have a good time. But that's all it is—I promise."

"I guess that makes sense," he said.

The sound of the doorbell ringing got their attention. She rose from the table, depositing both of their empty glasses into the sink.

"Draven's here," Daniel announced and took off for the door. She followed behind at a more reasonable pace.

The way Draven looked, standing in the doorway, stopped her in her tracks.

It dawned on her that this was the first time she had ever seen him dressed up. Their first date had been dressy casual, but this was something else. It made her heart race and her mouth water to see him looking so sharp and put together in that tux.

His eyes caught hers and the crooked grin that graced his handsome face made her knees weak. He winked. Damn him.

"This is usually the part where people start talking," Daniel said after they had been staring at each other for far longer than was normal. Olivia bit back a groan and Draven chuckled as he ran a hand through his hair.

"Sorry, kid. But your mom looks fantastic tonight," Draven said as his eyes landed on Daniel.

"That's okay," Daniel said. "At least you're better than Lucas. He usually just mumbles around Parker and he blushes a lot. It's kind of embarrassing."

"It really is," Draven said with a laugh. "I bet you won't be that way with Lola tonight."

"No way! We've got too much to talk about with the ..." Daniel trailed off before casting a glance at Olivia. "Well, you know, just everything."

"Well, if that's not a reason to get a move on, I don't know what is. Should we get going?" Draven asked.

Daniel agreed and ran out to Draven's car, leaving Olivia and Draven with a moment alone.

"Hey, you," she whispered as he took her into his arms.

"You look stunning, Liv. If I haven't already said that."

"You don't look so bad yourself," she said, trying her hardest not to blush. "This look suits you."

"I'm glad you like what you see."

She could not help herself. She pulled him in for a kiss. It was short and sweet, but it only served to remind her of what they would likely be getting up to later.

A 'hurry up' from Daniel got them moving out the door.

They stopped to pick up Lola, who lived only a few blocks away and headed for the gym. The place was packed full. Almost every town resident was in attendance. She was happy to see how much their hard work and planning these past few weeks had paid off.

After hanging up their coats, Daniel and Lola ran off to join some of their friends. Olivia and Draven went to grab some food. She, Rosa and Parker had spent the last few days making dozens and dozens of tamales. Along with gallons of Mexican hot chocolate.

They ate and ate until she felt like she would pop. Rosa and Janella chatted with Draven and Lucas about their mother. Olivia watched on with Parker at her side, happy to see how much Draven seemed to be enjoying himself.

Then Draven asked her to dance.

"I didn't know you could dance."

He laughed. "My mother taught me, actually."

"Well, she was a good teacher."

It was like a scene from a movie. Being here, surrounded by friends and family, there was an undeniable sense of security and joy. The aura around this whole place screamed Christmas and the general holiday spirit.

Swaying around the room in Draven's arms, knowing she had found someone to share these moments with, was like her wildest dream come true. She could have stayed here, with him, all night long.

But when the song ended and the next one began, he stopped dancing and leaned in to whisper in her ear, "I hate to steal you away when you're enjoying yourself. But I want to show you something and I think now's the time to do it."

"Okay. Lead the way," she said without hesitation. Maybe he was pulling her away from the crowd for a bit of privacy. Butterflies filled her stomach and her whole body suddenly felt warmer. She and Draven, in a small, dark space ... that could be fun.

On the walk from the dance floor, she caught the eyes of Parker and Jill. They had been dancing too but stopped to watch them leave. They were on the other side of the room, but she swore there was something resembling tears in Parker's eyes and Jill was grinning like a loon.

Something was up.

She was tempted to go over there and demand that they tell her what the hell was going on. But both of them sent her a thumbs up and waved her off. Okay, seriously? What was going on here?

She glanced over at Draven, but he was too focused on weaving his way through the crowd, so she could not get a good look at his face.

When they reached an exit door, Draven pushed his way through, pulling her along with him. What was going on? They would freeze out here. Her arms were already getting goosebumps.

"Uh, Draven. What are you doing? It's freezing outside."

She looked up as the door slammed shut behind them.

Snow, fluffy and white, was falling in the first flurry of the season. The sight brought a huge smile to her face. Ever since she was a kid, she had loved the snow. But only when it was like this, clean and light. Nothing could replace the feeling of peace that came over her when snow covered the earth, and everything was quiet.

Before she had a family, before she had found a home, she had this. Now that she had all of those other things, even if it seemed silly, the snow was even more special. She closed her eyes, breathing it in. Cool and crisp and perfect. A dreamy sigh escaped her lips.

After a moment, Draven's hand tightened in hers. She opened her eyes to look at him. He was looking at her with so much hope and so much love. It occurred to her that maybe the snow wasn't just luck.

"How did you know it would snow tonight?" she asked, shaking her head as she tried to make sense of it all. Red crept into his cheeks and his hand came up to cup the back of his neck. He smiled, but it wasn't his voice that answered her. It was Daniel's.

"We planned it that way, Mom."

Creating this moment had been a team effort by himself, Daniel, Jill, and Parker. Even Janella and Rosa had pitched in, conjuring up the snow. It was all worth it to see the look on Olivia's face right now—pure, unbridled joy.

"You two planned the snow?" she asked, her voice thick with emotion. Daniel nodded.

"That's so sweet. Thank you both so much. You know how much I love the snow, bud."

"I do, and that's what I told Draven. But that's not all, Mom. Not even close."

She looked back at Draven with a question in her eyes. He did not respond, watching her face as the horse-drawn sleigh pulled up behind him. He did not want to miss a second of her reaction.

"Oh my God. Oh, my God!"

Her grip on his hand tightened substantially as she took in the horse that led the old-fashioned sleigh. He grinned at how she could not seem to stop looking back and forth between their ride and himself and Daniel. It filled him with joy to see her in child-like wonder.

Daniel looked just as thrilled to see his mom happy. The horses had been his idea. Apparently, the two of them sometimes went riding together. Without the kid, none of this would have happened. He was the true mastermind.

"Ready to go for a ride?" Draven offered.

"Seriously?" she asked as he led her over to the sleigh.

"Seriously," Daniel said with a laugh.

She looked at her son and then to the sleigh that would only fit two people. The tiniest trace of concern creased her brow.

Daniel reassured her right away. This kid was so attuned to his mother it reminded Draven of himself as a kid. "Don't worry about leaving me behind; I have dibs on the next one with Parker."

"The next one?" she asked as Draven helped her up into the carriage.

"Well, it hardly seemed right to deny everyone this experience, given we planned this together. More sleighs are waiting to take everyone else on their own rides around town."

"God, I love you," she blurted out and he chuckled, bringing her hand up to his lips to kiss it lightly, loving the feeling of her warm skin against his lips despite the chill in the air.

"Hold on to that thought. It'll come in handy later."

She still seemed too shocked and excited to say much of anything as he rounded to the other side of the sleigh and got in. He did not mind, though, not when she looked as happy as she did right now.

Happy and cold. That was one thing he had overlooked. She was only in her dress, having hung up her coat when they arrived. Luckily, he knew each sleigh was equipped with a blanket. He pulled one out from under the seat and laid it across their legs. Their friends all exited from the dance, coming to stand with Daniel on the snow-covered sidewalks to wait for their own rides. They waved goodbye to Olivia and Draven as the sleigh moved off into the night.

They took a path around the gym and into the wooded area behind it, where everyone else would be taking a route around the square, down around Main Street and back. Draven had mapped it out himself earlier today.

The world around them looked like it had been retouched with movie magic, and it was breathtaking. Magic really was amazing. Jill and Parker had really managed to make a winter wonderland. That was exactly what Draven wanted for Olivia to have on this special night.

Parker had come up with the spell for the special snow, just for tonight. Then she and Draven had added it to the book together. She had even insisted he sign his name next to hers.

"What do you think of all of this?" he asked after a while of comfortable silence.

She just shook her head as she looked over at him and smiled. "I think I must be dreaming. I honestly can't figure out how you managed to do all of this without me noticing," she said as he brushed a strand of wayward brown hair from her face and tucked it behind her ear. She laughed. "I mean, I know it was magic, obviously. But you and me, us being here, having this. I never imagined my life could be like this. You know what I mean?"

"I do. You are a dream I never knew I always wanted, Liv."

She gave him a soft kiss and curled further into his side, soaking him through with a warmth and wanting that flowed throughout his entire body. No matter where they were or what they were doing, he always wanted her. Hopefully, things would only get better from here on out. His heart felt like it was going to fly out of his chest as the sleigh drew closer to the spot and the moment that could change his life forever.

He tried to keep his nerves under control as their driver took them down the less-traveled paths that had been carefully chosen for this night. All afternoon, Draven, his brother and their friends had worked to set up the twinkling lights and lanterns along the way. In the darkness of the night, they shone like bright stars. It all looked exactly as he hoped it would. The way it had all come together made it difficult for him to keep it together. This had taken a lot of planning, and he wanted it to go perfectly.

They arrived in the clearing Daniel helped him choose. It had reminded them both of something out of a fairytale. Once there, the sleigh drew to a stop, the driver climbed out and quietly retreated, walking back the way they had just come. Draven had arranged for him to be picked up by another sleigh so he would not have to stand around in the cold. Which he was now realizing was very considerate of him, but he had no idea how they were going to get the sleigh back.

A problem for later.

He helped Olivia down and his heart filled with satisfaction as she took in their surroundings. Her face radiated pure delight. He needed this to go well.

"I can't believe you did all of this," she said, pulling him from his thoughts. His hand was already reaching into his pocket, fingering the ring that rested there. Her brown eyes caught his, and he could see that she had finally put the pieces together.

"There is nothing in the world I would not do for you, Liv. But I was hoping tonight you might do something for me."

As he said the words, he dropped smoothly to one knee.

Her eyes widened, shining with tears.

Her right hand came up to cover her mouth, coincidentally leaving her left hand free. He pulled the ring from his pocket. Her eyes stayed firmly locked on his even when the ring was in plain sight.

Tears were now falling from those dazzling eyes that always saw right into his soul.

"Will you marry me, Liv?"

A giggle bubbled past her lips and he found himself laughing too.

"I realize that this is kind of fast. But that doesn't make it any less real to me. I never dreamed I would find someone like you, someone who understands me like no one else ever has. Someone who knows the world is full of magic and wonder, someone with a heart of gold. All I want is to spend the rest of my life loving you. You and that amazing kid of yours."

She closed her eyes for a moment, taking one deep breath and letting it out slowly. When she opened her eyes, they burned with intensity.

There she was, his brave beauty. "Yes, of course, I'll marry you. I love you, Draven. I love you so much. All I want is to be yours forever. Forever and always."

He stood up, grabbing her up into his arms and holding her tight.

Then he was kissing her. This kiss was a raging flame amidst a sea of falling snowflakes. A kiss so pure it touched his very soul. When they broke apart, he leaned his forehead against hers, trying to catch his breath.

He slid his grandmother's ring onto her finger, where it would now stay forever. It was a simple ring that spoke to Olivia's elegance, grace and beauty. It was as if the ring was made for her, which made him incredibly happy. He took it as another sign that she was the one for him.

She gazed down at the ring for so long, that he was sure she was going to say she hated it. But of course, he was wrong.

"It's perfect, Draven. It's just the kind of engagement ring I always imagined myself wearing. I love it."

"I'm so glad. It belonged to my grandmother. My mother left it to me. I know she would have loved you, loved that you were the one I gave it to," he said as he placed a kiss on her cold nose. "Now, as much as I wish we could stay here just the two of us for a while, there are some people who I'm sure will want to see you. Guess we'll see if I can drive a sled. I really didn't think that part through."

She laughed, shaking her head and then smiled fondly. "Daniel helped you plan all of this?"

"He did. We had a very serious talk a couple of weeks ago. He let me know the sooner I proposed, the better," he said, laughing at the memory of Daniel's very stern face throughout the entire conversation.

"Oh, I can believe it," she said with a laugh. "If Daniel had his way, we'd be married with a baby on the way already."

"Is that so?" he asked, his tone dropping into something a little more flirtatious at the mention of those next steps. If that was something they both wanted. Making babies meant sex, lots and lots of sex.

"Hold that thought, Draven," she said with a laugh. "Let's just take this one step at a time, all right? First, we have to tell everyone the good news."

"As per usual, you make an excellent point," he said, leaning in to give her a quick kiss on the lips. "Besides, I know your friends will never forgive me if I don't bring you to them soon."

"I can't believe they all knew," she mused to herself. "I mean, they're usually all so bad at keeping secrets and this one ... well, let's just say I can't believe they pulled it off."

"I think what kept everyone's mouths shut was that they wanted this whole thing to go well. You mean so much to them and all they wanted was for you to be happy."

"Well, it worked," she whispered as she held onto him, leaning in for yet another kiss.

Acknowledgments

Regina—For your endless encouragement, advice, and invaluable critiques. I have learned so much from you. Without you, this book would not exist. Thank you.

Alex and Tina—My amazing publishers and editors who have made this process so incredible. Thank you for championing my work. I will be forever grateful to you both.

Shannon—You met Olivia and Draven when they were the hottest of messes. Thank you for helping me wade through the chaos.

Matt and Jace—You are my heart, my home, my safe place. I love you, to the moon and back.

About the Author

Adrianna Schuh is a Mexican American author who writes romance of all kinds. Adrianna is a former librarian and stay-at-home mom. She lives in Wisconsin with her husband, son, and their seven pets. In her free time, Adrianna enjoys completing 2,000-piece puzzles and binging true crime podcasts. *Magic in the Air* is her first traditionally published novel.

Looking for more Romance? Check out Rising Action's other love stories on the next page!

And don't forget to follow us on our socials for cover reveals, giveaways, and announcements:
X: @RAPubCollective
Instagram: @risingactionpublishingco
TikTok: @risingactionpublishingco
Website: http://www.risingactionpublishingco.com

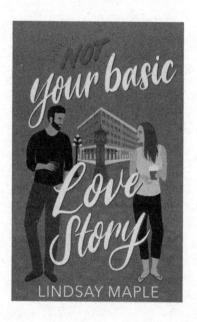

Stubbornly independent Becky isn't looking for love, but when sparks fly on a flight to Mexico she learns her carefully planned life might be the opposite of what she needs.

What begins as a fun vacation fling with a tall, sexy stranger turns into so much more. The problem? Dev and Becky couldn't be more different. Back home in Vancouver, Canada, their relationship grows, and their two worlds collide.

Can a roommate-hating city girl with a diet of chicken nuggets and cheap wine make it work with a vegetarian, non-drinking, Sikh man who lives with his rambunctious multigenerational family in the suburbs?

As Becky navigates her way through a culture she knows nothing about, she is faced with one of the most important decisions of her life: change her plans for how she'd imagined her happily-ever-after or walk away from love.

(Not) Your Basic Love Story is a RomCom about acceptance, compromise, and love being the only things that truly matter.

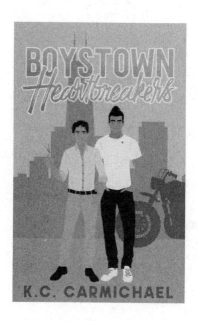

Chicago hairstylist Bastian Russo has only three things to his name: a pair of
$1,200 shears, a Boystown studio apartment, and a list of men's names written
on his closet wall.

His constant worry that he's not good enough and his chronic inability to trust are
what leaves him heartbroken time and again. After he adds the latest name, he
turns to his best friend, Andres Wood, for solace. But instead of treating Bastian
to dinner, drinks, and the usual effortless banter, Andres makes an interesting
suggestion: that Bastian should get over the breakup by dating ... Andres.

Sure, Andres is successful and attractive, but he also knows everything there is to
know about Bastian—including what an insecure pain in the ass he is. Meanwhile,
everyone in Bastian's life, from his mother to his co-workers, thinks he's an idiot
for not having dated Andres already. So, what could go wrong? Everything.

Now Bastian has to sort out his inadequacy and trust issues to prove he's worthy
of transitioning from Andres' best friend to his lover. Otherwise, it's a matter of time
before one or both of them end up on Bastian's list of Boystown Heartbreakers.

Despite saving people's lives every day as a successful trauma surgeon, nothing can mend Dr. Liliana Chase's heart after the loss of her husband and baby girl. When her mother convinces her to come back to Clear Springs, Idaho, for the first time in seven years, she intends to make the visit as short as possible. What she didn't expect was to wreck her car while avoiding a cow with a death wish.

Blake Richardson, a mechanic and single dad, isn't used to helping fiery physicians, but he can't leave Lili planted in a potato field and facing off with a cow. He swears he'll never let another woman into his world after the way his ex-wife left him, but something about Lili keeps him from seeing her as just another big-city doctor.

While Lili is stuck waiting for her car to be repaired in the tiny rural town, she can't resist the pull Blake has on her. Blake's fun-loving and genuine personality might be enough to make her believe in love again. But there's a secret weighing heavily on Blake, and his connection to the death of Lili's family will force them both to confront their fears of loss and abandonment, or risk being alone forever.

"A fun, fiery, and modern twist on a classic!"
— Abby Jimenez, NYT best-selling author of *Part of Your World*

ARDEN JOY

Keep This Off the Record

Abigail Meyer and Freya Jonsson can't stand one another.

But could their severe hatred be masking something else entirely?

From the moment they locked eyes in high school, Abby and Freya have been at each other's throats. Fifteen years later, when Abby and Freya cross paths again, their old rivalry doesn't take more than a few minutes to begin anew.

And now Naomi, Abby's best friend, is falling for Freya's producer and close pal, Will. Both women are thrilled to see their friends in a happy relationship – except they are now only a few degrees of separation from the person they claim to despise ... and they can't seem to avoid seeing one another.

Keep This Off The Record is a fun and fresh LGBTQIA+ story about the freedom to be who you are, even if that means falling for the person you hate.